Jesse Conway laid a hand on Anna Marie's shoulder. "Come, come, my dear. You're overwrought. Take a sedative and get a good night's sleep. Everything is going to seem very different in the morning."

She spat at him. "I've been telling myself that for days now."

"Now, Anna Marie." The warden sighed and rose to his feet. "We have a lovely guest room in my house. And in a few days you can leave, and——"

"*I'm leaving tonight,*" she said. "I'm leaving after midnight tonight. In a coffin, remember?" Her glance raked the frightened man. "I was promised that there wouldn't be an audience when I sat in the hot seat. No more than the necessary number of legal witnesses. You can fix it so they can be bribed. And then tell your reporters that Anna Marie St. Clair died in the electric chair at one minute after midnight or whatever the hell time it would be. If you don't, a lot of names are going to get dragged into the papers, in a very nasty way. So don't tell me you can't work it, because you can!"

Bantam Books offers the finest in classic and modern American murder mysteries. Ask your bookseller for the books you have missed.

Stuart Palmer

THE PENGUIN POOL
  MURDER
THE PUZZLE OF THE HAPPY
  HOOLIGAN
THE PUZZLE OF THE RED
  STALLION
THE PUZZLE OF THE
  SILVER PERSIAN

Craig Rice

HAVING WONDERFUL
  CRIME
MY KINGDOM FOR A HEARSE
THE LUCKY STIFF

Rex Stout

AND FOUR TO GO
BAD FOR BUSINESS
DEATH OF A DUDE
DEATH TIMES THREE
DOUBLE FOR DEATH
FER-DE-LANCE
THE FINAL DEDUCTION
GAMBIT
THE LEAGUE OF
  FRIGHTENED MEN
NOT QUITE DEAD ENOUGH
PLOT IT YOURSELF
THE RUBBER BAND
SOME BURIED CAESAR
THE SOUND OF MURDER
TOO MANY CLIENTS

Max Allan Collins

THE DARK CITY

Victoria Silver

DEATH OF A HARVARD
  FRESHMAN
DEATH OF A RADCLIFFE
  ROOMMATE

William Kienzle

THE ROSARY MURDERS

Joseph Louis

MADELAINE

M.J. Adamson

NOT TILL A HOT JANUARY
A FEBRUARY FACE

Richard Fliegel

THE NEXT TO DIE

Conrad Haynes

BISHOP'S GAMBIT,
  DECLINED

Barbara Paul

THE FOURTH WALL
KILL FEE
THE RENEWABLE VIRGIN

Benjamin Schutz

ALL THE OLD BARGAINS
EMBRACE THE WOLF

S.F.X. Dean

DEATH AND THE MAD
  HEROINE

Ross MacDonald

BLUE CITY
THE BLUE HAMMER

Robert Goldsborough

MURDER IN E MINOR
DEATH ON DEADLINE

Sue Grafton

"B" IS FOR BURGLAR
"C" IS FOR CORPSE

Max Byrd

CALIFORNIA THRILLER
FINDERS WEEPERS
FLY AWAY, JILL

R.D. Brown

HAZZARD

A.E. Maxwell

JUST ANOTHER DAY IN
  PARADISE

Rob Kantner

THE BACK-DOOR MAN
THE HARDER THEY HIT

Joseph Telushkin

THE UNOROTHODOX
  MURDER OF RABBI WAHL

Richard Hilary

SNAKE IN THE GRASSES

THE
LUCKY STIFF

Craig Rice

BANTAM BOOKS
TORONTO · NEW YORK · LONDON · SYDNEY · AUCKLAND

THE LUCKY STIFF

*A Bantam Book / published by arrangement with
the author's estate*

PRINTING HISTORY

Bantam edition / June 1987

ISBN 0-553-26221-1

Published simultaneously in the United States and Canada

PRINTED IN THE UNITED STATES OF AMERICA

O   0   9   8   7   6   5   4   3   2   1

THE
LUCKY STIFF

CHAPTER ONE

It was strange that Anna Marie should be able to sleep at all. Stranger still, perhaps, that she should dream.

When the prison chaplain went away, he whispered, "Try to sleep a little, my child." Anna Marie smiled wryly and said, "I'll have plenty of sleep, after twelve tonight."

But, surprisingly, she did sleep, falling back on the bunk in her cell. Perhaps it was because she'd been wide awake now for two nights running, through all those last-minute and hopeless attempts to obtain a stay of execution, a reprieve, a pardon. Now, with all hope gone, she did sleep, and she dreamed.

It was a dream she'd had before during these weeks in the prison, a dream with ever-changing variations, but always covering those last few minutes she would spend before they strapped her in the electric chair. This time it was laid in a beautiful room, lavishly furnished, with a thick, warm-colored rug, and big, soft chairs. She was there, waiting for the moment of her execution, and so were two or three other unfortunates—she was never able to remember their faces after she woke. They had nothing to do with her and were there to expiate their own crimes.

She was dressed in a brilliantly printed chiffon afternoon dress, with a full skirt and long full sleeves. It was as though she had just walked out from the fitting room in a dress shop, one side seam of the dress was caught with fitters' pins. Aunt Bess was in the room, and during one interval of the dream she told Aunt Bess she could have the chiffon dress, after *it* was over. Aunt Bess had been properly appreciative but uncertain as to when and where she could wear it in Grove Junction, Wisconsin. Anna Marie had had to give a little sales

1

talk about the dress, and point out how easily it could be fitted and made longer.

Then she'd told Aunt Bess not to mourn after her execution, because she'd be able to see Uncle Will now, and she'd be sure to give him Aunt Bess's love.

There had been a curious moment in the dream when all the prisoners had shed the coins from their pockets and thrown them on the floor. Anna Marie couldn't quite understand it, even in the dream, but she'd taken the sapphire bracelet Carl Black had given her off her wrist and let it fall to the rug. Then Uncle Will had come into the room, though Uncle Will had died two years before, and she'd asked him to promise that after she was dead, he'd get the coral necklace Roy James had given her long ago and put it around her neck, because she wanted it buried with her.

There seemed to be a shift in focus in the dream at this point, and suddenly all of the condemned ones were sitting in a semicircle on a thick Oriental rug, and a person who might have been a judge came and sat behind a big, carved mahogany desk and began to talk to them. That was when Anna Marie leaped to her feet and said, *"You must know that I'm innocent! Can't you tell by looking at me? I've never killed anyone——"*

That was when her own voice wakened her, as it always had in other dreams. For a few minutes she lay there, her eyes closed, her body cold with sweat. Then the warmth began to come slowly back into her veins.

"What a nightmare!" Anna Marie whispered to herself. "I thought I was going to the electric chair——"

Suddenly she sat bolt upright on the edge of the bunk, staring wildly at the barred door. Because it was true. She was going to the electric chair, a little less than three hours from now.

Over and over, in the past weeks, she'd told herself that it was impossible. An innocent person couldn't be arrested for murder, and tried, and convicted, and finally executed. But it had happened to her.

She'd been unworried and confident during the trial, almost gay. It was an absurd situation, and she'd laugh about it later, at parties. The jury's verdict had been a shock, but the sentence had seemed like a mere formality. They could never make it stick.

And then there had been one step after another, conferences with her lawyer, studying of the evidence, motions, appeals, all the rest. Little by little she'd become frightened. She *was* caught in a trap, after all. Then the fear had become stark terror, so that she'd sat for hours on her hard bunk, silent and motionless, so that the *Times* reporter had written, "Anna Marie St. Clair, convicted murderess of Big Joe Childers, seemed like a woman carved out of stone——"

At last there had been hopelessness. And dreams.

Anna Marie St. Clair, convicted of murder, sat up, stretched, and reached for the powder compact they'd allowed her to keep. Stupid thing, powdering her nose and fixing her hair to keep a date like this one. But the move was instinctive. She looked for a moment in the mirror at her smooth, warm-colored face, her gray-blue eyes that an admirer had once called "smoky," her full, dark red mouth, and her tawny hair. How was she going to look, after midnight? She wished she had enough time for one more shampoo and wave at Bettina's.

She stretched again, looking critically at her rounded legs and smooth, pale arms. Anna Marie had known since she was fourteen that she had a beautiful body, and she became even more aware of it now. Suddenly she thought that it was a pity, really, she had that date with the electric chair. The beautiful body still was capable of giving—and having—a lot of fun.

There were footsteps on the stone floor of the corridor.

Anna Marie's beautiful body stiffened. It couldn't be time. She couldn't have slept more than a minute or two. But the feet were slowing as they approached her cell. Could the chaplain's watch have been wrong? Impossible. There had to be those few hours left. It mustn't, it couldn't, it mustn't be *right now*.

There was the rattle of a key, and the cell door was opening. Anna Marie stood up. Remember what you swore, she told herself fiercely. A good front, right up to the last. A final statement, one that she'd rehearsed a thousand times in her mind. "I know I am innocent. Someday you will find out the truth." Someday they *would* find out the truth. But a lot of good that was going to do her, by that time.

One final wisecrack, just before they strapped her down. Something that would make Winchell's column.

The cell door opened, and one of the two guards who had come for her signaled for her to come out. She wondered about the chaplain while her numb feet managed those few steps out into the corridor. Maybe he was scheduled to join the procession later.

Nobody spoke. One of the guards took her arm, almost respectfully. She was conscious, as she walked, of the curious, silent interest in her from the other cells along the corridor. It seemed to be something from another world.

One of the guards swung open the immense metal door at the end of the cell block. Anna Marie stumbled through it, suddenly faint and nauseated. Remember now, she whispered, remember. *A good front.* Yet the cold sweat was beginning to bubble out on her face. In another moment, she knew, she was going to be sick, deathly sick.

"Hold her up, Luke," one of the guards said.

A strong hand caught her and kept her on her feet. Another hand grasped her other arm. Somehow her feet kept on moving, right, left, right, left, one step, then two steps, then a third, and a fourth——

There was another door, and another corridor, and an open courtyard, and still another door. Anna Marie walked, the guards supporting her by each arm, until the last door was opened, and she was shoved into a drab, brightly lighted room.

It was the warden's office.

Anna Marie St. Clair stood for a moment, half braced against the door, numb and trembling. The warden was there, at his desk, smiling at her, and so was Jesse Conway, her lawyer. Then Jesse Conway rose to greet her, hands outstretched, wreathed in smiles.

"Congratulations, my dear," he said. He caught his breath and said quickly, "It came just in time, didn't it?"

There was about two-thirds of a second before Anna Marie understood what he meant. Then she could feel the blood and the breath rushing back into her. And at last she managed to speak.

"Now, by God," she said, between tight lips, "now I *am* going to be sick." The warden's office whirled around and grew dark. She felt hands reach out to catch her. And then there was only darkness.

She could hear a soft throbbing, distant, but growing nearer, and voices so far away that she couldn't make out what was being said. It was a long while before she realized that she was on the couch in the warden's office, that the warden was holding a drink of raw rye whisky to her lips, that her eyes were open, and Jesse Conway was speaking to her.

"Everything's all right now," he was saying. "It's all right, my dear." Then he was looking up and talking to the warden. "Naturally, it's been a shock to the poor child. Good news can be sometimes. And after all this torture——"

The warden said indignantly, "This here jail is one of the best run jails in the United States."

"That wasn't what I was referring to," Jesse Conway said smoothly.

Anna Marie sat up and realized that she was, actually, alive. "What is it?" she whispered. "What happened?" The sound didn't seem to be coming from her own lips. "Did they find out that I didn't kill him?"

"Yes," Jesse Conway said. "Yes, they found out. You're free."

It was the warden who lighted a cigarette and put it between her trembling fingers. Then Jesse Conway told her.

The man who actually had killed Big Joe Childers had been shot during a little dispute over territory, something having to do with the numbers game. Believing himself at the point of death, he'd made a full confession, and that confession had been checked, rechecked, double and triple checked, and proved true. Anna Marie was completely exonerated. It had all happened during that little interval of time while she'd been sleeping, after the chaplain had left her.

There were, of course, a certain number of legal formalities to attend to, but at least Anna Marie would not be led to the electric chair at twelve o'clock.

"You're a very lucky little girl," Jesse Conway said in his most mellifluous voice.

Anna Marie St. Clair, farm girl from Wisconsin, photographers' model, chorus girl, night-club hostess, and mistress of several curiously important political figures, sat like a stone. Jesse Conway moved an eyebrow at the warden.

"We'll just move you over to my house," the warden said heartily. "Mrs. Garrity will get a room all ready for you. You'll be an honored guest, believe me."

Anna Marie said just one word. An unprintable one.

Warden Garrity gave a helpless and imploring look at Jesse Conway, who promptly took Anna Marie's ice-cold hands in his warm, moist ones, and said, "Now, my dear, we know this has been a bad time, but——"

This time Anna Marie said three words.

Warden Garrity's eyebrows signaled to Jesse Conway, *"We're going to have trouble with her."* Jesse Conway's shoulders signaled back, *"Leave it to me."*

"My dear little girl," Jesse Conway said, wiping the sweat from his forehead, "don't you realize what this means? You'll be able to leave here in a few days——"

"I'm leaving tonight," Anna Marie said. "At midnight. Remember?"

The two men looked at each other. Anna Marie laughed. It wasn't a pleasant laugh.

"How many people know about this," Anna Marie said, "except we three?" her eyes flamed at them. *"Answer me!"*

Jesse Conway stalled long enough to light a cigar. "Not many. Not the great big world, if that's what you mean. It hasn't been given to the papers yet. Why? Why do you care, Anna Marie?"

She smiled at him. "I care plenty." She rose and began walking gracefully up and down the long, narrow room, cat-like. "How many people, Jesse Conway, know that you came here tonight? How many know that this Garrity bastard must have been informed?"

There was a small silence. Jesse Conway laid down his cigar and looked questioningly at the warden.

"Well—" Garrity said.

Anna Marie laughed nastily. "*Were* you informed, Mr. Garrity?"

"Naturally," Garrity assured her, "only, you see——" He gulped, trapped. "Oh, hell."

"Only," Anna Marie said, "you had to get the straight dope before you were sure. Otherwise you'd have let me go to the chair."

Jesse Conway laid a hand on her shoulder. "Come, come, my dear. You're—well—overwrought. Take a sedative and get a good night's sleep. Everything is going to seem very different in the morning."

She spat at him, "I've been telling myself that for days now."

"Now, Anna Marie." The warden sighed and rose to his feet. "We have a lovely guest room in my house. You'll be very comfortable there. And in a few days you can leave, and——"

"*I'm leaving tonight*," Anna Marie repeated.

They stared at her. She stood, leaning against a gray-green filing case, a cigarette held loosely between her slender fingers, her eyes cold, not even angry.

"I'm leaving sometime after midnight tonight," she said. "In a coffin. Remember?" Her glance raked the frightened men. Then she smiled.

"I was promised that there wouldn't be an audience when I sat in the hot seat," she began, slowly and deliberately. "No more than the necessary number of legal witnesses. You can fix it so they can be bribed. Fix the whole thing any way you like, so it's convincing. And then tell your reporters that Anna Marie St. Clair died in the electric chair at one minute after midnight, or whatever the hell time it would be."

Garrity said, "*What!*"

"If you don't," Anna Marie went on, paying no attention to him, "there's going to be the damnedest suit for false arrest this state ever saw. And a lot of names are going to get dragged into the papers, in a very nasty way. Including you, and the D.A., and a lot of other people." She dropped her cigarette on the floor and stepped on it. "Don't tell me you can't work it, because you can."

"It's impossible," Warden Garrity said weakly.

"Oh, no it isn't," Anna Marie said. "Not if you want to hang on to your job. Fix it up. Bribe your witnesses. Turn on the juice in an empty chair. Tell the reporters I died happy. Hell, you can even load a coffin with concrete and hold a swell funeral if you want to be fancy. And meanwhile, Jesse here will take me back to town."

The warden and Jesse Conway looked at each other for a long moment. The warden shrugged his shoulders helplessly.

"She's got us," he said, his voice flat. He turned to Anna Marie, appeal in his eyes. "Look, sister. What do you want to do it for? You can't tell me that you just want"—his lip curled—"to bring a criminal to justice."

"Hell, no," Anna Marie said. "I don't mess with other people's business, just mine. But somebody's going to pay for what happened to me."

"Look here, Anna Marie," Jesse Conway said. "After all, you didn't die."

"You think not?" Anna Marie St. Clair said. "I died twenty-four times a day, for seven weeks."

She stretched herself to her full height, with an instinctive gesture, as though she were lifting a fur over her shoulder. Even in her drab prison clothes she was lovely, and dangerous.

Jesse Conway asked, "What are you going to do?"

She smiled at him. "Me? I'm dead. So what am I going to do? Guess. I'm going to haunt houses."

CHAPTER TWO

"But, Jake," Helene said, "You've got to do something. Somebody's got to do something. It's——" She looked at her ring watch and gulped. "Jake, it's almost eleven o'clock now!"

Jake Justus shoved his glass away and sighed. "Look,

darling. Just because we met at the scene of a crime, just because we became involved, against my better judgment, in a few other crimes, does not mean that every time a convicted murderess is going to the chair——"

"She may be convicted," Helene said firmly, "but she's no murderess."

"Have it your own way," Jake Justus said, "but it's none of our business." He reached out for her lovely, slender hand. It was icy cold, and it drew away from him in about fifteen seconds and opened a cigarette case. Jake leaned back in his chair and lit his own cigarette.

He was, he reflected, the most fortunate man in the world. Other men might be presidents, millionaires, movie stars, heroes. *He* was married to Helene.

For the moment he slid his worries off his mind and looked across the table at Helene. Smooth, shining, ash-blond hair. Delicate, lovely face, with that pale skin looking as though soft lights showed through it. The light green of her chiffon dress was like an ocean wave breaking over her white shoulders. And under the table there were those long, slender, beautiful legs.

This was their wedding anniversary. He couldn't even remember which one. It didn't really matter. All that mattered was the waking up every morning and seeing her long, silky hair spread out on the pillow, and her face, childlike in sleep, nestled in her arm. Coffee in the sunroom in the morning, Helene in her violet chiffon negligee, or her fluffy white robe, or her bandanna sunsuit, or, on special occasions, the blue satin house pajamas she'd been wearing the first time they met.

"Helene," he said, "every time I look at you I feel as if someone had just given my heart a hot-foot."

Her eyes warmed. "Darling," she whispered, "I didn't know you were a poet!" This time her hand reached out for his, and it wasn't icy cold.

Jake Justus, ex-reporter, ex-press agent, and, as he occasionally reminded himself, *definitely* ex-amateur detective, sighed again. Happily, this time. That unpleasant knot of anxiety in his stomach went away for a moment. After all, why should he worry? He was married to Helene, and he owned the Casino.

Across the table, Helene looked at him thoughtfully over the rim of her glass. There was a *Look* Jake got on his face when something bothered him. She could tell. He ran his fingers through his sandy red hair and twisted it into knots. He scowled. He wrinkled his nose. He lit cigarette after cigarette, and crushed each one out after a few puffs. He looked at something millions of miles away, and said, "Yes?" in an absent-minded voice when you asked him a question.

Her fingers tightened on his. She whispered, "Jake. Darling."

Jake blinked and said, "Yes?" And then, "What?"

"Oh, nothing," Helene said.

She knew from experience it wasn't any use saying, "What's the matter?" She'd only get a vague smile and a perfectly worthless assurance that nothing was the matter. After all, she reminded herself, she shouldn't worry. She had everything in the world to make her happy, including— especially—Jake. Just to look at his pleasant, homely, freckled face made her spine feel like a marimba in a rhumba band.

But she wasn't happy. Perhaps it was because a girl she'd never met, never even seen except in newspaper pictures, was going to the electric chair at midnight.

"Dance?" Jake said. He might have been speaking to a casual acquaintance, to an extra woman at a big and boring party.

"No, thanks," Helene said, in the same tone.

Jake lit another cigarette. He didn't really feel like dancing. Not with the thought that kept coming back into his mind in spite of the sight of Helene and the touch of her fingers. It would have been like—yes, like dancing on a new grave.

Forget it, he told himself grimly. You probably couldn't have done anything, anyway. Think about your wedding anniversary, think about Helene, think about the Casino. Think about everything else in the world.

The Casino. That was something worth thinking about. Jake looked around the big, softly lighted room; at the tables, the bar, the dance floor, the stage. The Casino had seen a lot of changes in its lifetime. First, a swank gambling joint, with the barest pretense of a night club for window dressing. Next, an exclusive night club with a dance floor the size of a prize ring, special entertainment in the bar, and the gambling discreetly moved upstairs. Then Jake had won it on a bet. Now the Casino, considerably remodeled, boasted the biggest dance floor in the Middle West, the best bands, the best entertainers, and was a place where a guy could bring his girl and have one whale of a good time for under five bucks, including taxi fare. It was making money, too.

He remembered the opening night of the new Casino. There had been worries on his mind then, too, but not like this one. A simple little matter of owing a lot of money, due on a day when he couldn't possibly pay it. That worry seemed pretty silly right now. And opening night had been something special, the place jammed with customers and crawling with celebrities of one sort or another. Big Joe Childers had had the table right over there, next to the dance floor, with his gorgeous girl friend Anna Marie——

Forget it!

For a moment Jake was afraid he'd said it out loud. He hoped that he'd only felt the shudder that racked his long, lean body, that he'd only imagined the cold sweat on his forehead. Most of all he hoped that Helene hadn't noticed anything.

"Jake, darling," Helene said. "There must be *something* you can do."

He looked at her and tried to pretend he didn't know what she was talking about.

"It's after eleven," Helene said. "Jake, telephone somebody. Get the mayor. Get the governor. Get Malone."

"Too late," Jake said.

"There's nearly forty minutes," Helene said. The skin around her lips was white.

"The mayor couldn't do any good," Jake said. "I don't know the governor. And I haven't the faintest idea where Malone is." He was talking as calmly as he could, in spite of that feeling in his stomach, as though someone had left a tray of ice cubes in it.

11

"Don't you *care?*"

"Stop being sentimental," Jake said coldly.

"I'm very sorry," Helene said, even more coldly.

Music ended, dancers stood still on the floor clapping wildly for more music. The beating of their hands sounded like rainfall. The band leader shook his head, smiling, and the pianist struck off a few chords. The floor emptied, and the lights changed.

"How can anyone dance, now, tonight?" Helene whispered.

Jake pretended he didn't hear.

There were a few minutes of quiet before the floor show started, just long enough for the waiters to pick up and deliver orders. Then a fanfare from the band, another change of lights, a few bars of music, and Milly Dale slipped out from between the curtains, tiny, sleek, smiling, tossing her long, dark hair back from her shoulders. The applause drowned out the band for a moment, then Milly Dale began to sing in her deep, sultry voice, and the big room grew still.

> *When I'm sitting in the gloom*
> *Of my lonely little room——*

Jake turned his back to the stage and tried to forget the first time he'd heard that song, in the old Haywire Club, now the Orchid Bowl, sung by a girl with an untrained, off-key voice, a girl with tawny hair and big, gray-blue, almost smoky, eyes. He signaled the waiter for two more vodka collins, then looked at his wrist watch. Twenty-five minutes to twelve.

The audience objected loudly to Milly Dale's leaving the stage, but they calmed down a little when the chorus romped down the steps onto the dance floor. They howled appreciatively at the comedians who followed the chorus. Then Milly Dale came back, in a black satin dress that fitted her like adhesive tape, struck a pose, and began to sing:

> *Dear jury,*
> *If you think I'm the girl with the gun,*
> *You can search me.*
> *Dear jury——*

"Jake!" Helene whispered. "I've just remembered—Jake, listen——"

"You can tell me when we get home," Jake said. He rose. "Finish your drink and let's get out of here." His voice was harsh.

Helene took one quick glance at his face, slid her wrap over her shoulders, and rose without another word.

They paused for a moment at the bar. Milly Dale had gone through half of her strip act before an imaginary jury and was now down to the black satin bathing suit.

If you think I hid those letters,
Try and find them,
If you think I——

"Darling, " Helene said. "That song. Doesn't it remind you of something——"

"It does," Jake said, "and shut up." It reminded him of that off-key voice. He said to the bartender, "A double rye, and quick."

Helene glanced at him and added to the bartender, "Same for me, and please have our car brought around to the side door."

When they left Milly Dale's voice followed them.

Dear Jury——
If you——

"Hell!" Jake said, and slammed the car door when they got in.

There was silence all the way to the apartment building, all the way through the lobby and up the elevator. Once inside the apartment Helene let the dark green wool cape slide off her shoulders. "Coffee?" she asked. "Champagne? Or just a drink?"

"Never mind," Jake said. He walked across the room and turned on the radio for the late news broadcast.

There was the buzz as the radio warmed up, and a commercial for a credit dentist. The station break, then the news announcer.

"*Anna Marie St. Clair died in the electric chair at one minute after midnight this morning, with a smile on her lips*——"

Jake switched it off and sank down on the couch.

"She was innocent," Helene whispered. "I could have proved it."

"A drink," Jake said. "Get me a drink."

He downed the glass of rye she put in his hand. Then he looked up at the pleasant, familiar room. There were flowers everywhere, the flowers he'd ordered and picked out for this occasion. There was, he knew, champagne being iced in the kitchenette. There was Helene in her pale green dress.

He hadn't wanted their wedding anniversary to be like this. He'd wanted roses and champagne and laughter.

If only he could tell Helene the whole story. Anna Marie. The Clark Street saloon on the night of the murder. But he couldn't. Not even to Helene could he give away the reason he'd kept his mouth shut all these weeks.

She looked at him, at the silent radio, and back at him again. Suddenly she caught her breath. So that *was* it. Helene made several unpleasant remarks to herself about being both tactless and an idiot.

"Jake. Darling." She sat down beside him. He looked at her, his eyes full of misery.

"Don't think about it. Don't brood about it. It's all over and done with." She paused to light a cigarette for him. "After all, you said yourself there wasn't anything we—you— could have done."

Jake turned away. "That's just the trouble," he said. "There was."

CHAPTER THREE

"You had us in a spot," Jesse Conway said, "and you know it. We had to give in to your crazy scheme. But what's in your mind? What comes next?"

"I don't know," Anna Marie said lightly. She sounded as though she didn't care.

She looked out through the window of Jesse Conway's limousine at the lights of Chicago's streets flashing by. Funny to see lights again. Lights and people and automobiles. There was the marquee of a theater. Perhaps tomorrow she'd go to a movie. Funny to be able to go to a movie. Funny to be out of the cell. Funny to be alive at all.

"What time is it?" she asked.

"Quarter of eleven," Jesse Conway said. "Now, look here, Anna Marie——"

"In an hour and fifteen minutes," she said with a little laugh, "I'll be dead."

Jesse Conway started to speak, changed his mind, and shrugged his shoulders. At last he said, "Well, where do you want to go?"

"My apartment first," Anna Marie said. "I suppose I can still get in."

Jesse Conway cleared his throat in an embarrassed fashion. "I still have the key, you know. Tomorrow I was to go in and get all your clothes, and send them to your Aunt Bess out in Grove Junction."

"I remember," Anna Marie said coldly, "and you can go ahead as per schedule. Only I'm afraid Aunt Bess will have to wait." She was silent for a few minutes, thinking. "I'll find a safe hide-out in the morning. You can bring me the clothes and some other things, and money. I don't suppose I can touch my own dough."

"Hardly," Jesse Conway said.

Anna Marie laughed. "That's the hell of being a ghost. Oh, well. You can advance me whatever I need, and I'll give it back to you when I'm through with this monkey business."

"Whatever you say," he said wearily. "But why the hide-out? Nobody'll try to take you back to jail."

"Because ghosts never appear in the daytime," she told him.

The car stopped in front of a modest apartment building. The street was dark and deserted, but Anna Marie glanced around for possible spectators before she crossed the sidewalk. Jesse Conway unlocked a side entrance on the ground floor and turned on the lights. Anna Marie paused just inside the door and looked.

There was a thin film of dust on the yellow brocade love seat, with its wickedly simpering carved cupids. There was dust on the thick pile carpet, on the deep-cushioned chairs, and on the built-in bar. Some news photographer had left a flash bulb on the gilt coffee table.

"Big Joe Childers did me proud," Anna Marie said. "Too bad some son-of-a-bitch killed him."

She told Jesse Conway to wait for her and went on into the bedroom, which she had perversely decorated with muslin and dimity, a young girl's four-poster bed, hooked rugs, and big, pale pink ribbon bows on the curtains. In it, her flamboyant beauty stood out like a firecracker in an old-fashioned garden, and she knew it.

While Jesse Conway waited impatiently and apprehensively in the next room, she poured handfuls of perfumed salts into the tub, ran in steaming water, and took a long, luxurious bath. Then she dressed, slowly and meticulously, reveling as much in the privacy as in the comforts of her room. To bathe and dress without one of those weasel-eyed female wardens watching—that was something!

Half an hour later she came back into the living room. Jesse Conway looked up, and gasped.

She wore a close-fitting, obviously costly, pale gray suit. The jacket was collarless, and fastened at her throat with a dull gold clasp. The skirt flared very slightly between her hip and her knee. Her tiny slippers were gray, and her incredibly sheer stockings were the exact color of her skin. There was a little gray pillbox hat on the back of her tawny head, and from it floated an immense, graceful, bright pink veil. She carried bright pink gloves, and the purse under her arm was made of wide, diagonal stripes of pink suede and gold kid.

"Good God!" Jesse Conway said. Then he took out his handkerchief, sponged his brow, and said, "But that's the—those are the clothes——"

"It's what I had on the night I was supposed to have shot Big Joe," she said, smiling. "Becoming outfit, isn't it?"

Jesse Conway said, "Very." He looked at her again, closely. She'd made up her lovely face so that it was very pale. The lipstick she'd used was almost lavender. There was a deep smudge of purplish eye shadow on her lids.

"You look white as death," Jesse Conway said. He bit the last word off suddenly.

"That's the idea," Anna Marie told him. "Now give me about twenty bucks and you can tell me good night. Tomorrow come in and get all my clothes out of here, and all the make-up and stuff I left on top of the dresser. I'll let you know where to send it, along with some more money."

He rose and stood looking at her, twisting his hat brim between his fingers. At last he said, "Anna Marie, you're insane."

"Maybe," she said lightly. She shrugged her shoulders, took a cigarette from her pink enamel case and lit it. "People have been known to go insane, waiting for weeks to be led to the electric chair." She blew out a cloud of smoke and looked at him through it, her eyes narrowed. "And you know, I bet you'd never have come near me tonight except for that lucky accident of the confession—which you had nothing to do with."

He tried to meet her eyes, failed, and sank down on the yellow brocade love seat, looking at the floor, wordless. Anna Marie stood for a moment, watching him. It was hard not to feel sorry for a man who seemed so anxious, so dejected—and so guilty.

Jesse Conway was middle-aged, well dressed, and dignified. His hair was gray, but it was still heavy, and carefully brushed. He had a handsome, deeply lined face, though the eyes were just a trifle bloodshot, and the lips twitched ever so little when they should have been in repose. A fine figure of a man, his friends said.

"Believe me," he muttered, "believe me, Anna Marie, it was none of my doing. I couldn't help it. I knew you were being framed."

"And you helped them frame me," she said without bitterness, almost gaily. "My own lawyer."

"No," he said, looking at the floor. "No, that isn't true. But my hands were tied, and you know it. Why, you were convicted before I was even engaged as your lawyer. And even then"—he crumpled a handkerchief between his palms, looked away—"you had the wrong lawyer, that's all."

Anna Marie remembered the weeks she'd spent in the death cell and laughed harshly. "That's no news to me."

"You don't understand," he said dully. "That isn't what I meant at all. There's one lawyer who might have spared you this. He's not afraid of anything or anybody. They say he's as crooked as a worm in an apple, but nobody can buy him if he doesn't want to be bought. At your trial the judge and the jury were fixed, but even with that he might have come up with something. I even thought"—he paused—"it's a damned shame that"—paused again and finally said, looking up, "I mean John J. Malone."

Anna Marie frowned. She sat down on the arm of a chair, swinging her foot. "I've heard about him."

"He's a little guy," Jesse Conway said, "short and stocky, with dark hair and a red face. Always looks mussed up. He's a souse and a dame chaser and a gambler, but he's a damn smart lawyer."

"Yes," she said, nodding slowly. "That's the one."

"He hangs out in Joe the Angel's City Hall Bar," Jesse Conway said. "He's got an office somewhere on Washington Street. The address is in the phone book, in case you ever need him." He smiled mirthlessly. "As you probably will, if you do what I think you're going to do."

"I'm not going to do any murders," Anna Marie said. She stood up and tucked her purse under her arm. Then she, too, smiled. "Unless scaring people to death counts as murder." Her eyes softened suddenly, almost with pity. "What are you being so damn helpful for?"

The gray-haired man looked past her, his face haggard, his hands clenched together between his knees. "Because," he said hoarsely. "Because. Today, all day. It was a kind of murder, you know. They were murdering you. And nothing I could do, not one damn thing." He sucked in his breath sharply. "It was an accident, you know. The confession. It just happened that way. It was a lucky accident."

"Sure," Anna Marie said, "and I'm a lucky stiff." Suddenly she laughed. "That's funny, you know. I'm a lucky stiff." She gave Jesse Conway a quick pat on the shoulder, walked to the door and flung it open. "Well, let's go, ghost."

The air outside was fresh and moist and cool. For a moment Anna Marie stood on the sidewalk, breathing deeply. Free, now. You know, free. Breathe the air, go to a movie, ride on busses, have fun, raise hell. Free, and alive. Just being alive, that wasn't so bad either. She looked at her watch.

Fifteen minutes to midnight.

She turned to the white-faced, shaken man. For a moment she'd felt pity for him. Now her heart hardened again.

If it hadn't been for that *lucky accident*, right at this moment she'd be in her cell, waiting for the footsteps in the corridor. She was alive now, and free, but it wasn't because of him.

"This insane scheme of yours," he mumbled. "Had to consent to it. Got us all on the spot, and you know it." His hand reached out to grasp the doorpost. "For God's sake, Anna Marie," he said, his voice rising desperately, "you're free, it's all over, it was all a mistake. If you want money I can get it for you, plenty of it. You're young, you're beautiful, you can have a happy life—" his voice trailed off into a gasping whisper. "What are you going to do?"

"Nothing illegal," she said. She looked at her watch. "In twelve minutes they'll inform the newspapers that I went to the chair with a smile on my lips. Then you're going to give out to the newspaper boys with that confession." Just one side of her mouth smiled. "It'll make a nice story. Girl executed for the murder she didn't do. Anna Marie St. Clair died at midnight, and then——"

"Don't!" Jesse Conway said. "I won't do it. I won't, I tell you."

"Oh, yes you will," she said. "You've got to. Or you and a lot of your friends are going to be very sorry. Give out with your confession story, Jesse Conway, but not until after the warden releases his statement. Or maybe you'll have ghosts in your attic, too."

She walked out to the edge of the curb and stood waving for a taxi. It seemed to her as though the blood was moving in her veins for the first time in all these weeks. There weren't going to be any footsteps in the corridor. No march to the electric chair. No wisecrack to spring from her lips at the last minute. The whole thing had been one hell of a bad dream—but *she* hadn't dreamed it.

A cab rolled up to the curb, the driver reached out and opened the door. Anna Marie paused, one foot on the step, then turned back to look at Jesse Conway.

He looked sick, old. Somehow he managed to cross the sidewalk with slow, shambling steps, managed to hold the door for her, to help her in with what seemed like a travesty of courtliness.

"Wait. Anna Marie," he said. It was a tortured whisper.

She smiled at him through the open cab door. Then she looked at her watch again.

"In eight minutes now," she said, "I'll be dead."

She threw herself back against the seat cushions and closed her eyes. A few blocks later she sat upright and called to the driver. Her face was bright, almost gay, and her voice was as clear as a bell.

"Joe the Angel's City Hall Bar," she said.

CHAPTER FOUR

"Leave him alone," Joe the Angel said, polishing a glass and putting it away back of the bar. "He's brooding."

It was an unnecessary caution. Anyone with half an eye could see that John J. Malone was brooding, sitting there alone at the far end of the bar, his head propped up on his right hand, his left hand nursing a glass of gin. The little lawyer's face was melancholy. One more gin and he'd probably burst into tears.

The tactful customers of Joe the Angel's City Hall Bar were leaving him to his sorrows. The bar stools on each side of him were empty. No one knew why John J. Malone was brooding, but the voices in the bar were unusually soft, and no one played the juke box.

Malone stirred and signaled to Joe the Angel, who came hurrying over. He pointed to his empty glass.

"Maybe you'd better just leave the bottle right here," Malone said. "I'm holding a wake."

Joe the Angel clucked sympathetically. "Friend or relative?"

"Neither," Malone said, shaking his head. "No one I ever met. You wouldn't understand."

Joe the Angel looked at him, sighed, and went away, leaving the bottle. It was true that he didn't understand, but then Irishmen like John J. Malone were subject to moods.

Malone looked up at the clock, winced, and looked away again. One minute to twelve. They'd have taken her into the death chamber now, and strapped her into the chair. He hoped she wasn't frightened, too terribly frightened. In a few more seconds now they'd turn on the infernal thing. He hoped it wouldn't hurt.

John J. Malone, criminal lawyer, went through this period of suffering whenever a convicted murderer went to the chair or was carried off to jail for life imprisonment. For that matter, he didn't like to see anyone go to jail for even the most minor offense against law and order.

The suffering had nothing to do with a lack of respect for law and order. Nor with any antisocial attitude toward crime. It wasn't even because he was a criminal lawyer and, as a matter of professional pride, always felt that if he'd been the condemned person's lawyer, the trial would have gone otherwise. It was simply that he always felt so damned sorry for the person going to jail or the electric chair, deservedly or not.

In this case, however, his suffering was unusually acute. In the first place the criminal was a woman, and John J. Malone had a deep-seated sense of gallantry which made the execution of a woman impolite, immoral, and unthinkable. In the second, he'd fallen in love with the newspaper pictures of Anna Marie St. Clair. He'd dreamed about her nightly during all these weeks leading up to her execution. And, finally, he had a horrible, and uncomfortable conviction that she was innocent.

He poured another gin and reviewed the circumstances of the case for the hundredth time. Anna Marie St. Clair had been provided for, lavishly, by Big Joe Childers. Possibly she'd been in love with him, though John J. Malone hoped not.

The day of the murder Anna Marie St. Clair had been informed, anonymously, that Big Joe was keeping company with another girl and was about to desert Anna Marie St. Clair. She'd admitted that at the trial, and admitted that she'd been upset, in fact, sore as hell.

She'd made a date with Big Joe to have it out with him. They'd met in one of the private rooms of a Clark Street bar.

According to a number of witnesses, the two had quarreled violently. At the height of the quarrel there had been the sound of a shot. People had rushed into the private room, to find Big Joe stretched out on the floor, and Anna Marie St. Clair standing over him, her face white, the gun in her hand.

Her story had been that, while they were quarreling, a man—she couldn't describe him, she hadn't had a good enough look at him—had rushed into the room, shot Big Joe, thrust the gun into her hand, and rushed out again.

Obviously, the district attorney had said, not only a falsehood but a ridiculous one.

The gun wasn't Big Joe Childers'. In fact, it was well known that Big Joe never carried a gun. That made it a premeditated crime.

The presence of Big Joe's widow in the courtroom hadn't helped Anna Marie's case any, either. Malone scowled at the thought of Eva Childers. She'd worn simple, inexpensive, almost shabby clothes. She'd been the perfect gentle, heartbroken, and helpless widow. Malone knew that she was a rich woman with social pretensions, and hard as nails.

If he'd been Anna Marie's lawyer, he never would have let her wear those gorgeous, becoming, and obviously costly outfits. He'd have gotten the Widow Childers on the stand, and somehow managed to show her up for what she was. He'd have—oh, he'd have done a lot of things.

John J. Malone sighed into his gin. Everytime he thought about the case, it seemed to him that there was some one thing that proved Anna Marie's story to be true. Only he couldn't put his finger on it. If he could have, perhaps he could have done something to save her. This time, though, his brains had failed him—and failed her. It was too late now. He looked up at the clock again and realized he'd been musing for an hour. It was all over now. A boy came in selling newspapers. John J. Malone bought one, almost against his will, and spread it out on the bar in front of him. Suddenly his whole body stiffened, his face whitened.

Anna Marie St. Clair had died in the electric chair at midnight. Less than half an hour later a dying gangster's confession had proved her innocence.

He had been right. Her story had been true. And it was too late, too late.

John J. Malone reached for the gin bottle, then pushed it away from him. He felt stunned and sick; the room displayed just a faint inclination to reel. Not because of the gin, either.

Through the blur in front of his eyes he saw Joe the Angel's face. He looked at it for a moment while it slowly came into focus, and while the room settled down again. Joe the Angel was white as a piece of chalk, his eyes looked like brown marbles. He was looking at something beside John J. Malone.

A soft voice said, "A double bourbon and water please." Joe the Angel nodded as though he were hypnotized. He mumbled something and rushed to fill the order.

John J. Malone turned slowly on the bar stool.

There she was.

It took a minute for his brain to function again. In that minute his eyes took in every detail of her pale face and wraithlike hands, her light, shining hair. He watched while she mixed the bourbon and water and drank it. He observed her clothes, the gray suit, the tiny hat with the veil, the gloves, and suddenly realized in what newspaper picture he'd seen them. In that moment she turned and smiled at him.

"No you don't!" John J. Malone said. He slid off the bar stool, overturning his glass, grabbed the gin bottle, and fled into the back room of Joe the Angel's City Hall Bar.

He sank into the farthest booth and sat there shuddering, his face in his hands. When he looked up again she was across the table from him, smiling.

"Go away," John J. Malone said. "*Go away.* You're not there. I'm drunk. It's a hallucination. Go away. I didn't do anything to you, did I? You know I didn't do anything to you. I could have saved your life." He drew a long, shivering breath.

"You didn't do anything to me," she whispered, "but you can help me now. You want to help me, don't you?"

"Anything," John J. Malone said. In the half-lighted booth, through the blur before his eyes, she seemed misty, all gray and shadows, and more beautiful than ever. "I'll do anything," John J. Malone repeated, and buried his head in his arms.

When he looked up again, she was gone.

Reason was what he needed, the lawyer told himself. Cold, hardheaded reason. And a breath of fresh air. And a long period of total abstinence.

He rose by bracing both hands against the table, caught his breath, and managed to walk out into the bar with a show of nonchalance. It was strangely quiet. Everyone seemed to be looking at him.

Malone nodded to Joe the Angel and said, "Put it on my bill." He started for the door.

"Wait a minute," Joe the Angel said hoarsely. "Where is she?"

"She?" Malone repeated. "Have you been seeing things?" Get a grip on yourself, he thought. There is such a thing as mass hallucination. He'd read about it once. "Good night, Joe."

But there on the bar was the glass from which she'd drunk her bourbon and water. Malone stared at it for a horrified moment, and fled out to the sidewalk, leaving a white-faced Joe the Angel, who promptly sent all his customers home, closed up his bar for the first time in nine years, and headed for the nearest church.

She was there, smiling at him, out on the sidewalk, beside the open door of a waiting taxicab.

Suddenly John J. Malone's fear left him. Anna Marie St. Clair was so beautiful. And she needed his help. She wasn't there to harm him or to frighten him; she was there because she needed him. And he was still in love with her.

He found himself smiling at her as he got into the taxi. He felt numb, numb all over, his skin was cold and damp, but he wasn't frightened.

"Where do you live?" she whispered.

Automatically he gave the name of the Loop hotel where he'd lived so many years. His heart began beating so hard he was afraid it might burst. She was going home with him, just as she had in a few of the more spectacular of his dreams.

Then he leaned forward and told the driver to go to the side entrance, the one near the freight elevator. The desk clerk in the hotel had been a trifle difficult lately, and he might not realize that Malone's companion was an illusion.

John J. Malone almost forgot that fact himself as he paid the cab driver, ushered Anna Marie St. Clair through the side door, and rode with her up the freight elevator. For the moment, she was just the most beautiful girl in the world.

He'd hung the "DO NOT DISTURB" sign on his door, locked the door, tossed his hat on the dresser, and said, "Can I give you a drink, dear?" before he remembered.

She was misty and lovely, standing there dressed in gray and pink and gold, smiling at him, encouraging him, perhaps even liking him.

He knew he should be afraid, but he wasn't.

"I like you, Mr. Malone," Anna Marie St. Clair said. There was a warm, almost an alive, note in her voice.

Malone stood there, looking at her, at every detail of her costume, the gray suit with its collarless neck and slightly flaring skirt, the tiny gray shoes, the skin-colored stockings, the hat, the veil, the purse, the gloves. Then suddenly it was as though an electric light bulb had flashed on in his brain.

"Now I know," he said hoarsely. "Now I know why you couldn't have killed him. The one thing I needed to realize. The proof. I can see it, now." He took a step nearer to her. "I can prove that you didn't kill him." Then there was a sob in his throat. "I *could* have proved it, I mean," he said, as he reached for her.

CHAPTER FIVE

He'd dreamed the whole thing.

The realization was a great relief to John J. Malone, lying there in bed with his eyes still closed. Because there were only two alternatives to its having been a dream, and he couldn't face either of them, especially at this hour in the morning. It didn't happen, he thought, and he wasn't crazy. Just a dream.

He regretted having wakened from it. It had been a beautiful dream, and an ecstatic one. "For a little while," he whispered, "I thought you were really here."

"I'm still here," a soft voice said, not very far away.

John J. Malone opened his eyes and sat bolt upright, clutching the sheet around his shoulders. There she was, Anna Marie St. Clair, sitting in the one easy chair, wrapped in his old bathrobe, her tawny hair loose over her shoulders, sipping a cup of coffee. And there on the floor was the newspaper, telling how Anna Marie St. Clair had been electrocuted last night at twelve.

"I phoned downstairs for coffee," she said. "I hope you don't mine. You'd probably like some yourself." She poured out a second cup and handed it to him.

He took it automatically and drank it, still staring at her, while his mind slowly snapped back into focus. Suddenly the empty cup slid from his fingers and rolled down to the floor, unnoticed.

"You had a double," he said. "I mean, *she* had a double. You were identical twins."

She laughed pleasantly and lit a cigarette. "Nothing like that. I'm Anna Marie."

Malone crossed himself hastily and instinctively. Then

he looked at her for a moment. Some of the details of what he'd considered to be a bright and colorful dream began to come back to him. "You're not ghost," he said, almost accusingly.

She laughed again. "Of course not," she said. "I never was one." Her face grew sober. "I'm terribly sorry, really. But I couldn't resist. I had to find out what the effect would be. If people would—believe in me. Really, you've no idea how glad I am that you did."

"But damn it," Malone said crossly, "you looked—" his eyes narrowed. Her face had been white, dead white, her eyes enormous and shadowy, her lovely mouth almost blue. Now, though there was a faint prison pallor on her smooth cheeks, her skin was alive and glowing, her lips red, her eyes bright. "Make-up!" he said. "For the love of Mike——"

He grabbed the newspaper, read hastily through the story of how Anna Marie St. Clair had died at midnight, a smile on her lips, protesting to the last that she was innocent.

"All right," he said. "Tell me." His voice was hoarse.

"The confession got there in time," she said. "Lucky, isn't it, that they broke the news to me before they gave it to the newspapers."

She told him the rest of it. The trial, the bland assurances that she had nothing to worry about, the verdict and the sentence, the appeal for a new trial, automatically refused, the long weeks in prison when no one, not even Jesse Conway, had come to see her and when she couldn't get in touch with anyone.

Malone already knew all the legal details, he'd read them again and again in the newspapers. And what she'd thought, and felt, during those weeks was something he'd not only guessed at, but lived through with her.

She told him about what she'd thought were going to be her last few hours alive, and the walk to the warden's office, and what had happened there.

"Now," she said, "I'm a ghost." She glanced at the tiny platinum watch on her wrist and said, "And a damned hungry one. It's eleven o'clock."

"I'm hungry, too," Malone said. He reached for the phone and said, "What do you want?"

27

"Anything, as long as it isn't lukewarm oatmeal, dry toast, and thin coffee."

The little lawyer shuddered, called room service, and demanded a rush double order of pancakes with sausage, scrambled eggs, hot biscuits with marmalade, coffee, half an apple pie, and a quart of cold beer.

'There's a lot more to discuss," he said as he hung up the phone, "but I dislike doing my discussing on an empty stomach." He managed a delicate operation of wrapping the sheet around him, squaw fashion, and getting out of bed, all at the same time. "I'm going to take a shave and a shower. There's all kinds of make-up and stuff in the top left-hand dresser drawer in case you want any. And if you want a drink, there's a bottle of gin under the clean socks in the middle drawer."

He stood under the shower for a long time, and lingered over his shave. He should have had a hangover, but he felt like a million—hell, two million—dollars.

He knew what Anna Marie was doing. He knew why she was doing it. Frankly, he didn't blame her. But maybe he could talk her out of it. Because if she went ahead with what was undoubtedly in her mind, she was going to blow the lid off a political pot that was already beginning to steam a little.

It would destroy a number of his best connections, if such a thing took place, but that wasn't his reason. He could always make new connections. It would ruin a number of his friends. Or were they his friends? Malone paused, razor in hand, and the lathered face that looked back at him from the mirror answered, "No."

It might bring about a reform administration in the next election, and he'd have to find a new place to play poker. That had happened before, and he'd always managed.

There would be danger to Anna Marie herself. Malone's razor paused again, halfway down one cheek, and he said, "Not with me around, there wouldn't."

But there would be trouble, big trouble, before the thing was through. Some of it he could anticipate, some of it he could sense. Murder, and suicide, and ruin, and political upheaval. Anna Marie was holding dynamite in her frail, lovely hands. Malone didn't like explosions.

He finished shaving and began rubbing lotion on his

face. Maybe he could talk her into giving up the whole thing. If she wanted to have a little fun with Bugs Brodie, or Butts O'Hare, or some of the boys at the City Hall first—well, he, Malone, was always willing to lend his hand to a practical joke. Then the whole thing could be explained as a joke. He grinned at the recollection of how Joe the Angel's face had looked, and sobered quickly when he thought of how his own face must have looked. All right, a joke was a joke.

Sure, that was the thing to do. Talk her out of it.

Malone patted talcum powder on his face and brushed his hair. He'd carried his clothes into the bathroom, and he dressed slowly, rehearsing what he was going to say to her.

And then, when he had talked her out of it——

He could make a lot more money than he did and manage his affairs a lot better. He might even be able to collect some of the money his clients owed him. He could reorganize his office arrangements and go after some really important cases. Why, with his brains, and his connections, he could be a rich man in no time at all!

There were some beautiful little apartments overlooking the lake, up on the drive.

Or maybe a pretty little house in Wilmette. Anna Marie might like a house. Just a tiny but perfect house, like a jewel box.

He'd reopen his charge accounts at Saks' and Blum's-Vogue. He'd make a lunch date for tomorrow or next day with that wholesale jeweler. And didn't that pawnbroker he'd successfully defended on an arson charge have a brother-in-law in the fur business?

Malone whistled happily as he tied his tie. From now on, everything was going to be wonderful.

He was glad that his brown suit had just come back from the cleaners, and that he had a new tie. He whistled a few more bars as he polished his shoes with the end of a towel and stuffed the towel behind the bathtub. Finally he gave his hair one last lick with the brush. Then he opened the door.

There was Anna Marie, standing before the dresser, smiling at him in the mirror. She'd dressed and made up her face. He stared at her.

The tawny hair rippled on her shoulders when she moved

29

her head. She was the most gorgeous girl Malone had ever seen, and he'd seen a lot of gorgeous girls in his time. The whole picture of what had happened to her ran through his brain, like the life history that's supposed to run through the brain of a drowning man. It took about ten seconds, but he saw all of it—the trial, the appeals, the long weeks in the deathhouse, the final walk to what she'd thought would be the electric chair. Someone had planned, deliberately, that it would happen to her, that way.

It wasn't going to be a practical joke. It was going to be something serious, and deadly. It was going to be dynamite. And, Malone told himself, he was going to love it.

"All right, baby," he said quietly. "We'll do it your way."

CHAPTER SIX

Ordinarily, John J. Malone preferred delicate-looking girls, with dainty, birdlike appetites. Possibly a hangover from the days when he was putting himself through night law school by driving a taxi. In those days a girl who said, "I'm not hungry, thank you, I'll just take a cup of coffee," was a rare jewel to be treasured. Or possibly it was because, in his later, and more affluent days, he liked his girls to pay attention to him, and not what he was feeding them.

This morning, though, he enjoyed watching Anna Marie at her breakfast. She'd been eating prison breakfasts for weeks now, and the little lawyer knew exactly how much graft was being collected from the food allowances. And even without the graft, oatmeal was a hell of a thing to face when you first woke up in the morning.

He managed, surreptitiously, to slide five of the pancakes onto her plate, and three onto his own. Most of the little sausages landed beside the five pancakes, and the sirup jug was pushed over to her side of the table. He watched, happily, while she wiped up the last drop of sirup with the last square inch of pancake. He gave her most of the scrambled eggs, and felt a warm, purring sensation when she piled gobs of marmalade on the biscuit. Finally, when she accepted most of the apple pie, and sighed over her coffee, his happiness was complete.

A fly would have starved to death on what was left on the table when breakfast was over.

Malone had been keeping the rest of the beer—he'd served some of it with the scrambled eggs—cool under the coldwater tap in the bathtub. Now he poured out two glasses, gave Anna Marie a cigarette, and said, "Well? Who framed you? Or is that what you want to find out?"

Anna Marie took a long, slow drag on her cigarette and said, "If I'd known, I wouldn't have started out by haunting *you.*" She gazed through the smoke and said, "I'm sorry I said that, this isn't any time to be funny." She paused. "What's more, I'm sorry I played that trick on you last night. I just couldn't resist——" She paused again. "And I'm sorry—oh, well, the hell with it."

She put down the cigarette and picked it up again. "I had to have someone to help. I couldn't manage a thing like this by myself. You were—the only person—— Well, if I'd had you at the trial, none of this would have happened. I was worried once, and I wanted—but they all kept saying, 'Don't worry, Anna Marie, we'll get you a good lawyer,' 'don't worry Anna Marie, we'll fix everything.'" She shook her head. "And then all of a sudden it was over, and——"

"Never mind," Malone said hastily. "That was yesterday."

"And there'll always be a tomorrow," she said automatically. She paused, stared at him, and suddenly laughed. "Every now and then I go on talking as if I were dictating something to sell to a confession magazine."

"And every now and then," Malone said, "I start answering as if I were reading one." He bit the end off a cigar. "There are certain things you want to do."

She nodded, and the "Yes" was a whisper.

Malone blew a shred of tobacco off his lip and reached for a match. "Why?"

"Well, because——" She looked up at him. "Are you my lawyer, or aren't you?"

"At least that," Malone said. "Unless I have been dreaming."

To his amazement, she blushed. Becomingly, too. He finally managed to get his cigar lit, and sent up a smoke screen between them.

"Revenge can be a lot of fun," the little lawyer said slowly, "but it can be a lot of trouble, too. Sometimes it's better to forget all the hell you've been through and pick up life at the beginning of the next chapter, and follow it through to the to-be-continued."

"A lovely sentiment," she said. "I wish I agreed with it." Her lips were pale under the make-up. "It isn't revenge. Not for me, I mean. Sure, it was a bad few months, but I'm alive. And Big Joe——"

Malone looked tactfully away, in spite of the smoke screen. A moment later he said, "Look out for that cigarette. Do you want to set the hotel on fire when it's the only home I have?"

She picked it up from the corner of the rug, brushed at the ashes with her fingertips, and said, "Sorry. Listen, Malone. Big Joe Childers had his failings, but he was a good guy. You know, a *good* guy. He was a crook, all right, sure, but he was one of the most honest crooks I've ever met, and I've met a lot of them. He wanted to live a long time, just like everybody wants to live a long time. Just like you want to, and I do."

"Ike Malloy killed him," Malone said, trying to sound disinterested.

Anna Marie jumped up from her chair. "Look, when some guy kills another guy, you don't arrest the gun he used, do you? Ike Malloy was a weapon, that's all."

"A very nice piece of reasoning," Malone said approvingly. "You have the makings of a lawyer." He glanced at her and added, "Though it would be a great pity for you to waste yourself on a legal career."

He picked up the newspaper and looked at it for a long time. "There are a few interesting facts about Ike Malloy's confession."

Anna Marie lifted a questioning eyebrow.

"It seems," Malone said, "an inquisitive cub reporter named Griggs got to the hospital about two jumps behind the ambulance bringing in Ike Malloy. It took him a little time to get to Malloy's room, because the press was definitely not invited. He got to the door just in time to hear Malloy demanding that the police take down his confession that he'd killed Big Joe Childers. But Ike Malloy's lawyer was informing the doctor and the policeman in charge that his client was obviously delirious and in no condition to talk." He paused. "Odd, isn't it, that his *lawyer* would be there, handling things."

"Go on," Anna Marie said through tight lips.

"Another item in the paper," Malone said, "states that one, Albert Griggs, reporter, is in St. Luke's Hospital recovering from head wounds received in an attempted holdup in an alley leading from his newspaper's parking lot." He laid down the paper for a moment. "They certainly were anxious to make sure that Ike Malloy's confession never saw daylight."

Her lovely mouth twisted into a wry smile. "I damned near was a real ghost."

"You can say that again," Malone said with feeling. "And the only reason you aren't is that this Griggs guy had sense enough to phone his paper from the public telephone in the hospital lobby before Ike Malloy's boss's hired hands kicked him out. Because the city editor got right on the job, and Captain von Flanagan, of the Homicide Bureau, was at Ike Malloy's bedside in fifteen minutes."

She sighed. "That was close."

"Ike Malloy told the whole works," Malone said. "Names and details. Von Flanagan checked fast. The two guys who drove Malloy to the saloon and waited outside, with the engine running in their car, broke down and talked. So did the waiter who let Malloy in the back way. In fact, Malloy only omitted one important detail."

"I know," she said. "He didn't tell who hired him."

"But," Malone told her, "the newspaper story does name the lawyer who said Malloy was in no condition to talk. He gave a statement later, by the way, to the effect that he had sincerely believed his client was out of his head, and that he was only anxious to protect his client from, quote, injudicious questioning, unquote. You can disbar a man for that, nor even publicly state that he's one of the damnedest liars since the snake in Eden."

"His name?" Anna Marie asked.

"Jesse Conway," Malone said.

There was a silence. Malone lit a cigar and looked thoughtfully at Anna Marie.

"I know a lot of people," Malone murmured. He might have been talking to himself. "You'd be surprised at some of the people I know. I'm surprised myself, now and then. I knew Ike Malloy, for instance. In fact, I was best man at his sister's wedding. Ike was a good, honest guy who obeyed orders and never killed anybody he wasn't told to kill. I know a lot of other people, including a couple of guys who could kidnap anybody you cared to name, and who could—using methods I wouldn't care to discuss—get information out of a mummy."

He paused, gazing at the end of his cigar. "I even know Jesse Conway. He used to be a pretty good lawyer. He used to be a pretty good guy, too. But something happened to him. I don't know what it was. He has plenty of money, but damned few clients. And he's gone soft. Soft, and worried."

Anna Marie said nothing. She was remembering Jesse Conway helping her into the taxi last night.

"Unless I'm very much mistaken," Malone said quietly, "it would take those guys I mentioned about five minutes to pry all the information you need loose from Jesse Conway. If you want it that way."

This time the silence seemed to stretch on and on. Then Anna Marie put out her cigarette and said, "I don't."

"Even if Jesse Conway told you the name you want to know, and all the details?"

She shook her head. "The one name isn't enough. Because I——" Her voice broke off. "I can't explain it."

"I know," Malone said. "You want to haunt houses. And I want to help you. And between us, we'll probably get into a lot of trouble, and I'm going to love it. Now, tell me, what made you trust Jesse Conway in the first place?"

She looked at the floor. "Malone, I had to trust somebody. It was——" She paused for a moment. "It happened so fast. I *was* angry at the time. Not because I was in love with Big Joe, I wasn't. Not because he provided for me—well, let's call it lavishly. Not because he was running around with another girl, even if she was one of my best friends. But because he would run around with another girl and not tell me. We'd always been square with each other, understand?"

"I do," Malone said. He aimed an inch of cigar ash at the ash tray and missed. "Who was the girl, or is it any of my business?"

"Milly Dale," Anna Marie said. "She's a singer. A swell kid."

Malone nodded and said in a very noncommittal voice, "I've heard of her."

"Big Joe swore he'd never been out with her in his life," Anna Marie said. Suddenly she lifted her head, and her smoky eyes grew brightly wet. "He was telling the truth. But I didn't know it then. And we got into a row. And then someone pushed open the door and shot Big Joe, and before I knew what was going on, he'd shoved the gun in my hand and was gone, and then the room was full of people, and the police came in, and——"

"Never mind," Malone said hastily. "I read all that in the papers." He wanted to put his arms around her, to comfort and soothe her, the way one would comfort and soothe a scared little child who'd not only been snatched from in front of a speeding truck but had dropped and lost an ice-cream cone in the excitement. Instead, he poured a little more gin in her glass and lit a cigarette for her. "We were talking about Jesse Conway, remember?" He glanced at her and added, "You can skip the next chapter because I can guess it. You were scared, and dazed, and sick, and you hardly knew what was going on. You were arrested and booked on suspicion of homicide, and then someone came to see you and said everything would be fixed up. Who was it?"

"Mike Brodie. Know him?"

"I do," Malone said. His mouth was grim. "Cousin of Bugs Brodie, the slot machine boss."

"He said everything would be O.K., and he'd been a good friend of Big Joe's, so I believed him. And he'd gotten me a lawyer, Jesse Conway, and I was to trust Jesse Conway and—and—" her voice broke again.

"And not worry," Malone finished for her. "And while you were two jumps from the chair, Jesse Conway was trying to hush up the confession that saved your life."

Anna Marie closed her eyes for just a moment. She was hearing Jesse Conway's voice—*"Believe me, Anna Marie—I couldn't help it——"* Don't get soft, she told herself. She looked at Malone and managed to smile brightly, almost too brightly.

"Let's get practical, Malone. I've got to find a hide-out. I've got to get in touch with Jesse Conway so he can get me whatever clothes and stuff I need from my apartment. Money, too."

"I can manage the hide-out," Malone said. He reached for the phone, called the manager of the hotel and explained that he had an important witness who had to be kept concealed for a few days, and how about that room around the corner from the freight elevator? Available? Fine. The usual procedure—all telephone calls to be switched to his, Malone's, room, and no maid service without fifteen minute notice from the switchboard. Thanks, pal.

"Sometimes," Malone told her, hanging up the phone, "I do have to hide out important witnesses. A couple of times I've had to hide out an important murderer. But this is the first time I've had to hide out an important ghost." He paused, scowled. "Suppose Jesse Conway or Garrity decide to confide in whoever was back of this business?"

"Right now," she said, "neither of them would dare. They're too scared."

Malone nodded. "That's true. You've got both of them nicely cornered. I'll get Jesse Conway for you." He picked up the phone again, called a number, and handed the phone to her.

She said, "May I speak to Mr. Conway, please. When do you expect him? Do you know where I can reach him? Thank you." She hung up.

"Let me try," Malone said. He waited a few minutes before calling again. A flat-voiced secretary at the other end of the wire informed him that Mr. Conway was out, no one knew when he would be in, no one knew where he was. Malone dug a little notebook from the drawer of the bed table and called the private line to Jesse Conway's apartment, then the desk of the apartment hotel where Jesse Conway occasionally visited. He made discreet inquiries of clerks in various Loop hotels and a number of night clubs. As a last resort, he called an intimate friend in the police department. Then he gave up.

"I have a feeling," he told Anna Marie, "that Jesse Conway has gone to Bermuda for a vacation. Or maybe South America. Or the Grand Canyon. Because he isn't in Chicago, and he hasn't been found dead."

She stared at him. "I might have expected it."

"I don't blame him," Malone said. "And don't worry. As far as clothes and anything else you need from your apartment are concerned, I had a client once who was an expert burglar, and he taught me a lot of tricks. And until you can walk right up to the counter of your bank and cash a check, as far as money is concerned"—he paused, swallowed hard, and said—"I can manage." At lease, he hoped he could manage.

"You're being damned helpful," she said, with just the right note of appreciation in her voice.

"The regular service to all my clients," Malone said. He slung his topcoat over his arm and reached for his hat. "I'll be back in a couple of hours. Don't answer the phone, and I'll hang out the 'DO NOT DISTURB' sign. And while I'm gone, you can be thinking of every bit of information that might be helpful to us."

She rose and smiled at him, her eyes warm. "Such as a list of the people who wanted to murder Big Joe?"

"No." His hands touched her shoulders, tightened there. "That would take too long," he said hoarsely. "Just make up a list of the people who wanted to murder *you*."

CHAPTER SEVEN

John J. Malone strode into the anteroom of his office in the dingy building on West Washington Street and said, "Good morning, Maggie," as blithely as though it weren't two o'clock in the afternoon. "Any calls?"

The black-haired office girl laid aside the book she'd been reading, looked at him coldly, and said, "Several." She picked up the list. "The bank called. It seems that——"

"All right, I'm overdrawn again," Malone said hastily. "I knew that."

"A Miss Fontaine from the Toujours Gai Lingerie Shop called, and that yellow chiffon negligee has arrived in the size sixteen you ordered——"

"Never mind," Malone said. "I don't want it now."

"A Mr. H. M. Wirtz called—a traffic violation case——"

Malone sighed. "Call Harry back, and tell him I'll get it fixed for him. Any more?"

"Francis Herman. His brother Mick has been picked up on another burglary rap."

"Get Fran Herman for me," Malone said, starting for the door to his private office.

Maggie looked up hopefully. "Are you going to take Mick Herman's case?"

"No," Malone said, "but I might want to borrow his tools." He swung open the door.

"Wait a minute," Maggie said. "One more. Jesse Conway has called three times."

Malone stopped, turned, and stood frozen in the doorway.

"He didn't ask you to phone back. He said he'd call again."

"If he does," Malone said, "I'm in, and don't spare the

38

horses. Or if you can locate him for me, I want to phone him back——"

She made a notation on the desk pad. "Anything else?"

"Just a minute," Malone stood, one hand on the door-knob, thinking. After all, he reminded himself, he was a businessman, and if he was going to turn over a new leaf and make a respectable fortune, this was a good time to start.

"Several things," he said. "Get hold of Herman and find out if he wants a lawyer or an alibi, and, in either case, how much he'll pay. Call Judge Seidel and fix Harry Wirtz's ticket, and send Harry a bill for twenty-five bucks. No, wait a minute, make it fifty." He paused. "Oh, yes. Call Miss Fontaine and ask her if she has that same negligee in gray chiffon, size"—and he did some quick mental calculations—"in size twelve."

Maggie sniffed and said, "Only one woman in a million looks well in gray."

"In this case," Malone said, "one in a million is an understatement."

The telephone rang before Maggie could answer. "Mr. Malone's office. Who's calling, please? Mr. Malone just went down the hall, I'll see if I can catch him for you." She looked up at Malone and mouthed, "Tom McKeown."

Malone grinned wickedly. "You caught me." He went on into his office, closing the door just as Maggie said, "One minute, Mr. McKeown."

The little lawyer slung his hat on the worn brown leather couch, dropped his topcoat on a chair, sat down at his battered desk, and leisurely lit a cigar before he picked up the receiver. "Hello, Tom. What's new?"

There were certain conversational formalities to be gone through. Nice to hear from you again. How's the family? What do you hear from Herb? Ran into a friend of yours in the LaSalle the other day. How about coming out for dinner some night? What do you say we have lunch a week from Thursday?

Through the formalities, Malone noticed delightedly, there was a strained, even anxious, note in Tom McKeown's voice.

"By the way, Malone, maybe you'd know. What's this

wild story some of the boys are telling around about something that happened in Joe the Angel's bar last night?"

Malone counted ten and said, "Story? What story? Have I missed something?"

He waited, grinning, while McKeown also counted ten. "Oh, some crazy business," McKeown said. "Someone said you were there and I thought maybe——" There was an even longer pause. "Tell me, Malone, did *you* see anything?"

"See anything?" Malone asked innocently.

"Well," McKeown said, "Harve Reed. You know how Harve is. He's half Welsh, and you know how those Welshmen are. Superstitious. Well, anyway, Harve, he thought he saw—something—in Joe the Angel's bar last night, and he talked to a few other guys, and"—Malone could hear McKeown gulping—"well, the story is all over town that Joe the Angel's bar is haunted, and you know how stories like that can spread, and how much harm they can do, and, well, Harve said you were there last night, and I just wondered——" His voice trailed off.

"Oh," Malone said. "Oh, *that*." He pictured Thomas J. McKeown gripping the receiver, waiting. "You know," he said in a thoughtful voice, "there *was* something strange. Just what did Harve claim he saw?"

"He——" Tom McKeown paused. "Malone, what did *you* see?"

"It's a funny thing," Malone said dreamily. "But—well, to be frank, Tom, I was a little high. Been to a wake. Fact is, I don't remember much. But I could swear I saw—— Oh, well, it's too silly to talk about."

"Malone, what *did* you see?"

"I saw—I mean, I thought I saw—a girl in a gray suit."

There was a long silence, and then Thomas J. McKeown said, "Imagine that. You must have been high."

"She was a darn pretty girl, too," Malone said. "Had on a cute little hat with a big pink veil. I'd like to meet her some time." He leaned back in his desk chair and propped the telephone on his chest. "It that the girl Harve was talking about?"

"I didn't say anything about a girl," McKeown said warily.

"Sorry," Malone said. "Must have misunderstood you. What did Harve see?"

"Oh, nothing," McKeown said. "You know how Harve is. I've been telling him for days he oughta go on the wagon. He passed out in Joe the Angel's bar last night, and woke up this morning with a wild story about seeing a ghost." A falsely hearty laugh came over the phone. "Poor Harve. I suppose it'll be a little green elephant next. Malone——"

"Huh?" said Malone, trying to sound as though he'd been deep in a thoughtful silence. "Oh. Oh, yeah. Well, frankly, I don't believe in ghosts, myself. Just a minute——" He leaned away from the telephone and said loudly, "I'm busy, Maggie. I don't care if it *is* the mayor's office. I'm talking on the other phone." Then, back at the mouthpiece, "Sorry I was interrupted. Don't forget, lunch a week from Thursday. Let's meet at Joe's, O.K.? My regards to the wife. Thanks for calling."

He hung up and yelled, "*Maggie!*"

She stuck her head around the corner of the door and said in a resigned voice, "My name is *not* Maggie."

"All right, Marguerite. Make a note to remind me to call Tom McKeown a week from Wednesday and break a lunch date."

"Yes, *Mr.* Malone. And Lew Altman is on the wire."

Lew Altman didn't waste any time getting to the point. "Hello, Malone? Say just what the hell *did* go on in Joe the Angel's bar last night?"

"Weren't you there?" Malone asked warily.

"No, but a pal of mine was."

"Well," Malone said, "as a matter of fact, I've been wondering myself what did go on——"

He used the mayor's-office-on-the-wire routine to get rid of Lew Altman and, a few minutes later, of Butts O'Hare. In the meantime he congratulated himself, he'd been just properly vague about the curious occurrence in Joe the Angel's City Hall Bar. He'd just finished using it on Ed Bateman and was relighting his cigar when Maggie came all the way into the office and said, "Mr. Malone, the mayor's office on the phone."

"That's very funny," Malone said, tossing the match toward the wastebasket. "But stop listening in on my telephone conversations."

She looked at him disapprovingly for a moment and said, "The mayor's office *is* on the wire."

Malone stuck his cigar in the ash tray and grabbed the phone.

It wasn't the mayor. It was Herb Shea, one of the mayor's confidential secretaries. Nice to talk to Malone again. Stinking weather lately, wasn't it. Say, did Malone know a cop named Klutchetsky?

"Him? Sure," Malone said, picking up the cigar again. "Known him all my life. Went to St. Joseph's with him, two terms. Threw him in the drainage canal once. Swell fella."

Klutchetsky had gone crazy. Maybe Malone could straighten him out. It seems that last night——

Malone listened to the end and then said gravely, "Herb, I don't want this to get around. Klutchetsky isn't crazy. I saw the same thing." He waited a minute and then said, "How did he say she looked?"

"Misty," Herb said in a small voice. "Just misty. Says he could see right through her. Says she seemed to sort of melt into the air, like cigar smoke."

"Yup," Malone said. "That's how it was. Tell me, Herb, this girl didn't have anything against Klutchetsky, did she?"

"Hell, no," Herb said. "He was kind of sweet on her, in fact. Used to take her cigarettes in jail."

"You just tell him to quit worrying," Malone said reassuringly. "She wasn't there to bother him." He certainly didn't want a good guy like Klutchetsky to go around unhappy. "Tell him to pray for her soul." No harm in that, either. Anna Marie might need a few prayers before she was through. "Better keep this quiet, Herb. You know how it is when people get to talking."

"Oh, sure, sure, sure," Herb said. There was a short pause and then, "Malone, have you any idea who—it—*was* looking for last night?"

"None at all," Malone said with what he hoped sounded like a forced and hollow laugh. "Maybe it was me."

He sat for a while, tipped perilously back in his desk chair, gazing at the ceiling. It hadn't taken long for the story to get around. Now, the trick was to produce Anna Marie, looking misty, at just the right time and place.

Maggie came in and reported.

"I got Mr. Wirtz's ticket fixed. I sent Mr. Wirtz a bill for seventy-five dollars. He'll pay at least forty of it. Fran Herman says his brother is innocent, he never was near the place, nobody saw him, and he didn't leave any fingerprints. He wants an alibi. I've already arranged with Mrs. McDonald to fix him up, and I told Herman I'd let him know the cost as soon as I found how much trouble and expense it would be to you. Miss Fontaine does have that negligee in gray, size twelve. Do you want rose, blue, or green ribbon ties, and do you want it wrapped as a gift?"

"Green," Malone said, "and just tell her I'll wear it home. Maggie, you're wonderful."

"You mean invaluable," she said icily, "and my name is not Maggie. I've not been able to reach Jesse Conway, and Mr. Justus is waiting in the office."

"You're fired," Malone said cheerfully. He bellowed, *"Jake!"*

The tall, red-haired man came in slowly, almost wearily, and closed the door. He said, "Hello, Malone," in a dull voice, and sat down heavily on the couch. He fumbled for a cigarette.

Malone looked at him thoughtfully. He'd known Jake for a long time. In fact, since quite a while before Jake had met Helene. He'd seen Jake through a number of things, ranging from murder to matrimony. He was going to have to see Jake through something now, he sensed, and he crossed his fingers that it wouldn't be anything serious this time. "Something on your mind?" he said calmly.

"Damned right," Jake said. He lit the cigarette, took one puff, and put it out again. "Malone, I'm—look, I couldn't tell Helene anything about it because she wouldn't ever agree with my handling it that way, and I know now she'd have been right, but it's too late. And nobody hates the protection racket worse than I do, but you know how it is, once in a while a guy gets in a spot where he can't fight, at least I didn't dare take the chance, because I want Helene to have everything she wants in the world, but believe me, Malone, I would have fought it even if I'd lost the Casino and everything else if I'd known the girl was going to die. Understand?"

43

"Perfectly," Malone said.

"Malone," Jake said. "Believe me. I'm haunted."

Malone jumped in spite of himself. He stared at Jake. The ex-reporter's face was pale and haggard, his naturally unruly red hair was mussed more than usual, his eyes were tired and red-rimmed.

"That's no haunt," Malone said with forced cheerfulness, "that's a hangover. What you need is a drink."

He rose and started searching his office. There should be a half-full bottle of gin somewhere in the file drawer marked "Unanswered Correspondence." Before he could locate it, Maggie came in quietly, a paper in her hand.

"Here's those figures you wanted, Mr. Malone."

Malone looked. The scribbled note read: "Mrs. Justus phoned she's on her way here and if Mr. Justus should call you not to let him know."

The little lawyer nodded. "Those look all right to me. Let me check them over to make sure." He dug through his pockets, found a chewed pencil stub, and wrote hastily, leaning on the filing case. "Stall her in the anteroom until he's out of here." He handed her the paper and said, "Yes, those are right," smiled at Jake and said, "just some important investment of mine," and went on searching for the gin. Finally he located it in a file marked "Contracts," rinsed out a couple of glasses, and poured two drinks.

Jake took his, held it between his hands, stared at it.

"Are you going to drink that," Malone said crossly, "or pretend you're a crystal gazer?"

Jake put the drink, untasted, on the table by his chair. He took out another cigarette. After wasting half a dozen matches that shivered out in his shaking hands, he threw it away.

"You see, Malone," he said hoarsely, "I knew all the time who killed him."

CHAPTER EIGHT

Helene dressed slowly, and with special care. She always did when there was something on her mind. Somehow an extra job of make-up and hair-do seemed to help her think.

She glanced through the window at the heavy, late autumn fog. One of those combinations of dampness, dreary darkness, and unseasonable, almost oppressive, warmth that sometimes struck Chicago at this time of year. It might rain, and it might not. She decided on the tan suede coat with the wide belt and long, slightly flaring coat. The high-heeled calfskin oxfords with the matching gloves and purse. The broad-brimmed tan suede hat that went with the coat.

No, the combination was much too drab. She studied it for a moment. Then she knotted a flaming scarlet scarf around her throat, tucking the ends behind the lapels of her coat, and changed the purse and gloves for a pair that matched the scarf. She brightened her lipstick a trifle. There. Much better.

Damn Jake. When anything worried him and he decided to keep it a secret, you might as well try to get clam juice out of a turnip, as Malone would say.

After that one admission—if she could call it that—last night, he'd shut up and refused to say another word. She'd coaxed. She'd reasoned. She plied him with champagne and then with scotch. She'd even tried that old gag of pretending she knew all about it anyway and only wanted to discuss certain aspects with him. Nothing worked.

At last she rose and surveyed herself appraisingly in the full-length mirror. The effect was wholly pleasing, marred only by the slight frown between her eyebrows.

"I am not," she told herself firmly, "the kind of wife who pries into her husband's personal and business affairs." Except, of course, on an occasion like this. Whatever Jake was brooding over was obviously serious, and it was up to her to find out what it was.

Something to do with that girl, Anna Marie. Helene stood thinking for a moment, tapping a cigarette against her thumbnail. Something that had been going on for a long time, and growing in intensity. Since—suddenly she frowned, remembering when Jake had first begun acting strangely, pretending not to be worried and going off on unexplained errands. That had been *before* Big Joe Childers had been murdered.

Was Jake mixed up, somehow, in Big Joe's murder? No. In that case, he'd have gone straight to Malone. Or would he? There was no predicting what Jake might or might not do. That, she reminded herself, was one more reason why she adored him.

On a sudden impulse she called Malone's office, looking at her watch as she reached for the receiver. After two o'clock. The little lawyer ought to be in now.

Mr. Malone was on the other wire. Would Mrs. Justus care to wait?

"No, thanks," Helene said. "Just tell him I'm on my way down."

She went down the corridor and into the elevator, deep in thought. The operator remarked that it sure was a terrible day outside, and Helene absent-mindedly agreed with him, yes, it was warm for this time of year.

Jake's anxiety had begun before Big Joe Childers' death, but it had something to do with Anna Marie St. Clair. Therefore, the murder was the starting point for thought.

She paused at the desk long enough to ask if Mr. Justus had left a message as to where he was going and when he'd be back. Mr. Justus had not. Thank you, Ed. She went on out to the street and walked through the fog to where she'd parked the gray convertible the night before.

What was the name of that saloon where Big Joe Childers had been killed?

She sat for a moment behind the wheel, trying to remember. Happy something. She'd noticed that at the time of the murder, and had reflected that it hadn't been a happy place for Big Joe. She'd noticed something else, too, at the time. She'd been reading the newspaper and looking at the pictures, and some one thing had struck her as proof that Anna Marie hadn't shot Big Joe. Jake had shut her up and changed the subject quick. She'd become too concerned over the way Jake had spoken to think any more about the murder, and since then she'd never been able to remember what it was.

That wasn't important now, anyway, except as something to puzzle over in the long winter nights. Even if she could remember, it wouldn't help Anna Marie now.

She drove down to Division Street and turned into Clark, moving slowly through the fog. Happy Hour? No, that wasn't it. She passed Bughouse Square, crossed Chicago Avenue. Clark Street was drearier than usual in the smoke-laden fog; pawnshops, cheap clothing stores, tawdry night spots, saloons.

There it was. *The Happy Days*. Silly of her to have forgotten.

She parked the convertible around the corner on Ontario Street.

What on earth was she going to say or do when she got inside? March up to one of the waiters and say, "Look here, how is my husband mixed up in Joe Childers' murder?" What the devil did she expect to see or find?

Helene shivered in the damp air. A flashily dressed man looked at her hopefully. She pushed open the door to The Happy Days and told herself firmly one thing she expected to find was a drink.

The Happy Days didn't pretend to be anything but a cheap joint. A bar along one side of the big room. Brown-painted booths on the other. A few tables scattered in between. Pinkish lights. A juke box. A door at the end of the room leading to the "Private Dining Rooms," the office, and the toilets. A sign over the bar reading, "Whisky, 30¢ a drink. Double 50¢." And, at this hour of the afternoon, very few customers. A bored-looking bartender sat reading the *Racing Form*.

Just an ordinary North Clark Street joint. But Helene shivered again, this time it wasn't from the fog. Nor even from the fact that Big Joe Childers had been murdered in one of those back rooms. Just something—she couldn't tell what it was—indescribably sinister about this place.

She slid onto one of the bar stools, said, "Hello," in her brightest voice, and gave the bartender her best smile.

He looked at her coldly and said, "Yeah?"

"A double rye. Isn't it a horrid day?"

"Yeah." He poured the rye, collected fifty cents, and proceeded to ignore her.

"Tell me, didn't you used to be at Brownie's, on Division Street?"

He shook his head.

Helene smothered a sigh. She was justly famous for her way with bartenders, but she certainly wasn't getting anywhere with this one.

"That's funny. I could have sworn I saw you there. Weren't you there about a year ago?"

He didn't rise to the bait and say, "No, I was here a year ago." He simply shook his head again.

Helene sipped the rye. It wasn't as bad as she had expected. "It must have been somewhere else then. Where were you about a year ago?"

This time he looked up long enough to say, "Why?"

"Just curiosity," Helene said. She could feel her cheeks reddening. For a while she sat in silence, looking at the reflection of the dingy room in the bar mirror.

At the far end of the bar was a morose young man drinking gin rickeys. One of the tables was occupied by a plump man with a newspaper and a bottle of beer. A couple were in one of the booths: a man with sleek, dark hair, a sallow face, and expensive clothes; a smallish woman in a black Persian lamb coat and a tiny black hat with bright green feathers. The woman's face was hidden, but there was something vaguely familiar about the set of her shoulders and the way she carried her head. Helene puzzled over it for a moment and then dismissed the thought. It wasn't likely anyone she knew would be in The Happy Days.

There was a thick-set, red-faced man lounging in a chair near the rear door. He, too, seemed curiously familiar. Helene regarded him for a while in the mirror. Stiff yellow hair, little blue eyes, a blotchy nose. Then she remembered. He had been an important witness at the trial of Anna Marie St. Clair. Helene felt a little flutter of excitement.

The rye was about half gone when she had a sudden inspiration. She looked at her wrist watch, shook it, and called out to the bartender. "Please, I'm afraid my watch has stopped. Do you know what time it is?"

He looked at a clock back of the bar and said, "Ten after three."

"Oh, *dear!*"

The tone she put into it did make him look at her.

"Please—I was supposed to meet my husband here at two o'clock—I didn't know my watch had stopped and I'm afraid I was late—do you know if he's been in—and gone?"

"Don't know your husband," the bartender said.

"Oh, but you must. He's tall and he's got red hair and freckles. His name is"—she hesitated only a fraction of a second—"Jake Justus."

The bartender laid down his paper and looked at her silently for a long time. It was a look that Helene didn't like. "Don't know him." There was another silence. "Maybe Jack knows him." He rose, waddled out from behind the bar to confer in whispers with the red-faced man. He came back and said, "Jack don't know him, either."

"Well, thank you," Helene said.

She saw the red-faced man start down the corridor towards the back rooms. The room seemed very still, and everyone in it was looking at her. The bartender. The plump man with the beer. The morose young man with the gin rickeys. The couple in the booth.

If she were to walk across the room and out through the door, would anyone stop her? She wasn't sure. She finished the rye, and it warmed her a little.

Then she saw the face of the woman in the booth. Joe Childers' widow.

Her hunch had been right. For a moment she forgot about being afraid. Somehow, Jake was tied up with the murder of Big Joe Childers. Obviously, his name was known here. Mentioning the name of a perfect stranger wouldn't cause all this commotion.

The man named Jack came back and resumed his lounging. The couple went on with their conversation. The bartender turned to page three of the *Racing Form*. Everything seemed back to normal, then a man walked out from the back rooms, a man Helene recognized on sight. Bill McKeown.

She'd had him pointed out to her a dozen times or more, the big, burly man who was so unexpectedly suave in dress and manner. He'd tried to buy the Casino once, and Jake had turned him down. He owned a lot of places, but she hadn't imagined that The Happy Days might be one of them.

When he came over to her side, she pretended, successfully, not to recognize him.

"Were you looking for somebody?"

Helene's eyes could be wide, innocent pools. They were now, as she repeated the story she'd told the bartender.

"Justus?" He shook his handsome head. "Don't know anyone of that name here."

"That's funny," Helene said in an anxious, almost childlike voice, "I thought he came here all the time."

"Sorry," Bill McKeown said. "You must be in the wrong place." His tone and his manner were friendly, but a glint in his eyes said, "You *are* in the wrong place, and you'd better get out right now."

"Oh," Helene said. "I'm sorry I troubled you."

"No trouble at all," Bill McKeown said. He paused for just a moment at the door and said several words, with a gesture to Jack. The gesture, which Helene caught in the mirror of her compact, indicated that Helene was harmless.

Helene waited until the bartender had served another gin rickey to the morose young man and a pair of bourbon highballs to the couple in the booth. Then she turned on her best smile.

"I think I'll wait a few minutes longer, just in case. Will you give me another double rye while I wait, please. And I believe I'll sit over in a booth."

No one was paying much attention to her now. She walked across the room and slid into the booth behind Mrs. Childers in time to hear a fragment of conversation.

"You've got to listen to reason." That was Mrs. Childers.

"Four murders." That was the man.

"Four?"

"The girl was murdered, too. It's a kind of murder."

The bartender paused for a moment on his way to Helene's booth, and the conversation ended as though it had been on a radio suddenly clicked off. Helene said, "Thank you," very sweetly as she paid the bartender, her heart wishing him all the bad luck in the world. A moment later the couple got up and left.

Four murders. She knew of only two. Big Joe, and Anna Marie—because the man with Mrs. Childers had been right, that *had* been a kind of murder. Wait—there was Ike Malloy. But who had been the fourth victim?

Was Jake all right?

She lit a cigarette. Of course Jake was all right. Jake could take care of himself. He was in trouble, but he hadn't been murdered, and she knew that by the same intuition by which she knew he was in trouble.

The door to the corridor was ajar. From where she sat, she could see most of it, including doors to some of the private rooms. The newspaper account of how Ike Malloy had come in and out was pretty complete, but she wanted to see for herself. Well, that was easy to manage.

Helene finished her drink, picked up her purse, walked over to the red-faced man, and said, "Where is the——?"

He jerked his head toward the corridor and said, "Third door on your right."

There were two "Private Dining Rooms" on the right and one on the left. Helene peered in as she went by. This, the first on the right, was the one from which the "reliable witnesses" had heard the quarrel and the sound of the shot. The one on the left had been unoccupied when Big Joe was killed. It contained a round table, a sideboard, a number of chairs, and a green-shaded light. It looked well used, too. Helene wondered where all the poker players had been on the night of Big Joe's murder.

The room where Big Joe had been killed was small, soiled, and sordid. A table, a couple of chairs, a wicker floor lamp, a few ash trays, a lumpy couch with a faded cover, and a few gaudy pictures on the walls. Helene was satisfied with one quick glance.

It wasn't the first time she'd seen a room where someone

had been killed. But there was something about this one that made her shudder. Big Joe had been a rich man, a lavish spender. He owned a five-acre estate in Highland Park, and when he came to the Casino he always acted as though he were slumming. And Anna Marie had been a girl who would have insisted on the best of everything.

Why had they picked this tawdry room, in the rear of a cheap saloon, as a meeting place?

Or had it been picked for them—without their knowledge? Who had picked it, and why?

It had been damned bad stage setting on somebody's part. That fact alone fairly yelled of a frame-up. What *had* been the matter with Anna Marie's lawyer?

There was a murmur of voices at the end of the corridor. Helene went on a few steps. There were two more doors on the right, marked with enameled signs. *Ladies. Gentlemen.* The door on the left was marked *Office*, and it was just slightly ajar. That was where the voices were coming from.

"—and I don't care if the song was specially written for you, you aren't to sing it again, anywhere, understand?" That was Bill McKeown's voice. A pause, and he went on, "I'm only trying to save *you* from a lot of trouble. See?"

A feminine voice called Bill McKeown an objectionable name.

"Don't you lose your temper with me," Bill McKeown said.

There was a silence. On a sudden impulse Helene pushed open the door marked *Office*. Bill McKeown sat behind a grimy golden-oak desk. The angry and sulky girl who was slumped in the one armchair was Milly Dale. She didn't look up.

Helene muttered. "Sorry. I was looking for the——"

"Across the hall," Bill McKeown snapped.

She said, "Thank you," turned and entered the room labeled *Ladies*, and bolted the door. Suddenly she was scared, more scared than she had ever been in her life. Everything seemed to be tying up together. The murders, and everything else, certainly had something to do with The Happy Days. And here she was barricaded in the ladies' room of The Happy Days, after having been entirely too nosy for her own good.

She heard the corridor door close. There was a firm, deliberate sound to the closing. The face that looked back at her from the mirror was pale.

It could still be her imagination, she told herself. Perhaps the door was customarily kept closed. Or it had blown shut. Perhaps no one was noticing her.

There was one way to find out. She added a touch more lipstick, tilted the broad-brimmed hat to an even more gay angle. Then she went back into the corridor.

The door to her right, leading to the alley, was padlocked and bolted. It had been, she remembered, the night Big Joe Childers died. A waiter working for The Happy Days had opened it and let in Ike Malloy, while a car waited in the alley. But no waiter was going to open it for her right now.

She noticed that the door to the office was wide open, and the office was empty.

Helene squared her shoulders, marched down the corridor, and tried the door. It opened. She walked through the bar and out to the sidewalk. No one stopped her. No one noticed her. A minute later she was in the convertible, lighting a cigarette.

There had been something strange about that room when she passed through on her way out. A different bartender looked bored behind the bar; the man named Jack had been replaced by a thin boy with a pallid face; the two customers had disappeared, and several others had come in. True, bartenders and bouncers did go off duty, and customers did come and go, but it had been a very quick and complete change for so short a time.

She started the convertible and headed for Michigan Avenue. At the same moment a black sedan slid away from the curb. Not until she'd reached State Street did she wonder if it was following her. A few experimental turns—Ohio, to Rush, to Huron, over to Wabash, back on Erie toward Michigan. The black sedan stayed discreetly half a block behind.

Helene's lovely mouth set in a firm line. She slammed on the brakes, and the black sedan slid up almost bumper to bumper. She couldn't recognize the man at the wheel from what she saw in her rearview mirror, but there was no mistaking that hat with the bright green feathers.

Losing the black sedan would be easy. She'd once lost the police department of the city of Chicago by the simple expedient of taking the lower level of the Michigan Avenue bridge.* But Helene had a better idea. She drove at a leisurely pace down the Avenue, turned into the Loop, and stopped at Marshall Field's, where an attendant took her car for parking.

The great store was already a blaze of light and color with Christmas decorations. Helene stood behind an ornamental Christmas tree and waited. A few seconds later the Widow Childers came in, and after that it was only a matter of playing hide-and-seek, or squirrel-around-the-tree.

She was able to get a good look at Joe Childers' widow. A pretty, early middle-aged, perfectly groomed woman who, right now, looked irritated and vexed.

It wasn't long before Eva Childers gave up and went out into Washington Street. This time, it was Helene who followed. The sidewalks were crowded, but the bright green feathers were like a beacon. Across State Street, straight on west past Dearborn and Clark. The building Eva Childers entered was a dingy one, with a soiled tile floor and one rickety wire-cage elevator.

Helene waited until the elevator came down again. "Hello, Bill," she said to the shabby old operator.

He grinned at her. "Hi, Mrs. Justus. Going up?"

"Maybe, maybe not. What floor did that woman go to—the one who just came in?"

"Eleven, Mrs. Justus."

Helene said, "Thanks. I guess I will go up."

There were, she knew, three offices on floor eleven—two vacant and one occupied. The occupied one belonged to John J. Malone.

*The Corpse Steps Out.

CHAPTER NINE

"The protection racket is a stinking one," Malone said through a cloud of cigar smoke. "It's making a guy pay for something he never gets. It's blackmail when you haven't done anything to be blackmailed for." He paused and scowled sternly at Jake. "But, of course, when guys are dumb enough to fall for it——"

Jake said, "All right, I'm dumb. But I thought *you* were smart. My mistake."

"You can take your choice," Malone growled. "Keep your temper, or give me back that drink. When the muscle boys came around, why didn't you tell them, in a delicate manner, exactly what they could do with their protection?"

"Because," Jake said, "that's just what they wanted me to do."

There was a brief silence. Malone rose, strolled over to the window, gazed for a moment across the Loop roof tops. He relit his cigar and said, "Yes?"

"The Casino makes a lot of money," Jake said. "It could make a lot more if I wanted to run it a little differently, but I don't. To some people, it could be a gold mine. To me, it's just a little tiny gold mine, but it's the only gold mine I've got. And if anything happened to it, I'd be just another press agent out of a job."

Malone nodded. "Of course," he said, "if it burned down, or blew up, or was robbed, or someone threw bricks through the windows, you do have insurance."

"Sure," Jake said. He grinned wryly. "Only that isn't the angle. Nothing quite that crude."

"Begin at the beginning," Malone said. "It's customary."

"It began with a telephone call," Jake said. "Salesman for

a protection agency. You know the routine. One grand a month, and nobody will drop stink bombs down your chimney. I told him to go to hell. Two days later a couple of guys came to call. They"—again he grinned wryly—"quote, urged me to reconsider my decision, unquote. I kicked them out. Then one of the bartenders—George, you know him, the fat guy with the bushy eyebrows—was caught selling liquor to a minor."

Malone pursed his lips, laid down his cigar, and sat up straight. "Why didn't you call me?"

"Turned out I didn't need to," Jake said. "George swore he didn't know the kid was under twenty-one, and I still believe him. I paid the fine and thought I'd be stuck with a threat of having the license revoked. But the whole thing was settled, slick as a whistle. Then comes another call, telling me that was just a warning. The price had gone up to two grand a month. I lost my temper and said a bad word over the phone. Two days later one of my waiters was picked up for selling reefers in the Casino."

He paused, lit a new cigarette, and said, "That time, I damn near did call you. Because I'd never hired that waiter. He was a plant."

"I'd guessed that," Malone said. "Only you couldn't have proved it in court. In a pinch you couldn't have proved that you didn't know all about it."

"And——" Jake began.

"Shut up," the little lawyer said crossly. "I can tell the rest of it. If you hadn't paid protection money, there would be more arrests. Finally, an injunction closing the Casino, and you thrown in the jug. After that, you'd be approached—sell the Casino for a small sum, the injunction would be lifted, and you'd be sprung from the can. After which, you'd go back to being a press agent, and someone would own a gold mine."

Jake crushed out his cigarette and said, "How the hell do you know all this?"

"Because," Malone said, "the Casino isn't the only night club in Chicago, and you aren't my only client. And this isn't the first time this racket has been worked. It's a damn slick trick, I wish I'd thought of it myself. Somebody owns a lot of saloons by now, and has a tidy sum of money tucked away. How much did *you* pay, and who to, and where?"

A dull red color crept into Jake's cheeks. "Damn it, Malone. What else could I do?"

"Nothing," the lawyer told him, "and answer my question."

"Two grand a month," Jake said. "I've had to go into debt. I paid off to a guy named Ambersley, who met me at The Happy Days bar. A white-haired guy with a broken-down face. Looked familiar to me, but I never could figure where I'd met him."

"The Happy Days bar," Malone said thoughtfully, "is where Big Joe Childers was killed."

"And I was there," Jake said. "I was sitting in a booth, waiting for Ambersley. I saw the man in the corridor—I know now it was Ike Malloy. I heard the shot. I—— *Malone!*" He ran his lean brown fingers through his unruly red hair.

"Never mind," Malone said. "I'd have done the same thing myself." He poured a little more gin in Jake's glass. "In your place, I'd have ducked out quick before the cops broke in, because you couldn't be caught in a joint like The Happy Days on a pay-off trip. What's more, I'd probably have kept my mouth shut afterward. So stop worrying."

"I'm not worrying," Jake said. "Only you see, afterward Ambersley talked to me. He said the whole thing was fixed up, and I didn't need to worry. After that girl was convicted, I was warned to go on keeping my mouth shut. I had to. Because, you see, there's Helene——"

"Yes, yes, yes, I know," Malone said quickly. "Helene, and the Casino, and all the rest of it. You don't need to go on. You don't even need to tell me that if you hadn't believed, right up to the last, that Anna Marie St. Clair would be saved, you'd have told your story, warnings or no warnings."

Jake looked at the floor and said, "Well you see—well, yes, that's it. But then at the last—when it began to look as though the girl was really headed for the chair—I couldn't stand it, Casino or no Casino. Something had to be done."

"You could have gone to the police," Malone said quietly.

"Would you mind letting me tell this in my own way?" Jake said. "I went to The Happy Days saloon and sat there in a booth nursing a beer and hoping someone would come and contact me. Eventually, Ambersley showed up. Maybe he just dropped by, or maybe someone there sent for him to come and talk to me. Anyway, he told me two things. One, that Anna Marie St. Clair was scheduled for a reprieve and a new trial. Two, that if I didn't keep my mouth shut in the meantime I was just as likely as not to be a widower."

"They threatened Helene," Malone said, chewing on his cigar, "and you fell for it."

"They did, and I did," Jake said grimly. "Those guys don't play."

Malone said, "Neither does Helene. God help them if they ever mix up with her."

"Yesterday," Jake said in a low voice, "I went to the D.A.'s office. They laughed at me. They called me a liar. And when they asked me how I happened to be on the scene and why I hadn't come forward before, I couldn't tell them. Because"—he paused, gulped—"if anything ever happened to Helene——"

Malone said, "Never mind. And you're still paying off."

"At this rate," Jake said, "I'll be broke in six months. But that isn't the reason. After last night—" he paused, gulped. "That girl was murdered. I'd like to lay hands on her murderer. I'd like to know who's running this racket. I thought it was Big Joe Childers, but he's dead, and I'm still paying."

"Are you suggesting," Malone said, "that you'd like to engage my services?"

"Look, Malone—" Jake began.

"I hate to bust up a good racket," Malone said, "because for all I know, I may be getting income from it, through one source or another. But since it's you," he added coyly, "my services can be had, for a small sum, of course."

"Helene mustn't know about it," Jake said. "She's got to be kept out of it."

"Naturally," Malone said. "Or else she'll do the job herself and I'll lose a fee. Now tell me about this guy Ambersley——"

The door opened. Maggie said helplessly, "Mr. Malone——" A small woman in black, with a green-feathered hat, marched imperiously into the room. She nodded to Maggie, said, "Thank you, my dear." Then, to Malone, "I'm sure you don't mind my coming right in. It's really quite urgent that I see you, immediately." She gave Jake a glance indicating that he was as welcome as a stepchild with scarlet fever.

Malone rose. "Glad to see you, Mrs. Childers. You know Mr. Justus?"

She raked him over with a glance and said, "Delighted."

"Delighted to meet *you*," Jake said. "Have a drink?" He absent-mindedly held out his own glass.

"Thank you," she said. "I don't drink."

"Suit yourself," Jake said. "Do you smoke, swear, spit, or what *do* you do?"

Eva Childers looked away and said, "Mr. Malone——"

The little lawyer cleared his throat. "If you don't mind, Jake——"

There was a slight commotion behind the door, and it opened again. Maggie said in a despairing voice, "Mr. Malone, I simply couldn't——" Malone said wearily, "You're fired," as Helene walked leisurely into the room, peeling off her gloves.

She stood there, a tall, lovely, slender figure. For a moment Malone forgot all his problems and gazed at her. He observed that there was a faint pink in her cheeks and that she was slightly out of breath. He braced himself for trouble.

Helene said, "Jake darling, I'm so sorry I was late. I waited in that bar for an hour. It's my fault, my watch had stopped."

Jake opened his mouth to say, "Huh," caught a signaling wink from her, and shut it again.

"Mrs. Childers!" Helene beamed. "How *nice* to see you again! We met at Mrs. McClane's garden party, remember?"

"Oh, yes. Yes, of course," Eva Childers said. She certainly did remember that garden party. It had taken a lot of doing to wangle an invitation to it. Her dark eyes narrowed. Maybe she'd been mistaken in her suspicions of Helene. After all, she'd been Helene Brand, heiress, only daughter of one of *the* families. Eva Childers concentrated on looking friendly, charming, and, of course, ladylike.

"I've wanted *so* many times to call you," Helene gushed

on, "but I'd lost your phone number. Wasn't that silly of me? I'd simply *adore* to have lunch with you someday soon."

"That would be——"

Before Eva Childers could think of a synonym for "wonderful" Helene had gone on. "How about tomorrow noon? One o'clock? Pierre's? Oh, grand. I'm *so* glad I ran into you here. Is Mr. Malone your lawyer, too?"

"Well—" Eva Childers began.

"Aren't you *lucky!* He's simply *marvelous!* Oh Mrs. Childers, I'm *insane* about your hat! You must have had it made specially for you. It's the most becoming thing——"

Malone said, "If you please——"

"Oh, I'm *so* sorry," Helene gasped. "I'm keeping you from talking business. Jake, angel, *did* Mr. Malone settle that point about Uncle Arthur's will?"

Jake swallowed hard and said grimly, "Yes, dear. We can't break it. The Associated Dog and Cat Clinic get every penny of it."

"What a shame," Eva Childers said sympathetically.

"*Mrs. Justus,*" Malone said. He was fighting off a conviction that in thirty more seconds he was going to lose his mind.

"I *do* wish we could all dash out for a drink or something," Helene said, oblivious of interruptions, "but Jake and I are simply hours and *hours* late—remember, darling, Lady Leiber's tea——"

"Oh, yes," Jake said. He drank the last drop of gin in his glass. "Mustn't disappoint Lady Leiber."

"By all means, don't," Malone said. "And I'm sorry I couldn't have been more helpful about Uncle Arthur's will."

"Don't forget, Mrs. Childers," Helene cooed, at the door. "One o'clock, at Pierre's."

Jake resisted an impulse to bang the door shut. He grabbed Helene's arm. "What's the idea, or do you know?"

"Sssh! I want to hear what she has to say to Malone, and so do you." Helene punched the elevator button. "That's just so she'll think we did go downstairs. In case she's listening, and she will be, she'll hear the elevator come up and go down." She led the way down the hall. "Malone can't afford a dictograph, so the office next to him is vacant, in case he wants Maggie to take down a conversation unobserved." She opened the door.

"How did you know it was unlocked," Jake whispered, "and how did you know you could hear——"

"Because," she whispered back, "I caught the tag end of your conversation with Malone. Just what is it I've got to be kept out of? Whatever it is, I'm in it already. And," she added sternly, "I think you were very, very rude to poor Mrs. Childers."

CHAPTER TEN

Eva Childers sat straight up in the big chair. Her tiny feet just touched the floor. She accepted a cigarette from Malone like a little girl accepting a lollipop from a stranger, and held it delicately between her fingers as though, Malone thought, she was about to pick up a hammer and drive it into the wall. She glanced toward the door Helene had closed behind her and said, "Lovely girl, isn't she?"

"Very lovely," Malone said, striking a match for her. His sharp ears had caught the faint sound of a door closing, and he had a good idea who was in the "listening office." He cleared his throat and said loudly, "Lovely, but quite crazy, unfortunately. Too bad. Beautiful girl, if you like that washed-out blond type. Should have been committed years ago. But you know how it is. Influence. Sad, sad affair. Just between us, and I know you won't tell a soul, she's a pyromaniac."

"What a shame!" Mrs. Childers clucked sympathetically. "She has such pretty white teeth, too. I suppose she'll have to have them all pulled. And her husband?"

"Oh, he's just a petty crook," Malone said, raising his voice a little. "Nice guy, in his way, but just a good-for-nothing drunk, gambler, and woman chaser. Runs a high-class saloon for a living. Believe me, if his wife knew one-half of what I know about him!"

That ought to hold Jake and Helene for a while, he told himself. He concentrated his attention on Mrs. Childers. If she was consulting him as client, there might be a fat fee. And he'd seen a bracelet Anna Marie would love to have.

"Now, my dear Mrs. Childers. What's troubling you?" Even if there wasn't a fee, he was interested in what Eva Childers had to say.

"My conscience," Eva Childers said. "I feel as if I'd murdered that girl."

Malone let that hang in the air for a moment. Then he looked sympathetic and said, "Come, come."

"I told the truth," she said simply. "I thought it was right at the time. And it was so kind of the lawyers not to ask me to testify. I just had to testify at the inquest, and, of course, he *had* been—what's the word—*keeping* her." She reached for a lace-edged handkerchief.

"There, there," Malone said, in what his friends, enemies, and grateful clients described as his best cell-side manner.

"It was a great mistake," she murmured, "my marrying Mr. Childers. I was too young to realize what he was like. He had what seemed a great deal of money, and his attention flattered me, and—oh, you know how it is——"

"Indeed I do," Malone said. "Your poor, poor little girl."

Eva Childers managed a faint, tremulous smile. "He was always very kind to me. He gave me everything I wanted. He left me a—a—well, a fortune, Mr. Malone. But—oh, the ways he made his money—and—these other women——" She bowed her head in the lacy handkerchief.

Malone sighed, rose, walked around his desk and patted her thin, delicate shoulder. "You've had a bad, bad time, my dear, brave little woman. But you must put it all out of your mind. You must remember, you have a long, happy life ahead of you."

"Oh, Mr. Malone," she breathed, "you're so understanding!"

He patted her on the other shoulder and said, "Now, what can I do to help you?"

"That girl," she said. "I do feel so guilty. I want to *do*

something. Not that I could bring her back. But—she must have a family somewhere. A father and mother, maybe, brothers and sisters. I'd like to find them. I'd like to provide for them. Not that I even dream mere money will make it up to them. But—that's the only thing I can do. Oh, Mr. Malone——"

She clasped her hands and gazed up at him with tragic eyes. "If you'd only just drop everything you're doing and devote yourself to finding her family! I'd pay you anything—*anything!*"

The little lawyer pulled a fresh cigar from his pocket, lit it, and began pacing up and down the room. He wondered how large a bill he could send for *anything*. He felt a slight stiffening along his spine and a prickling of the nerves. Something was going on here, something more than finding Anna Marie's bereaved family. "Drop everything . . . devote yourself . . ." He began speculating about what he might be doing that Eva Childers wanted him to drop. Would, indeed, pay him *anything* to drop.

"My dear Mrs. Childers," he said suavely. "Tell me. Why haven't you gone to the young woman's lawyer—Jesse Conway, I believe his name is. He might be able to give you the information without having to—conduct an expensive investigation." He got that "expensive" in loud.

She looked hurt and said, "Naturally, I thought of that. But Mr. Conway has gone on a vacation. There doesn't seem to be any way of reaching him."

"Oh, he's gone on a vacation, eh?" Malone said. "H'm. Well, in that case——"

"Of course—you'll want a retainer——" She began digging through her black moleskin purse. "I brought a thousand dollars. If that would be enough——"

"I'll have to think about it," Malone said. He sat down behind his desk again.

He owed a month's office rent, and he owed Maggie two weeks' salary. He was overdrawn at the bank again. And he'd promised to provide Anna Marie with whatever money she needed, to say nothing of a few comforts and luxuries he'd thought of himself. There was exactly eleven dollars and fifty-five cents on his person, and heaven only knew when any more would come in. He looked thoughtfully at Eva Childers for about fifteen seconds.

"A retainer won't be necessary in a case like this," he said smoothly. "If I succeed in finding the girl's family, and arranging things the way you want them, I'll send you a bill. I'd much rather do it that way."

"Oh, but please," she said. She laid ten one-hundred-dollar bills on his desk.

"Please, no," Malone said. His fingers ached as he pushed them away.

"If it isn't enough," Eva Childers said, "I could make it *much* more." She opened the purse again.

"No, no, no, no," Malone said. He added, *"No!"*

They argued about it delicately for a moment or so. Then she slid the bills back in her purse with a regretful gesture and rose.

"Believe me," Malone said, holding her hand, "I'll drop everything and devote myself—heart and soul—to this little problem of yours."

He had, he reflected later, never spoken a truer word.

After she'd gone he sat for a few minutes, his forehead resting on his fists. Even after paying Maggie's back salary, and a few other important debts, and a slight installment on the rent, he'd be able to provide for Anna Marie out of what was left from a thousand dollars. He'd promised her that he'd "manage." His head sagged into his hands. He began humming absent-mindedly, "I wish I had never known sunshine—I wish I had never known rain——"

Maggie came in and said, "Did you want something, Mr. Malone?"

"I want a lot of things," Malone said, "and right now one of them is to be left alone."

"Mrs. Childers left this with me," Maggie said. "Your retainer. She said to call her if you required more." She laid the ten one-hundred-dollar bills on his desk.

Malone sat up and stared at them. He imagined them changed into fifties, twenties, tens, fives, and slot machine money. He thought about all the things they could buy. He thought about Maggie's salary, and the rent, and Anna Marie. And that small bill at Joe the Angel's bar.

He looked up at Maggie. "Mrs. Childers left that here by mistake," he said. "Put that money in an envelope and mail it to her. Registered mail, return receipt requested."

"But Mr. Malone—" Maggie began unhappily.

"That isn't a retainer," Malone said. "That's a bribe."

Maggie sniffed, said, "It wouldn't be the first time," and picked up the money.

"Maggie," Malone said in his sternest voice, "there are bribes *and* bribes."

"That gray chiffon negligee," Maggie said, "is going to cost you seventy-five bucks. Plus sales tax."

Malone winced, but he looked her right in the eye. "Honesty is the best policy," he said. "Or at least I've always heard it spoken of very highly. Also, there's such a thing as my duty to my client, and I don't believe in being bribed into neglecting it."

"Who *is* your client?" she demanded.

"You'd be surprised," Malone said, grinning. He reached for his hat. "If anyone wants me, I'll be at the crap game in back of Joe the Angel's."

"I thought you'd given up gambling," Maggie said, following him to the door.

"I did," Malone told her. "But I've got to pay the rent and your salary somehow." And a few other things, he reminded himself.

There was one chance in a thousand he'd be able to slip down the hall, take the stairs to the floor below, and ring for the elevator without encountering Jake and Helene. And he missed it. They pounced on him the moment he'd closed the office door.

"Malone," Helene said happily, "Jake has told me everything."

"Yeah," Jake said. He caught Malone's eye over Helene's shoulder. "I told her all about how I was trying to bust an extortion ring and had to keep under cover, and how now I'm still trying to bust it and at the same time find out who hired Joe Childers' murderer and framed Anna Marie St. Clair."

"Well, well," Malone said, "so everything is straightened out now. Fine. And if you'll excuse me——"

Craig Rice

Helene grabbed his arm. "And I told Jake all I'd found out," she said. "About how there have been four murders, but who could the fourth victim have been? And——"

Malone blinked. "This is all very interesting," he said, "but I have a very important business appointment."

"We know," Helene said. "We heard you. And another thing——"

"Eavesdroppers," Malone said smugly, "always come home to roost." He punched the elevator button.

Helene said, "You mean, chickens never hear good of themselves."

"I know what I mean," Malone said. "I mean, don't count your birds in the hand before they come out of the bush."

The elevator stopped, the wire door rattled open. A big man in a well-fitting brown suit and a slouch hat stepped out. He could have worn a Roman toga and the word "cop" would still have been written all over him.

"Hi, Malone," he said. "Just the guy I was looking for."

"Hello, Lou," Malone said with false heartiness. "Sorry, I'm just leaving to keep an important business engagement."

"That's O.K.," Lou said. "It can wait. Von Flanagan wants to see you, and he's in a hurry. Your phone was busy a couple of times he called, so he sent me up for you."

Malone said, "Well——"

"That's fine," Lou said. He punched the down button for the elevator.

"Yes," Malone began, "but I——"

"That's all right," Lou said. "He won't keep you long."

"We're coming with you," Helene said.

"Oh, no you aren't," Malone said.

"Oh, yes we are," Helene said cheerfully.

Malone looked at her for a moment. There was a look in her eyes that he recognized. It meant trouble. He knew there was no use arguing. Besides, a sudden idea had hit him. He was going to need Jake and Helene.

"You're more than welcome," he said. "And what's more, do you have a date for this evening?"

Jake and Helene looked at each other. "Nothing we can't break," Jake said.

"Fine," Malone said. "You have one now."

The elevator arrived, the door opened, and Bill said, "Wish you folks would make up your mind. Fella gets tired, riding this thing up and down."

"That's life," Malone told him. "Just——"

"Fella gets even more tired of that same old gag," Bill said. "Wish I had two bits for every time I've had to listen to it. When a fella gets to my age——"

He slid open the door. "First floor. All out." He caught Malone by the sleeve, nodded his head toward the plain-clothes man. "Trouble with the cops? Need any help?"

"Not yet, Bill," Malone said.

Lou consented to ride in Helene's car. He sat in back with Malone.

"Have a cigar," Malone said. "How's your boss?"

"He ain't so good, Malone," Lou confided. "Last few weeks he's had the office full of head doctors."

"Head of what?" Malone asked.

"Not head of anything," Lou said. "Just, head doctors. We used to call 'em crazy doctors when we was back in school. Just between us, Malone, I wonder——" He paused. "Acts funny, too. Now, this here business."

Helene had slowed up for a stoplight. The convertible slid to a stop. Lou's next words sounded unexpectedly loud.

"Don't you let on like I talked to you, Malone," he said, "but he's got trouble. He said I should come and fetch you and he said it was something about"—the plain-clothes man paused, swallowed hard, and went on—"a murder that no-body knows where it was committed at, and nobody knows who it happened to."

CHAPTER ELEVEN

"I never was one to worry," Captain von Flanagan growled, "and a nice simple murder I can understand. Most murderers are dumb anyhow, and they don't give me no trouble. Like this babe a few months ago. Got sore account of this guy was running around with some other babe, and she stuck a bread knife in his ribs. Dumb thing to do. Now, if she'd of stuck the bread knife in the other babe's ribs, it could of done her some good. Some smart lawyer, like you, f'rinstance, Malone, could of got her off, and she could of had the guy, with the other babe out of the picture. But no, murderers are dumb. They gotta do everything the hard way."

"The hard way for you," Malone said, "the easy way for them. Damn few murderers take into consideration the problems of the homicide squad. Or," he added, sliding the cellophane off a cigar, "the way the victim happens to feel about it. Most people don't want to be murdered."

"Like I don't want to be a cop," von Flanagan said gloomily. He leaned dangerously far back in his swivel chair and scowled. He was a big man with thinning gray hair and a round red face that turned purple in moments of great emotional stress. It was beginning to turn purple now.

"Like you went to court and had the 'von' added to Flanagan so you wouldn't even sound like a cop," Helene said.

He tried not to smile at her, and couldn't help it. "As a matter of fact," he confided, "I've had enough of it. I'm retiring. Going into a line that's really profitable." The purple receded from his face, he relaxed and accepted one of Malone's cigars.

"That's nice," Jake said. "Last I knew, you were going to study magic and go on the stage."

"Gave that up," von Flanagan said, with a majestic wave of his hand. "Overcrowded profession. No, this time I'm on to something really good." He leaned forward and clasped his hands on the desk. "I'm gonna be a psychoanalyst." He pronounced it correctly and very carefully.

"A what the hell?" Malone said.

"Look," von Flanagan told him, "you know about psychology. Here in the police department we use it all the time, one way or another. Well, you know my sister-in-law—Joe's wife?"

"Sure," Malone said. He lit his cigar. "The one that's sick all the time."

"There you are," von Flanagan said, beaming. "Only she isn't sick, see? She's—well, she's not nuts, she hasn't any buttons missing, she's just—well"—he made a significant gesture with his right forefinger—"turns out she's just a little bit *mashugga*. So Joe, he sends her to a psychoanalyst. And what does *he* do?"

"What?" Helene said. "I'm fascinated."

"He don't do a damn thing," von Flanagan said. "He just sits and she talks. And he gets twenty-five bucks an hour for it, five times a week. Not that Joe can't afford it, the way his garbage collection business is doing these days, but look at the dough those guys make. So me, I'm just gonna brush up a little on my psychology, which I know anyway in a job like this, and I'm gonna rent me a swell office and set up in business. Just figure it up. Twenty-five bucks an hour, five days a week. Hell, a guy could just work half days and be rolling in dough."

"That's wonderful," Jake said. "Only a psychoanalyst has to have a doctor's license."

Von Flanagan waved a hand. "Nothing to it. With my City Hall connections, you think I couldn't get a license inside of twenty-four hours? And for a guy like me, with what I know about psychology?" He drew a long breath. "F'r-instance, here's what I mean. If I'd of been in Joe the Angel's bar last night, nobody would of got upset. I'd of used psychology."

Malone sat tight for a moment. This was the moment he'd been dreading with Jake and Helene. He looked at the end of his cigar and said thoughtfully, "Who got upset in Joe the Angel's last night, and why?"

"There's your psychology right there," von Flanagan said. "Some drunk in there thought he saw a ghost. O.K. One guy thinks he sees a ghost, so everybody there thinks he sees a ghost. Now, if I'd of been there——"

"Funny," Malone said frowning. "I was there. I didn't notice anything."

"Huh?" von Flanagan said. "The way I heard it, she——" He broke off, looked at Helene, and said, "Sorry. I didn't mean to scare you."

"I'm not scared," Helene said through clenched teeth, "but whose ghost was it?"

"Oh, that girl," von Flanagan said, "the one who went to the chair last night."

Jake gave a tiny groan. His face was gray.

"Perfect nonsense," Malone said briskly. "Just as you said, von Flanagan. Psychology. Some drunk had been looking at her picture in the newspaper, and instead of seeing little green men with pink wings crawl out of his glass, he thought he saw *her*. So he sells all the other customers on the idea."

"That's how I figured it," von Flanagan said. He looked relieved. "You see now what I mean, there's a great future in this psychoanalyst racket. Fact is, I've been talking to one of the big shots. Ellsworth LeGeorge, his name is. Doctor LeGeorge. Swell guy. Drives a Cadillac half a block long, and lives in a two-story apartment on Lake Shore Drive. He told me I ought to go through the business myself first, but hell, you can't pay out any twenty-five bucks an hour on a cop's salary."

"Tell me," Jake said with elaborate carelessness, "just who was the guy who saw that ghost?"

"Who cares?" Malone said quickly. "And what's on your mind, von Flanagan, besides your promising future?"

The police officer launched into a long dissertation on the fact that everybody tried to make things hard for him. He went on, "And here's this guy being murdered, and it isn't enough he doesn't tell his name, he has to ask for you, Malone."

Malone said, "Huh?" Helene sat up very straight. *The fourth murder?* she thought.

"Who was being murdered," Jake said, "and where?"

"If I knew," von Flanagan said, his face beginning to turn purple again, "I wouldn't have to ask Malone who he was. But this guy——" He thumbed through a bunch of reports on his desk, pulled out one, and read: "At two-twelve this afternoon an operator call was received which was immediately transferred to the police. A male voice was calling 'Help! Get the police.' As received at the police switchboard, the call proceeded, 'Help me, I'm going to be killed. Tell Malone.' The police operator heard a slight confusion at the other end of the line and what appeared to be the sound of a shot. At this point the receiver was evidently replaced at the other end of the line. As the call came from an automatic dial telephone, it is not possible for the telephone company to trace the call."

He laid the paper down and said, "See what I mean about when a guy is going to kill some other guy, he goes to work and makes it hard for the cops?"

"I see exactly what you mean," Malone said. "How about somebody playing a practical joke on the police?"

"Uh-uh," von Flanagan said. "Unless some guy is one hell of a swell actor. Account of I talked to the desk man who took the call. When that guy hollered 'Help,' he meant '*Help*.' " He leaned across the desk and bellowed, "But why did he holler, 'Tell Malone'?"

"Damned if I know," the little lawyer said. "Maybe he was a friend of mine. Or maybe he thought I'd like to defend his murderer."

Von Flanagan said nothing. He punched savagely at a buzzer on his desk. When the door opened he roared, "Send in the guy who took that call this afternoon." Then he glared at Malone and said, "There's more to it than that."

A good-looking, nervous young cop came in.

"Tell this bastard what you told me," von Flanagan said. He caught his breath, turned to Helene, and said, "Pardon me."

"I——" The young cop paused, gulped. "Well, it seemed silly to me. It didn't go in the report. Actually, it might have been my imagination."

"Psychology," Helene murmured.

"Shut up," Malone said amiably. He added, to the cop, "What did you hear?"

"Well. I thought this man said—'I'm going to be killed.' And then——" He paused again.

"Go *on*," von Flanagan said.

"Then—'Tell Malone—*Anna Marie*—' and then there was noise, and the shot." The young cop looked pale.

The room was very quiet. Everyone looked at Malone. No one moved until at last the little lawyer knocked a half-inch of ash off his cigar with elaborate care, just missing the ash tray.

"I still say someone was playing a practical joke on the police," he said.

"That's all, Dugan," von Flanagan said to the young cop, who went out, closing the door softly. He looked long and reflectively at Malone. "I have enough trouble as it is, without having trouble from you. Some guy's been shot. Most likely killed. I don't know who he was, or where his body is, or who killed him. Don't do a thing until his body turns up, probably in a trunk in the Kansas City freight office. So if you know anything about him, and you don't tell me, so help me, I'm going to toss you in the can for obstructing justice."

"Believe me," Malone said, "I don't know any more about him than you do."

"For your sake," von Flanagan said, "I hope you're telling the truth." He pulled a newspaper from under his desk and waved a headline at them. "Look at that!"

MYSTERY MURDER CALL
BAFFLES POLICE

"Thank heaven," von Flanagan added, "that 'Anna Marie' crack didn't go on the record. Or all hell would have broken loose."

Malone also thanked heaven, but silently, and not for the same reason. He rose and said, "I've got to see some men about some investments of mine. Is that all you wanted?"

"Isn't it enough?" von Flanagan demanded. He sighed. "Malone, you wouldn't lie to me about this?"

"I would not," Malone assured him. "I haven't the faintest idea who called and said he was being murdered. And evidently *was* murdered. But I'll promise you this, if I find his corpse, I'll give you a ring."

Downstairs on the sidewalk Malone dug through his pockets, found an old envelope in one and a pencil stub in another, and carefully wrote down a few words. He gave the envelope to Jake.

"You two meet me there at nine-thirty tonight, and don't ask any questions."

Helene grabbed his arm. "Malone, I'm going to ask a question, and you're going to answer. Last night—at Joe the Angel's—tell me, did you——"

He looked her straight in the eye and said, "I cross my word. I mean, I give my heart. Anyway, so help me. I did not see the ghost of Anna Marie St. Clair in Joe the Angel's last night, nor any other ghost."

He went on down the street while they stared after him. There was a problem on his mind right now that was just a bit more serious than the supernatural. Who had been murdered who knew that there was any association between Malone and Anna Marie? And even more important, how much did his murderer know about it?

CHAPTER TWELVE

"I'm glad you like it," Malone said. "It's just a little trinket, but I thought it would look well on you."

Anna Marie twirled the bracelet on her pale, slender wrist. "You really shouldn't—" she began. She paused, smiled at him, and said, "You're doing so much for me already."

'No one could possibly do enough for you," Malone said. He added, "And besides, it really *is* just a trinket. Inexpen-

sive little thing I happened to see in a window." After all, he
reflected, it was always wise to be honest about the price of
presents. Anna Marie would probably have it appraised. He
adored Anna Marie, but he knew women. "One of these days
I'll find something really worthy of you. Meantime, how is
the steak?"

The look she gave in answer was almost a purr. They
were dining from a tray in Malone's room, a meal Malone had
chosen carefully for a girl who'd been eating prison food for
weeks. Steak, fried potatoes, fresh peas, sliced tomatoes,
beer, lemon pie, and half a gallon of coffee. For the second
time that day he decided that never before had he so much
enjoyed watching a girl eat.

"Tomorrow night," he said happily, "fried chicken and
ice cream."

She smiled at him again, and he felt as though the little
room had been flooded with sunshine.

Everything, for the moment at least, was rosy. It turned
out he'd been quite justified in his choice of crap games.
Later there had been a brief poker session in a Randolph
Street hotel room. Now there was a bracelet on Anna Marie's
wrist, steak on her dinner tray, and a spare two hundred
dollars in his pocket. He was going to use all of it for good
purposes, too, except a week's salary for Maggie. The bank
and the office rent could wait. For just a moment he thought
regretfully of Eva Childers' ten one-hundred-dollar bills.

He waited until Anna Marie had polished off the last scrap
of lemon pie and sighed ecstatically over the last drop of coffee
before he lighted her cigarette and asked very casually, "Have
you any idea why Joe Childers' widow would want to pay me a
big hunk of money to find your bereaved family?"

Anna Marie stared at him incredulously. "Do you know
what you're talking about?"

"If I don't," Malone said, "I've been dreaming all afternoon." He went on to describe the interview. "I didn't take
her money," he finished, "because I had a pretty good idea
she had a hunch I was nosing around to find out who did
arrange Big Joe's murder, and she wanted me to drop it. It
was just a polite way of offering me whatever dough I cared
to name to lay off."

"Do you think that she——" Anna Marie frowned. "I don't know. She might have."

"Or," Malone said, "she might know who did. Or, I might have been all wrong and it wasn't a bribe. She might have been telling the truth."

Anna Marie grinned wickedly. "Why don't you take her up on it? Take the retainer, locate my only relatives, and send her a bill for a big fee?"

"I never thought of that," Malone said, looking at her admiringly. "It never occurred to me that you can tell me who they are."

"Not *they*," Anna Marie said. "*She*. Aunt Bess. She's all my family, now that Uncle Will is gone."

Jack St. Clair, her father, had been a tent-show actor. Her mother had run away with him from Grove Junction, Wisconsin. After Anna Marie had been born, St. Clair disappeared. In time her mother had married again, a side-show barker who didn't want to be bothered with a baby, and Anna Marie had gone to live with Aunt Bess and Uncle Will. She'd been sixteen when her mother died, leaving her a collection of cheap jewelry and a little under a hundred dollars in cash.

"We were definitely wrong side of the tracks," Anna Marie said. "Uncle Will ran a livery stable, and prohibition came in about the time livery stables went out, so he took up bootlegging. Aunt Bess ran the business end of it. Then prohibition went out, and they opened up a tavern. It never made a lot of money, but it was a living. They were wonderful, both of them." There was a little catch in her throat. "You can't even guess how good they were to me."

"I can," Malone said, unwrapping a cigar. "Just the same, you couldn't have been very popular with the mammas and pappas of Grove Junction."

"Definitely not." She smiled. "But I had plenty of dates."

"I can imagine that, too," Malone said.

"They sent me away to school, my last year in high school. I stuck it out for a term, and then I ran away and got a job singing with a dinky little dance band. Eventually I landed in Chicago at a cheap night spot, and you can pick it up from there if you want to look over the newspaper accounts of my trial."

"I know them by heart," Malone said. He lit the cigar. "Shall I find Aunt Bess and take Mrs. Childers' dough?"

"Name five good reasons why not."

The little lawyer said nothing. He gazed at the ceiling, his short legs propped comfortably on a chair, and puffed out a great gray-blue cloud of cigar smoke.

"All right," Anna Marie said, "name one."

"I'll name one," Malone said almost dreamily. "I'll probably get in a lot of trouble, and I'm in enough trouble as it is. But on the other hand"—he gazed thoughtfully at the end of the cigar—"I might as well, and trouble be damned. O.K., I'll have Maggie telephone her in the morning and say that I've changed my mind about the retainer. Then I'll go through the motions of locating your Aunt Bess, and send Mrs. Childers a suitable bill."

One thousand dollars, and his conscience clear about taking it! His creditors would never know how much they owed to Anna Marie's fine, logical mind.

He poured two glasses of brandy and lit another cigarette for Anna Marie. "I knew Big Joe Childers," he said in a reminiscent tone. "A tall, heavy-set, stoop-shouldered guy. Looked ill. A good guy. I remember him. Worked in a shoe store, and went to the same night law school I did. He was older than I was. Fact is, he quit that school about eight years before I went into it, and started package-running for a second string bootlegger."

Anna Marie said furiously, "He had to. You don't understand——"

"Shut up," Malone said pleasantly. "I'm doing the remembering this time. He quit that school and took that job because he had a widowed mother with—with what was it, Anna Marie?"

"Dropsy," Anna Marie said. Her lips were pale. She held the brandy glass tight.

"This is a success story," Malone went on in that same dreamy tone. "Big Joe fought it out a few times with the cops, and with rival gangs. But, like the Rover boys, he always won out. So let's skip ahead a few years. Quite a few years. We find Big Joe a rich man, with a rich and socially ambitious wife, and a beautiful girl friend."

Anna Marie said sharply, "That's enough!"

"I told you to shut up," Malone said. "Do you want me to bribe you, or threaten you? Anyway. Big Joe wouldn't have"—he paused, decided not to go into details of the kind of protection frame-up that had been worked on Jake. "Well—he wouldn't. Anna Marie, who would have wanted to arrange Big Joe Childers' murder—and *your* murder?"

"His murder? Plenty of people, Malone. People who wanted him to go into things he didn't want to go into. Look, Malone. Big Joe was a racketeer, but he was honest. Understand? People who owed him money. People who were afraid of him. Any number of——" Suddenly she leaned forward, elbows on her knees, her eyes very bright. "Malone, for weeks I sat there in that grimy cell and asked myself, who would have wanted to murder Big Joe. And I made up a list of people as long as a pair of arms. But somehow I couldn't see any of them planning it. I was stuck, and I'm still stuck. I wish to heaven I could lay my hands on—oh bust it, is there any more of that brandy?"

"Plenty," Malone said. He poured two more drinks and retrieved his cigar from under the end table. "You haven't answered, who would have wanted to arrange *your* murder?"

She let the glass sit on the table and stared at him. "I don't know. Honestly, I don't know. Hell, everybody makes enemies, I suppose, but an elaborate frame-up like that——" Her breath caught in her throat.

"Drink that drink," Malone said harshly, "and get set to answer a bunch of questions. Tough ones."

She drank it obediently, tried to smile at him, and said, "Go ahead, you're the doctor."

"I'm the lawyer," Malone said, finishing his own drink. "There's a difference." He relit his cigar. "Pretend you're on the witness stand, babe, and don't answer anything you don't have to."

He rose and waved the cigar at her.

"Did you ever know Ike Malloy?"

"I don't think so. I may have met him."

Malone noticed how her back stiffened as she began answering questions. She'd been through a lot of this at the trial. He hoped the misery in his heart didn't show through his eyes.

"What was Bill McKeown to you?"

"Nothing. He said he was in love with me. But I never——"

"You never what?"

"I never did. I couldn't. Because——" She drew a long, almost gasping breath. "Malone, what *is* this?"

"A brief cross-examination," Malone said. "Did you ever know a man named Ambersley?"

She frowned, looked blank in thought for a moment, then shook her head. "Never heard of him."

"Sure?"

"Malone, do you think I'd lie to you?"

"Could be," Malone said laconically. "Girls do tell lies. That's why lawyers study up on cross-examining." Suddenly he rose and began pacing up and down the little room. "This isn't a rehearsal for a vaudeville act, you know. I may seem to be asking silly questions, but you're suppose to give back serious answers. Why did you lie to me about Ike Malloy?"

She stared at him, her lovely eyes wide, her lips turning pale.

"I didn't lie to you, Malone. I didn't know Ike Malloy. I said—I may have met him."

"Ike Malloy was a bouncer at the old Haywire Club when you were singing there," Malone went on relentlessly. "You saw him a dozen—hell, a hundred—times. Didn't you?"

"Yes, Malone."

"Damn it," Malone said, keeping his eyes away from her tortured face. "Don't look at me in that tone of voice. You're still on the witness stand. Now answer yes or no, and no nonsense about it. Would you have recognized Ike Malloy?"

"Yes." It was a whisper.

"Talk louder," Malone said, "the jury can't hear you. Why didn't you recognize him when he came in and shot Big Joe Childers?"

"I——" Her mouth opened with a gasp, then shut like a trap.

"He wasn't wearing a mask," Malone said harshly, "and your eyesight is good."

She gave a little moan and covered her face with her hands.

"Don't mind me," Malone said. "I'm just your lawyer. Remember, this hurts me worse than it does you." His tone was light, almost gay. "One reason was that it wouldn't have done you any good. Is that right?"

She nodded. Then she said, "I could have said I saw Ike Malloy come in and shoot him, or I saw Joe Jackson McGillicuddy come in and shoot him—and it wouldn't have made any difference. Because nobody would have believed me. And whoever I named would have had an alibi. Those things are arranged—very carefully."

"Right," Malone said. He puffed at his cigar and stood staring at her. "But there was one other reason why you didn't name names. You were assured you were going to be all right. And you knew, or thought you knew, who'd hired Ike Malloy."

He took one quick glance at her dead-white face and added hastily, "Never mind, you don't have to answer any more questions. For the love of little potatoes, don't faint now. Because we've got to go out and haunt a house, remember? And," he said with unexpected cheerfulness in his voice, "you don't know it yet, but you're going to haunt a couple of my dearest friends."

CHAPTER THIRTEEN

"It's nine thirty-five," Helene said. There wasn't anyone to overhear within half a mile, as far as she knew, but she whispered it just the same. "Jake, I don't like this."

Jake frowned. He said, "I wish you'd taken my invariably sound advice and stayed home."

"He said *both* of us," Helene reminded him. She shivered. "Jake, is Malone mixed up in something, or is he just a little——" She paused, took out a cigarette, and began tapping it against the back of her slender hand. "Why the blazes doesn't he get here?"

They'd been at the meeting place in Lincoln Park ten minutes early, and the waiting time had seemed almost unbearably long. Helene had parked the convertible a block away from the intersection of the two paths that Malone had described in his note, a gloomy corner shadowed by elm trees and, right now, eerie with fog.

"But why Lincoln Park?" Jake complained. "Why couldn't we meet him at Joe the Angel's, or his office, or damn near anywhere except here?"

"Maybe he's being followed," Helene said. "Or maybe he has a client who's discovered a pneumonia cure, and he wants to try it out on us." She sneezed.

Jake said, *"Sssh!"*

There were slow, cautious footsteps crunching up the gravel walk toward them. Then a pause. Then more footsteps. A longer pause. Malone's voice, low-pitched and hoarse.

"Jake? Helene?"

"Here," Helene said.

Malone breathed a sigh of relief that all but blew twigs off the leafless elm trees. He emerged from the shadowy mists, disheveled, gasping and pale.

"Is she following me?" he demanded in an anxious whisper.

"She?" Jake and Helene said in unison.

Malone glanced cautiously over his shoulder and gave a low moan. "Jake. Helene. My dearest friends. Do you—see anything?"

"I warned you about that two-buck-per-gallon prune brandy," Jake said crossly, "even if you do know the guy who makes it." He took another look at the little lawyer's face. *"What is it?"*

Jake looked. There were dark trees, there was a wide space of shadowed lawn, there was a street lamp far in the distance, there was darkness, laced with white wisps of fog. He shuddered in spite of himself.

"You'd better go home to bed, Malone," he advised.

"No. That girl."

"Who?"

"Her."

"Where?"

"For crying out in the night," Helene said, "let's get away from here and go get a drink. Anyway, you're doing that routine wrong. It's a dramatic poem. Bear. Where? There. Near? Here——" Her voice broke off into a weird gurgle. "*Jake!*"

One minute there had been darkness and shifting mist. The next, there was a ghost, pale gray, transparent, floating. It moved halfway across the lawn and paused.

Jake held Helene's hand, tight. "Don't believe it," he muttered. "Shut your eyes. It'll go away."

"Perfect nonsense," Helene said. "How can it go away when it isn't really there?" She turned to look at the little lawyer. "Malone!" He was grinning.

"That black raincape with the hood was a wonderful idea," Anna Marie's voice came across the lawn. "Look."

Jake and Helene looked, in spite of themselves. The ghost vanished. A moment later it appeared again, and a silvery little laugh came echoing through the trees. "Good night, Malone," Jake said. "This has been a lot of fun, but we have a very important engagement——"

"Wait," Malone said.

Anna Marie walked through the mists, dressed in the gray suit and the little hat with the floating veil, carrying the black raincape over her arm. She paused where a ray from the street lamp struck her face, and took a cigarette from her purse.

"Go away," Jake said, his teeth clenched.

"I won't," Anna Marie said pleasantly.

Malone lit a match for her cigarette and said, "She doesn't have to go away. She's my client."

Helene choked on an indrawn breath. She said, in a dangerously calm voice, "Malone, are you——"

"Do I have bells in my battery?" the lawyer asked. "No. Please don't be disturbed." He lit a cigar, the glare of the match throwing a weird orange glare over his face. "Did I ever tell you about my apparition?"

"Damn you, Malone," Jake said. He stared at Anna Marie for a minute and then demanded, "Are you real?"

"Sure I'm real. I'm alive, too. If you don't believe it, pinch me."

"My wife doesn't like me to pinch girls *or* ghosts," Jake said. He had an uncomfortable feeling that he was losing a mind, and he hoped it was someone else's, not his.

Helene said, "I don't know just what this situation is, but whatever it is, it calls for a drink. There's a bottle in the car. In the meantime, Malone, if there *is* an explanation——"

The explanation had been made, in detail, by the time they were comfortably settled in the convertible.

"So you really are a ghost." Helene said at last. She reached into the glove compartment, pulled out a bottle of rye, uncorked it, and passed it to Anna Marie. "Why did you haunt *us?*"

"We had to have a rehearsal," Malone said, gallantly holding the bottle for Anna Marie. "Besides, we need you."

"I won't be haunted," Jake said stubbornly. "I *won't,* understand? Go pick on somebody else. Go on, disappear, will you?"

Anna Marie obligingly pulled the raincape over her head and vanished. Jake groaned.

"Stop scaring my husband," Helene said indignantly, "or else give me back my rye. Where to, Malone, and what next?"

"There's a very nice club on Cicero Road," Malone began, "where——" He paused, cleared his throat apologetically, and gave the number of Anna Marie's apartment. "But we have a little burglary job to attend to first." He added, "If a ghost can't break into her own apartment——"

"First time I ever heard of a ghost needing a skeleton key," Helene said. The convertible moved away from the curb and headed for the near north side.

Jake stole a glance in the rearview mirror. Anna Marie's face was pale, but definitely flesh and blood. It seemed to him that several thousand tons had slid away from his conscience. A miracle—yes, it *had* been a miracle—had saved her life. Yet he wasn't completely happy. He had an unpleasant premonition that there was going to be a lot of trouble before this business was finished.

As the convertible swung into Lake Shore Drive, the fog deepened. Cars crept along through the gray-white darkness.

"If you had to be a ghost," Jake said, "you certainly picked the right weather for it."

Anna Marie giggled. It was a warm, reassuring giggle, and it made him feel much better. "An old friend of mine works in the weather bureau."

"Oh, of course," Jake said. "And you got in touch with him via Ouija board."

Helene turned right, then left, and stopped the convertible in front of the apartment building whose address Malone had given her. "What now, Malone."

"Let me get out of this stuff Mick Herman lent me," Malone said, going through his pockets. "Smart guy, Mick. Married the daughter of one of the best locksmiths in the world. She was thirty-eight, a spinster, and looked like the other side of a mud fence, but he treated her like a princess and gave her everything her little heart desired. The lock hasn't been made his keys and tools can't open."

"Handy person to know," Helene said. "But what do you want us to do?"

"Park here where it's fairly dark, wait for us, and watch for trouble," Malone said.

Anna Marie added, "The other apartment in the building is empty. If you see anyone going in, honk."

"I'll do *this*," Helene said, "with the horn." She drummed out the first eight notes of the "Habañera" on the steering wheel. "And if someone does go in, and if I do do this"—she repeated the rhythm—"what next?"

"Start your motor, hold the car in gear, and be ready for anything," Malone said.

"Meanwhile, you'll be doing what?" Jake asked.

"We'll burn down that bridge when we come to it," Malone said, helping Anna Marie out of the convertible.

A moment later they disappeared into the building. Jake snuggled close to Helene's shoulder. "Why did I marry a girl who loves trouble?" he complained.

"Because I'm irresistible," she told him. She sighed. "Jake, she *is* beautiful."

"M'm-h'm," Jake said. "Not like you, though."

"I don't blame Malone a bit."

"Huh? What about Malone?"

"You mean you haven't noticed?" Then a whisper. "Jake!"

A short, slender man in a gabardine raincoat and snap-brim hat had paused in front of the apartment building, and started up the steps. Helene played the "Habañera" on the horn, started the motor, and put the car in gear. Jake held open the door.

Moments passed. A lot of them.

Suddenly Malone came down the steps, in a hurry. His round face was pale.

"A man in a tan raincoat went into the house."

"Hell," Malone said. He scowled. "We didn't see or hear anybody. Never mind that now. Come inside."

Helene shut off the motor. They followed him across the sidewalk and into the building.

One dim light showed in Anna Marie's parlor, making it look as half-real and ghostly as Anna Marie herself. But it was bright enough to show Jesse Conway lying on the thick, pale blue carpet, a bullet hole in his forehead.

"He's been dead a long time," Malone said.

Jake stared at the body, and then at the little lawyer.

"In case you don't recognize him," Malone added, "it's Jesse Conway."

"No it isn't," Jake said suddenly. "That isn't Jesse Conway. That's—*Ambersley!*"

CHAPTER FOURTEEN

Helene said, "Never mind the guy's name and address right now. As far as I'm concerned, he can be Judge Crater." Her voice was calm, but Malone suspected that her teeth were getting ready to chatter. "The B of I boys are pretty efficient. Let them find out who he was. We saw someone come in this house, and I have a hunch we ought to find out where he is, and what he's doing."

"She's right," Malone said. He had an unpleasant feeling that in another minute his own teeth were going to chatter. "Jake, you want to go upstairs and take a look around?"

"No," Jake said firmly. "Do you?" He added, in a milder tone, "All right. We'll both go."

The little lawyer said, "Well—but I think someone ought to stay here and protect the women."

Helene said one very rude word.

"All right, all right," Malone said hastily. "But I'd feel better if I had a gun. Anna Marie, you don't happen to have one tucked away somewhere here?"

She shook her head.

"Gun!" Suddenly Helene's eyes blazed blue fire. "Wait! Anna Marie! Don't move!" She stood there for a moment, staring at Anna Marie. "*Now* I know!"

"*What?*" It was Jake and Malone at once.

She shook her head. "Never mind. It can wait. I won't forget it again. This isn't a time to discuss, it's a time to act. And as soon as——"

She stopped almost in the middle of a word. There were soft, slow footsteps coming down the stairs, and just a faint creaking of the stairs themselves. The footsteps came down the hall and paused just outside the door.

"Duck!" Anna Marie hissed, pointing to the bedroom door. Jake, Helene, and Malone ducked, just as Anna Marie switched off the light.

There was the sound of the door being slowly and cautiously tried, then of a key being slowly and cautiously inserted in the lock. They held their breaths.

Through the crack in the bedroom door they could see the hall door opening, letting in a faint greenish light from the hall outside. They could see Anna Marie, a misty, pale gray figure. She seemed to be suspended in the air, almost a foot above the floor.

The man in the tan gabardine raincoat shrieked, then fled. They could hear his racing footsteps on the sidewalk outside as he tore past.

Anna Marie stepped down from the footstool, shut the door, turned on the light, and prophesied calmly, "He won't be back. Not for a while."

"You have great presence of mind," Jake said, wiping his brow. "Who was he?"

"I don't know."

"Neither do I," said Malone.

Helene said, "I do. He's the young man who was in The Happy Days saloon this afternoon with Mrs. Childers. But what was he doing here? And why did he go upstairs first, instead of here?"

"I don't know, and I don't care," Jake said. "All I know is we promised von Flanagan a corpse, and we've found him one. The one that called up and said he was being murdered, and added 'Tell Malone—Anna Marie——' "

"That's right," Malone said. He took out a cigar, started to unwrap it, glanced at the late Jesse Conway, and put it back in his pocket. "It can't be anyone else. Jesse Conway knew that Anna Marie was alive. He knew she was going to get in touch with me. Furthermore, he tried to phone me and couldn't reach me."

He scowled and said, "I never liked Jesse Conway much, but now I wish that he'd succeeded."

"Nobody could have saved his life," Anna Marie whispered. "Not even you, Malone."

"I might not even have tried," Malone said. He took the

cigar out again and managed a nice compromise by unwrapping it and holding it unlighted. "But anyway, his fingerprints are probably on the telephone receiver and"—his eyes narrowed for a moment—"there's even a chance that his murderer's will be."

"I tell you, his name was Ambersley," Jake said, a little wildly. "The guy I——" He started to say, "Paid off to," caught himself in time, and finished, "—met that time I told you about."

"One and the same man," Malone said, quickly and smoothly. "I should have recognized him from your description this afternoon." He added, "But why did he get himself murdered in this particular apartment? Why was he here, and why was his murderer here?"

"And why did the man in the tan raincoat go upstairs?" Helene demanded. "We're getting a lot of whys and no wherefores, Malone."

The little lawyer turned to Anna Marie. "What was—what *is*—upstairs? Whose apartment?"

"Nobody's." She sat down on the arm of a pale rose brocade chair. "Big Joe rented it. With me here, he wanted to have the whole building. Not that he was so damned exclusive, but you never know what you may draw in the way of neighbors."

"Did he rent it just to keep it vacant?"

"That was the main reason," she told him, "but he did use it. He had a few odds and ends of furniture up there, and once in a while if he wanted to talk business with someone—in private—he'd arrange a meeting upstairs."

Malone scowled. "Let's go up there and take a look." He led the way into the hall and up the stairs.

There was dust everywhere, thick gray dust, and cobwebs. Helene touched the stair rail once and drew her hand away, shuddering.

The door to the upstairs apartment was not only unlocked, but partly ajar. Malone pushed it open a little wider and peered in cautiously. Beyond was a dark and frightening cavern. The little lawyer felt Anna Marie's fingers tighten, ever so lightly, over his own. He turned his head and saw that Helene was very pale.

"Come on in," he said cheerfully. "Remember, it's four of us against none of *them*. Only," he added wistfully, "I wish we'd brought along a flashlight."

Anna Marie said, "The lights must be on here, if they're on downstairs. The whole building is on one meter."

She reached around the doorjamb and clicked the switch. Lights blazed. She went on into the apartment, Jake and Helene close behind her.

Malone gripped the edge of the door and stood there for a moment, his stomach contracting, his hands suddenly ice-cold. It was like seeing a stage set from which the furniture and props have been removed, the actors long since gone. Because it was the twin of Anna Marie's apartment—and completely empty.

After coming up from the rooms downstairs, it was like looking at the corpse of some familiar friend. There were the windows, there was the little fireplace, there were the alcoves above the bookshelves. But there were no draperies at the windows, no logs in the fireplace, no books on the shelves, no amusing little ornaments in the alcoves. And Anna Marie—he glanced at her.

He shut his eyes and held tight to the edge of the door.

"*Malone!*" Helene said sharply. "What's the matter with you?"

"I—nothing!" He realized he'd started to say, "*I thought I saw a ghost!*" He opened his eyes, looked around and said, "Somebody has been doing a very nice job of searching."

There was dust here, too, but it had been recently and thoroughly disturbed. The drawers had been yanked out of the built-in window seat, and there were knife marks along its top. Similar knife marks showed around the window frames and sills and the edges of the doors.

They went into the bedroom. It, too, was empty of furniture, but there were the same signs of a recent and desperate search. A built-in mirror had been wrenched off its frame. The pale green carpet had been ripped up from the floor. Malone noticed that the carpet looked new and unused. Anna Marie must have been telling the truth about the two apartments.

In the bathroom the medicine cabinet had been pried

from the wall. The toilet tank cover had been removed and not replaced.

The kitchen was a shambles.

"Someone *has* done a very nice job of searching," Malone repeated admiringly. "Look, he even pried along the edge of the baseboards to see if any of them came loose." He finally lit the cigar he'd been carrying. "Too bad he didn't find what he was looking for."

"Do you know," Helene demanded, "or are you guessing?"

"With me," Malone said, "a guess is as good as a gander." He blew out his match, dropped it on the floor, and looked at it thoughtfully. "I might add, the guy in the raincoat didn't do the searching job. He just stopped by to inspect it."

Jake sighed and said, "If you keep this up you'll be competing with Dunninger. Or do you expect *us* to read *your* mind?"

"It's perfectly simple," Malone said indignantly. "Mr. Raincoat, to give him a name, was only here a few minutes. This searching job must have taken a couple of hours, at the least. If whatever had been looked for had been found, no one would have come back. The guy who did the searching wouldn't have come back, because he'd already done everything except tear the paper off the walls."

"Malone—" Helene began.

"Shut up," the little lawyer said pleasantly, waving her aside. "Don't derail me when I'm on a train of thought." His eyes narrowed. "Mr. Raincoat came back here to make sure that Mr. Searcher hadn't missed a trick. As anyone with half an eye can see, he hadn't. Therefore, Mr. Raincoat decided that the downstairs apartment should also be investigated."

He knocked a little ash off his cigar and said to Anna Marie, "What the devil did Big Joe have hidden around here? The Great Mogul diamond, a complete set of plans for blowing up the Tribune Tower, or a life pass on the El?"

"I don't know what he was hiding. It was none of my business." Her white little face seemed to have turned to stone.

Malone looked at her thoughtfully and said, "All right, the defense rests. Let's go downstairs, where there's a corpse

Craig Rice

to keep us company and a nice comfortable place to sit down."

"Wait a minute," Helene said. "Malone. why did your Mr. Searcher come up here first?"

"Maybe he believed there's always room at the top," Malone said. "Or maybe he was smart enough to have a better reason." He flicked a nonexistent ash from his cigar by way of gesture. "He may have reasoned that Big Joe was a smart enough cookie to have his hidey-hole where his girl friend wouldn't stumble on it accidentally or intentionally." He shot a glance at Anna Marie and added, "Am I right?"

"You're right," Anna Marie said harshly, "but *he's* wrong." She leaned against the doorjamb. Her face was like a shadow against the darkness. "Maybe you just don't understand about guys like Big Joe. If a dog gets a bone there's ten dogs after him. If a guy gets a sweet racket there's fifty guys after him. And if he happens to have the kind of nature Big Joe had, he's got to trust somebody, and if he can't trust his girl friend, then who the hell——" She broke off suddenly.

Malone said hastily, "We understand." He chewed savagely on his cigar for a moment. "Then Big Joe did have a hiding place, and you do know where it is."

"Know!" Anna Marie laughed. It wasn't a pleasant laugh. "I should know. Because I made it for him." She sighed. "He told me that he wanted a good safe place to keep valuable papers, and sometimes money, a place nobody could find. He didn't trust wall safes or movable floor boards or any of the usual places."

"From the looks of this room," Jake said, "he had the right idea."

A wry smile crossed her face briefly. "This whole damn building could be torn apart, roof to basement, and no one would ever find what he was looking for. When Big Joe told me that, I remembered—in grandmother's house, back in Grove Junction——"

She paused. Her eyes softened. She smiled.

"O.K., come downstairs. I'll show you where it is."

"The important thing isn't *where*," Helene said, "but, what's in it?"

They all looked at Anna Marie.

90

"I think he used to keep important business papers there," she said, almost in a whisper. "And sometimes I think he kept money there, quite a lot of it. For a while he kept a diary, and he kept it there. But not long before he—before Ike Malloy shot him—he burned the diary. As far as I know, he never put anything else in the hiding place."

"As far as you know," Malone repeated. "Didn't you ever look?"

"Of course not," Anna Marie said. She sounded shocked. "Whatever he put there wasn't any of my business."

Malone revised his opinion of Anna Marie. She was, he decided, one in *two* million.

"Look, my dear," he said. "It is your business now. There may be something there, something important. It might tell who murdered him and tried to frame you. That's something you want to know." He added, "You don't need to show what you find there to us, or to anybody else, if you don't want to."

Helene sighed and said, "This is a very pleasant tea party. But tempus is fidgeting, and someone who doesn't believe in ghosts may decide to search that downstairs apartment. And while this is no time to bring it up, Malone, you really ought to ring up von Flanagan and tell him you've found his murder victim."

"Business before pleasure," Malone told her. "A place for everything, and everything in its time. I say, let's get the hell downstairs and find the missing emeralds. Besides, Anna Marie has to pack her other toothbrush."

At the door to Anna Marie's apartment he paused and looked at her, one hand on the doorknob. He was remembering the fleeting expression on her face when she'd realized that Jesse Conway had tried to hush up the confession that had saved her life. It hadn't been anger, or shock, or even surprise. It had been a kind of anguished sympathy for the once brilliant man who had been forced into a deal like that. And right now, Jesse Conway was lying dead on her pale blue carpet.

"Maybe," he began hesitatingly.

"Don't be a sentimental fool, Malone," Helene said in an unexpectedly sharp voice.

He glanced at Helene, saw that her blue eyes were very wide and bright, and that she had one arm linked through Anna Marie's. He flung open the door and said, "Ladies first," as he ushered them into the room.

Anna Marie hurried into her bedroom and began tossing things into a suitcase, talking about the house in Grove Junction while she packed. It had been Grandmother's house once. Grandmother's husband had been a wealthy farmer, and the house was a good substantial one, with fine woodwork and the best of hardware. Glass knobs on the downstairs doors and furnace heat. Aunt Bess used to take her there to visit. Then Grandmother died, and Aunt Bess had expected to inherit a lot of money. But the old house was heavily mortgaged, and the hiding place had held only a garnet necklace and a pair of silver earrings.

"Aunt Bess got the jewelry," she finished, "and I learned how to make a hiding place nobody could find. Frankly, I think I got the best deal."

Malone had been prowling silently and restlessly around the living room, chewing on his dead cigar and being careful not to touch anything that would register a fingerprint. He took the suitcase she handed him and carried it out to the hall. Then she took a footstool to the kitchenette door, climbed up, and ran her fingers along the top of the door. A thin strip of wood lifted up.

"It's very simple," she said. "The top of the door is hollowed out. Then a piece of wood is fitted in. If anyone runs his fingers along the top of the door, it feels perfectly smooth."

She climbed down from the footstool. There was a piece of notepaper in her hand.

"This is all there was."

"Put it in your handbag," Malone said, "and read it later. Let's get out of here."

"Wait," Helene said. There was a thoughtful look in her eyes. "There's no hurry. Maybe we ought to look at that paper before we leave. It may not be as easy to break in here a second time."

"The key!" Anna Marie said unexpectedly. They stared at her.

"That's right," Malone said scowling. "The young man in the raincoat had a key to the apartment. How did he get it? And"—he nodded toward the late Jesse Conway—"how did he get in?"

"The young man—his key—" she paused. It was a good half minute before she said, "There's only two people he could have gotten it from. Jesse Conway, and—Big Joe."

"That's nice," Malone said. "And neither of them is going to tell us a thing. How many keys were there to this apartment?"

"Only two," she said. "Big Joe had a special lock made. A pair of them, just alike, one for the back door and one for the front. He had—well, there were people who didn't like him. He enjoyed feeling—safe!"

She paused again, and there was an awkward silence. Finally Malone said with forced cheerfulness, "Well, maybe that's why he didn't get murdered long before."

Anna Marie smiled at him, a faint smile. "There were two keys made. Very special ones, with engraved initials. His on one, mine on the other. And a little design in chip diamonds."

Malone decided immediately that if he was ever able to manage that little house in Winnetka or Wilmette for Anna Marie, he'd do something fancy in the way of door keys. Only he wouldn't use little chip diamonds.

"I gave my key to Jesse Conway," Anna Marie said, "when I went to—jail."

Malone knelt beside the body with a faint grimace of repulsion. "There's a chance he may still have it." A moment later he added, "He did."

He handed the ornamental little key to Anna Marie and said, "Then the young man who dropped in to visit must have the key that belonged to Big Joe. I think it's safe to assume Big Joe must have been carrying the key when he was killed. What happened to it after that?"

"That question can wait until later," Helene said firmly. "Personally, if that piece of paper Anna Marie found is worth that searching job upstairs, I'd like to know what it is."

They looked expectantly at Anna Marie. She unfolded the paper, looked at it for nearly a minute, and frowned.

"It doesn't make sense," she said at last. She gave the paper to Malone. It was an ordinary piece of inexpensive notepaper. At the top was written, "Dear Anna Marie." Tha: had been scratched out. A few lines below was, "Dearest Anna Marie: If I weren't ill——" That, too, had been scratched out, and still farther down the page, "Anna Marie, my darling—forgive me for what I must——" That was all.

"Big Joe's writing?" Malone asked.

Anna Marie nodded. "But I don't understand——"

"It looks like the first draft of a letter," Malone said slowly. "Evidently a letter to you. I'd say that probably he was interrupted before he could finish it, and stuck it away in the hiding place so that no one would see it before he had a chance to finish it." He handed the letter back to her. "For the last time, let's get out of here. We can talk somewhere else."

"You've got to call von Flanagan," Helene reminded him again.

The little lawyer nodded and said, "Yes, but not on this telephone. I don't want to ruin what may be a lovely set of fingerprints."

Suddenly Jake said, "Furthermore, Malone, *you* aren't going to call him." His eyes were flickering with excitement. "Maybe you've all forgotten my profession before I became a respectable saloonkeeper."

He turned to Anna Marie and put a friendly hand on her shoulder. "My dear ghost—what you need now is a good press agent."

CHAPTER FIFTEEN

"There are some things some people know more about than some other people," Jake said. "And one of the some things I know some more about than some people I could name is publicity."

"You mean, *some* publicity," Helene said scornfully, swinging the convertible into Clark Street.

"No," Malone told her, "he means, you can fool all of the people all of the time, and you can fool all of the people all of the time, but you can't fool all of the people all of the time."

"Jake knows what he means," Helene said. "Malone, you're drunk."

"I'm not," the little lawyer said indignantly, "but it's not a bad idea. Anna Marie——"

"Later," Anna Marie said. "Right now I've got to talk to my press agent."

"Right now," Jake said, "you've got to talk to von Flanagan. Where's the nearest telephone booth?"

Helene answered by slamming on the brakes and skidding the convertible to a stop in front of a corner drugstore. "There you are, smart guy. Now, does Anna Marie wear her rain cape, or does she change with me?"

"Neither," Jake said. "That's what I mean by her needing a press agent. Right now, Anna Marie could stroll in there walking on her hands, with a rose in her teeth, and nobody would notice her."

Anna Marie stepped out of the car, waved her eyelashes at Jake, and said, "Mr. Justus, you underestimate me."

"My apologies," Jake said. "I meant, nobody would recognize you. And my friends call me Jake. Let's go make that phone call."

It was a dinky little drugstore, four stools in front of the discolored marble soda fountain, flyspecked displays of bath salts, antiseptics, toothpastes; a few shelves of cheap liquors, a green-curtained doorway leading to the prescription department, and one phone booth. Nobody noticed Anna Marie. Jake bought a handful of phone slugs for her and a lemon coke for himself. From where he stood he could hear every word from the phone booth.

"Captain von Flanagan, please." Pause. "But it's very important. I must reach him right away. About a murder." Pause. "This is Anna Marie St. Clair calling." Long pause. "From a phone booth." Another long pause. "Whose murder? Mine, of course." Very long pause. "His home phone number? Thank you."

Jake sipped his lemon coke and grinned, imagining the confusion at the other end of the line.

Anna Marie had a little trouble after that. Captain von Flanagan wasn't at home, he was at an anniversary party. He'd left the anniversary party with one of his in-laws. He wasn't at the in-law's house, he'd gone to a night club in Cicero. No, he was at a friend's apartment in Rogers Park, and there she got him on the phone.

"Captain von Flanagan?" Anna Marie's voice was smooth, mellow, and soft. "This is Anna Marie St. Clair. Jesse Conway has been murdered, in my apartment. I thought I'd better call you direct."

Jake shoved away the lemon coke and wished with all his heart that he could hear what von Flanagan was saying.

"But this *is* Anna Marie St. Clair. Don't you recognize my voice?"

That ought to get him, Jake reflected. Anna Marie did have a voice that no one could forget.

"It's Jesse Conway. He telephoned the police just before he was killed and said he was being murdered. How do I know? He told me, just now. Captain, I think you'd better get right over there. Good-by——" The last word trailed off into an ethereal whisper.

Out in the car Jake said, "It's a good thing von Flanagan's psychology-conscious these days. He'll be able to practice it on himself."

"How about tipping off the newspapers?" Helene asked, starting the car.

"Not yet. I know what I'm doing. Just because you married a press agent doesn't mean you are one."

"Every woman is a born press agent," Helene said. "But you're the boss. Where to?"

"The Casino," Jake said happily, "and leave everything to me. Anna Marie, can you still sing that song—'My Lonely Little Room'?"

"I could sing it in my sleep," she assured him.

The ensuing scene at the Casino was a memorable one. Jake, Helene, and Malone were at their usual table. The lights were dimmed for Milly Dale's first number. She slipped out from between the curtains, smiling at the audience.

Then there was a scream, Helene's scream, above the applause. The orchestra automatically went on playing, but another voice took up the song.

When I'm sitting in the gloom—
Of my lonely little room—

Milly Dale looked in the direction of the voice, then fainted. The audience didn't notice her. They were staring at the doorway to the left of the stage.

The instruments of the orchestra stopped one by one. The lovely voice began to grow softer, dying away into the faintest shadow of a sound. Then it was gone completely, and so, in the same instant, was the vision.

The Casino was deathly still for a minute. Jake jumped up from his chair, raced to the doorway and on into the hall that ran along backstage. Then everybody in the room began to talk at once, but nobody got up to leave. The headwaiter had the presence of mind to carry Milly Dale off the stage, but he took her to a couch in the ladies' lounge instead of her dressing room.

A moment later Jake reappeared. He was mopping his brow and he looked pale. There was another sudden hush.

Jake said loudly, "I assure you, there's no one—nothing—backstage. It must have been an optical illusion. Something about the lights." He paused. "I regret that Miss Dale will not be able to finish her appearance tonight. The floor show, however, will continue as scheduled."

The orchestra began to play, a little shakily at first. The chorus came out on the stage. Its members didn't dance particularly well tonight—or any night, for that matter—but no one paid much attention to them, anyway. The buzz of conversation all but drowned out the music. A few minutes later Jake, Helene, and Malone slipped out through the side door. Anna Marie was waiting for them in the car.

"You even convinced me," Malone told her. "And you looked beautiful."

"Tomorrow night," Jake said, "the Casino will be jammed."

Helene sniffed. "I thought that press-agenting job wasn't purely altruistic. What do we haunt now?"

"Home," Jake said. "Fun is fun, but there's no point in overdoing it. Besides, there's a lot of things that need to be talked over."

"And," Malone said, "I need a drink."

They took Anna Marie up the back elevator. The telephone was ringing when they reached the door. Jake answered it.

"Sorry," he said after a moment of listening, "no statement." Another moment, and, "Yes, Harry, I know we're pals. But there's no statement I can make. I don't even know what I saw. Besides, I don't believe in ghosts myself."

As he hung up the receiver he said contentedly, "That was the *Examiner*." The phone promptly rang again, and as he reached for it he said, "That will the the *Trib*." It was.

All the papers had called by the time Helene came out from the kitchenette with a tray of dishes and a golden brown omelet that sent out an aroma of bacon, onion, tomato, and green pepper. Malone began mixing drinks.

"Everything is going fine," Helene said. "As long as nobody gives the show away. We won't, and Jesse Conway can't. But——"

The telephone rang again.

Jake said into it, "Hello, von Flanagan, what are you doing up at this hour of the night? Malone?"

The little lawyer shook his head furiously.

"Sorry," Jake said. "I don't know where you could find

him. He left the Casino with us, but—he wasn't feeling very well."

The sound of von Flanagan's voice could he heard all over the room, a profane roar. Jake said, "I'll be damned!" and, "You don't tell me!" and, "I'll try to locate him for you!" and, "Well, it's pretty late—suppose we drop in tomorrow morning?" and finally, "Yeah, that's right. Just psychology." He hung up.

"I take it," Helene said, serving the omelet, "that von Flanagan has found the late Jesse Conway." She glanced up, saw Jake's face, and said, "*What?*"

"Von Flanagan has not found the late Jesse Conway," Jake said. His face was pale, his eyes very bright. "Von Flanagan was tipped off—he doesn't say by whom—that Jesse Conway had been murdered. But when he got to the scene of the crime, Jesse Conway—the *late* Jesse Conway—wasn't there."

No one spoke for a good sixty seconds. Then Helene said, "Impossible."

"But," Jake went on, "there was blood on the carpet in the place where he was supposed to find the late Jesse Conway. And he's removed the telephone for fingerprint tests."

Malone scowled. "Whoever moved Jesse Conway's remains may have had the presence of mind to wipe off the telephone."

"That isn't all," Jake said. "Von Flanagan has a very important murder on his hands." He reached for a drink, gulped it down in one breath. "The wreckage of a car was found by state police on the highway south of Gary. It looked at first as though the driver had been killed by the wreck. But it turns out there was a bullet hole in his body."

"Who?" Anna Marie demanded.

"Warden Garrity," Jake said.

The room was very still. Helene pushed aside her plate and lighted a cigarette. "Well," she said, "*he* won't give the show away, either."

"That's just the point," Malone said. "Two people knew Anna Marie is alive. Both of them have been murdered." He frowned and said, "That may mean—that there's somebody else——" He didn't need to finish the sentence.

CHAPTER SIXTEEN

"It probably doesn't mean a thing," Helene said. "Just because someone happened to murder Jesse Conway, and someone happened to murder Garrity——" She paused and began refilling glasses.

"Your tone of voice lacks conviction," Malone said. He chewed on his cigar for a minute. "But I'll play along with your theory. Purely coincidence, that's all. In spite of the fact that Jesse Conway was killed in Anna Marie's apartment, and Garrity seems to have been rushing to Chicago immediately after Conway's murder. These little coincidences are happening all the time. I remember once in St. Louis——"

Helene made a brief, unflattering remark about Malone, then said, "All right, we'll play it your way. Who knows that Anna Marie is alive?"

"More to the point," Jake said, "who knew that Conway and Garrity knew it? And——" He caught the look on Malone's face and was suddenly silent.

"I can think of a lot of questions beginning with *Who*," the little lawyer said gloomily. An inch of cigar ash landed on his vest, he brushed at it ineffectually, and went on, "Now, if I could only think of the answers to them, I could go home and get some sleep."

"They can wait until tomorrow," Anna Marie said.

Malone shook his head. "Not these questions."

"And I never knew the day," Jake said acidly, "when his needing sleep couldn't wait until tomorrow, or even the day after tomorrow."

"Or even the week after next," Helene added.

"I'm becoming a respectable businessman," Malone told her firmly. "Bookkeeping. Office hours. From now on, it's early to bed for me. Remember about the early worm turning over a new leaf."

Helene said, "You mean it's a long worm that has no turning."

"Don't rattle me," Malone said. "I know what I mean. It's the healthy bird—I mean the wise worm—hell! I mean, the early leaf——"

"You mean," she said, "the old worm is turning over the last leaf."

"That's right," he said. "No——!" He paused. "Never mind."

He looked at his watch. Two-fifteen. He remembered his resolution to get to the office every morning at nine and shuddered. Maybe he was making a big mistake. Then he looked at Anna Marie, sitting in the exact center of Helene's pale blue satin sofa, and became twice as determined about the resolution as he'd been before. After all, he reflected, he could just stay up all night for the first few times, until he got used to the new routine.

"The important question beginning with *Who*," Anna Marie said, "is who hired Ike Malloy?"

"Uh-uh," Malone said. "That's important, but it's only one question. I've got a whole set. Who planned an elaborate job of framing you? Who shot Jesse Conway? Who shot Warden Garrity? Who has been running the protection racket? Who sent Mr. Tan Raincoat to search that building?"

Helene said, "One name might answer all those."

"Might," Malone said. He relit his cigar, "But not necessarily. In fact, I have a feeling that it's going to take more than one name to answer those *Who* questions."

"How do you know?" Helene demanded.

"I don't know. I told you it was just a feeling."

"It's bad enough you have to be a respectable businessman," Jake said in a complaining tone, "on top of that, you have to be psychic."

Malone ignored him and went on. "The most important *Who* to me is still, who might have hated Anna Marie enough to have arranged this whole thing so that she would not only die, but be tortured for weeks before she died?"

He looked across the room at Anna Marie. Her lovely face was pale, and this time it wasn't a matter of make-up.

"I don't know," she whispered. "I simply don't know. Why would anyone hate me that much?"

Helene brought Anna Marie a fresh drink, handed her a cigarette, and said, "How about Eva Childers?"

"Possible, but only remotely," Malone said. "I doubt if Big Joe meant that much to her. And, anyway, even if that were the motive—getting rid of a rival—it seems to me like an awfully roundabout way for a woman to go about it."

"If she doesn't have something to do with it," Helene insisted, "why was she in The Happy Days saloon with the young man in the tan raincoat? And why did she show up at your office later with a bribe?"

The little lawyer said, "I don't know, and that goes for both questions. But that reminds me, I've got to call her first thing in the morning to tell her I've decided to take the bribe." He sighed deeply. "This business of becoming a respectable and prosperous businessman is going to be a terrible strain on me."

Helene grinned wickedly and said, "If it's a good enough bribe it ought to be worth the effort."

Malone glanced at Anna Marie and said, almost dreamily, "It's worth it, all right. And don't bother me, I'm thinking."

After a few minutes of silence Jake yawned and said, "Maybe what we all need is a good night's sleep."

Helene shushed him and refilled Malone's glass. It was empty again. A fresh cigar had been lighted before the lawyer spoke.

"Why should the unfinished first draft of an unwritten letter be so important?"

This time it was Helene who sighed. "He thinks for twenty minutes," she complained, "and all he comes up with is another question."

"Shut up," Malone said amiably. He turned to Anna Marie. "That is, if it was unwritten. Did he ever finish it and send it to you?"

Anna Marie shook her head. Her lovely eyes were puzzled.

"He wrote—'If I weren't ill——' Do you know anything about the state of Big Joe's health?"

She shook her head again. "I never knew him to be sick.

If there was anything the matter with him, he never told me."

Malone scowled and puffed furiously at his cigar. "It simply doesn't make sense," he said. "Not just the letter but the fact that someone apparently went to considerable trouble trying to find it. Or," he went on, "was something else the object of the search. Did Big Joe have something else hidden? And if so, what?"

"And if he did," Helene said, "why didn't we find it when we found this?"

"Because it had already been taken away," Malone hazarded.

Helene said, "But you said yourself that whoever took the place apart couldn't have found what he was looking for."

"How can I think when you're heckling me?" Malone roared indignantly. He added in a milder tone, "Maybe somebody else got there first and took it away."

"Who?" Helene asked. "And what did he find? And where is it now? And how did he get in if there were only two keys?"

"I don't know and I don't know and I don't know," Malone said savagely. "It could have been Jesse Conway. He had the other key. But I went all through his pockets and I didn't find anything that had anything to do with the case except Anna Marie's key. Maybe he found whatever it was on some previous visit and took it away. But then, why did he come back? And who murdered him? And who took his body away? And why?" He drew a long breath. "Maybe Jake's right. Maybe I do just need a good night's sleep."

Helene said, "I've figured out a possible answer to one question all by myself. The question of how the young man in the raincoat got his key." She leaned back on the apple-green cushions, looking like a smugly pleased child.

"How?" Jake demanded.

"He got it from Mrs. Childers," Helene said calmly. She added, "Of course."

Malone stared at her for a moment. "That could be it," he said thoughtfully. "Big Joe's effects—whatever he happened to have in his pockets at the time—would naturally be turned over to his widow as soon as the police formalities were over, and she——"

"She is having lunch with me tomorrow," Helene said, "and I have a feeling that Mrs. Childers and I are going to be great, great friends."

Jake was on the point of saying that he didn't like the idea. Not from any objection to Mrs. Childers, nor to Helene's motives for cultivating her, but because he suspected Mrs. Childers was involved in something not only unpleasant, but quite probably dangerous to anyone prying into it. He was interrupted, however, by a thunderous knock at the door, and von Flanagan bellowing, "Open up!"

Helene grabbed Anna Marie's hat, purse, and rain cape and carried them into the bedroom. As Anna Marie followed, she whispered, "Make yourself comfortable," and closed the door.

Malone carried Anna Marie's glass into the kitchenette as Jake opened the door. "I'm looking for Malone," von Flanagan said, slamming the door behind him. He used a few adjectives before "Malone," of which "lying scoundrel" was the most complimentary. "He's not at his hotel. He's not at any of his hangouts, and if he isn't here, you two can just come along and help me find him." He spotted Malone coming out from the kitchen, and his face turned an ominous shade of magenta.

"I'm sorry you had to look for me," Malone said. He added smoothly, "I haven't been here long. Jake told me you'd called, but I didn't know where to reach you. What's up?"

"I ought to arrest you for obstructing justice," von Flanagan roared, "and don't tell me you don't know anything about these murders, because you do."

Malone said nothing and looked innocently curious.

"First Jesse Conway dies saying 'Tell Malone,'" the big police officer said, breathing heavily, "and now Garrity——"

Malone said quickly, "I didn't even know Garrity was dead until"—he caught himself just in time—"Jake told me."

"Since you don't know anything about it," von Flanagan said with acid politeness, "I'm delighted to be the first to inform you that when Garrity was murdered he was on his way to Chicago—to see you."

CHAPTER SEVENTEEN

"There's some perfectly logical explanation," Helene said. She gave von Flanagan the special smile she reserved for policemen and cab drivers. "You look so tired. Sit down—no, here, this chair—and I'll make you a drink. And how about some bacon and eggs?"

Von Flanagan relaxed in the most comfortable chair in the room, sipped his drink, sniffed the odors from the kitchen, and remarked at length on the fact that Jake Justus didn't half appreciate what a wonderful little woman he had for a wife.

Jake refrained from answering. He'd have found it difficult to keep the word "Delilah" out of the conversation.

Helene was back with the bacon and eggs and steaming coffee before von Flanagan got back to business. She put the tray in front of him, beamed, and said, "Now don't say another word before you've finished every scrap of that!"

At last von Flanagan handed her a completely empty tray and accepted a second drink with, "Well, since I'm not officially on duty." He added wearily, "I shouldn't be, at this hour. Why the hell can't more people get murdered in the daytime?" That reminded him of his errand. He glared at Malone and growled, "And you, making it hard for me. There's laws about keeping secrets from the police in a murder investigation."

Malone hung for a split second between a bland, "I don't know what you're talking about," and an irate, "Prove it!" The latter won.

"Now, Malone," von Flanagan said in an unexpectedly soothing tone. "We been friends for a long time. We been friends since I was a rookie cop and you was pushing a hack and going to night law school. This is just a friendly little visit, nothing official about it, and I'm asking you for old times' sake, do you know anything about Garrity's murder."

"That's using the old psychology on him," Helene murmured under her breath.

Von Flanagan didn't hear her. "And if you lie to me, Malone, so help me, I'll toss you in the can."

"Believe me," Malone said, "I don't know anything about it. I don't know anywhere near as much as you do."

"Why was he coming to see you?"

"I don't know," Malone said. "How do you know that he was?"

"Because," von Flanagan told him, "before he left his office, he got one telephone call and made two. The one he got was from a Chicago pay station. Then he called your hotel. You weren't there, and nobody knew where you were. Nobody knew when you'd be back. He finally located that black-haired secretary of yours. She didn't know where you were, either, but he told her to start looking for you and he'd call her again as soon as he got to Chicago. He didn't get to Chicago."

"That last statement," Malone said, starting to unwrap a fresh cigar, "is the only dramatic touch to a very dull story."

Von Flanagan's broad face began to turn purple.

"Why the hell," the little lawyer went on, as much to himself as to von Flanagan, "did Garrity want to see me, and why was he in such a hurry that he got my secretary out of bed to look for me, and started driving here in the middle of the night?"

"I came up here to ask you that," von Flanagan said.

"And I don't know," Malone said, "The last time I saw Garrity was at a testimonial banquet for Butts O'Hare, two years ago. I never knew him very well, and the closest I ever had to having any business dealings with him was when I got a couple of traffic tickets fixed once for a cousin of his."

"Well, damn it," von Flanagan said, "he certainly was in a sweat to get in touch with you tonight. And that coming on top of Jesse Conway trying to leave a message for you——" His eyes narrowed. "I don't suppose you know anything about that, either?"

Malone did, but he felt this wasn't the time to discuss it. He evaded the issue neatly by saying in a deeply earnest tone, "If you find out why Conway wanted to reach me—what message he wanted to get to me—I wish you'd let me know."

"If I ever do find out," the big police officer said gloomily. "The trouble with my job is that people go clear out of their way to make it hard for me." That launched him on the subject of his not having wanted to be a cop, and this time he went way back to the fact that he never would have been a cop, he'd have been an undertaker like he'd always intended to be, only somebody at the City Hall owed one of his relatives money. Every promotion he'd had during his twenty years on the force he'd looked on as an injustice and an injury.

"And another thing," he said at last, "people do play jokes on the department, and it ain't right. Like tonight."

Jake, Helene, and Malone listened breathlessly.

"Some dame calls me up on the phone and says she's Anna Marie St. Clair," he said. "For a minute she really had me rattled. I'm not superstitious, y'understand, like some Irishmen I could name. But it sounded so much like her voice, it really—yeah, really had me rattled. Now that's where my knowledge of psychology comes in handy."

"I bet you knew immediately it was somebody playing a joke," Helene said admiringly.

He beamed at her. "I just told myself I was tired and maybe been working too hard, and it did sound like the same voice, and so for a minute she darn near had me believing in ghosts. Especially since she'd called up to tell me Jesse Conway was dead."

Malone signaled Jake with his eyes. Jake said, "That reminds me. When you called up before, you said you'd gone to where Jesse Conway's body was supposed to be, and it wasn't there. How do you know he's dead?"

"I don't know," von Flanagan said. "It's a deduction. Psychology and deduction, they go together like the Smith Brothers. There wasn't a body, but there was blood on the rug where a body could of been. And Jesse Conway seems to have been missing since last night. So my theory is he's been murdered, only I got to wait till his corpse turns up to prove it. Maybe it will, maybe it won't. And one of my boys dug a .38 bullet out of one of the window frames."

"I suppose you turned it over to ballistics right away," Malone said casually.

"I did," von Flanagan said. "It came out of the same gun that killed Garrity." He rose. "I don't like these murders. They're mixed up with politics. Big Joe was an important guy. Tom McKeown is a big shot nowadays. He and Big Joe got Garrity his appointment, and his brother Bill is running some kind of a racket. And Big Joe got killed in a joint Bill runs."

Jake and Helene glanced at each other briefly. Malone relit his cigar.

"Brodie," von Flanagan went on, "was mixed up with the whole bunch of 'em, and for a while Brodie damn near ran this town. Still runs his ward. And Jesse Conway owed Brodie a hell of a lot of dough. I don't like it. When politics and murder gets mixed up together, there's likely to be trouble."

He turned to Helene and said formally, "Thank you for your hospitality, Mrs. Justus."

"It was a pleasure," Helene murmured.

At the door the police officer paused, one hand on the knob. "You know," he said thoughtfully, "I never believed that girl killed Big Joe."

Malone jumped and said, "What?" Then, "You arrested her."

"I know it," von Flanagan said in an unhappy tone. "But I didn't think so even then. Psychology again. Her story sounded so phony it didn't seem reasonable anybody would make it up if she was guilty. But I couldn't do anything about it. After I made the pinch, it was out of my hands."

"Don't worry about it," Helene said. "It wasn't your fault."

"I know it. But—well, there was another thing. All the time it seemed to me there was something proved her story was on the up and up. Only I never could quite figure what it was. Couple dozen times it seemed like I almost had my finger on it. Maybe if I had——"

He sighed deeply and said, "Well, good night. And you, Malone, if any more guys get murdered on their way to see you or while they're talking about you, I'm going to run you in."

After he'd gone, Jake said, "That was all very interesting. Who shall Anna Marie haunt now, Tom McKeown, Bill McKeown, or Brodie?"

"I vote for von Flanagan," Malone growled. "Him and his cracks about superstitious Irishmen!" He added in a milder tone, "That's a funny thing—his talking about *something* that would have proved Anna Marie was innocent. Because I've had the same feeling all along, and I can't quite figure out what it is, either."

"I can," Helene said serenely. "I can, and I have."

While they stared at her, she rapped lightly on the bedroom door, then opened it. Anna Marie had been curled up, half dozing. She rose, stretched like a sleepy kitten, and smiled at them. Her smooth cheeks were pink.

"Look at her," Helene said.

"I am looking at her," Malone said. He almost added, "With all my heart."

"Were you carrying a wrap—any kind of wrap—the night Big Joe was murdered?" Helene demanded.

Anna Marie shook her head, bewildered. "I wore just exactly what I have on now. And my hat and purse, of course."

"Good," Helene said. "Now, Malone, look at the way that skirt fits. Look at the way the jacket is cut, and the way *it* fits."

"What *is* this," Anna Marie asked, "a fashion show?"

"A fashion show," Helene said grimly, "that should have been put on for the jury at your trial."

Malone nodded. "I think I get the idea." He looked at Anna Marie. "Turn around. All the way around."

She pirouetted, half posing. The pale gray suit, close-fitting save for the very slight flare between her hip and her knee. The tiny pillbox hat with its floating pink veil. The pink and gold purse, just big enough to carry a compact, a small cigarette case, and money. Not much money.

"Yes," he said, "I do get the idea."

"But it took a woman to point it out," Helene gloated. She smiled at Anna Marie. "The crazy fools. Where the devil did they think you carried the gun?"

CHAPTER EIGHTEEN

Malone tucked the sheet under Anna Marie's chin and stood looking at her for a moment. In sleep, her face was the face of a very young and very happy little girl, the tawny hair rumpled on the pillow, the long, curling lashes, the slightly parted and smilingly curving lips, the faintly flushed cheeks.

She'd fallen asleep in the taxi, relaxing first against his shoulder and then into the curve of his arm like a tired and trusting child. He'd carried her up the freight elevator and through the hall to her room. He'd unpacked her suitcase, carefully arranging dresses on hangers and making a neat little parade of cosmetics on top of the bureau. He'd selected a gossamer-thin pale orchid nightgown and its matching robe, and tucked her in bed, carefully folding the robe over the nearest chair.

He glanced around the room to see if there was anything else he could do for her. Suddenly the thought occurred to him. There should be flowers when she woke.

Flowers in the room, a bed-tray with fruit, coffee, and the morning paper. Roses on the bureau, a vase full of hyacinths on the desk, and a bowl of violets on the table by her bed.

Malone looked at his watch. Fifteen minutes to five. A difficult time of the morning to find roses, hyacinths, and violets. But he'd manage somehow. He'd met and coped with harder problems in his lifetime.

He took one more long look at the sleeping Anna Marie. He considered kissing her, very lightly, on the forehead. No, that might waken her. He contented himself by whispering, "Sleep well. I'll be back soon," and tiptoed out of the room.

Out in the hall he considered the immediate problems at

110

hand. Here it was nearly five in the morning, and he had to be at his office by nine. For a moment his resolution weakened. He reminded himself that if he had eight hours of sleep and got to the office at three in the afternoon—*no*, he'd made up his mind and he wasn't going to change it now!

Roses, hyacinths, and violets, and where to find them. Jesse Conway, Garrity, and the man in the tan raincoat. Eva Childers and her bribe. Getting to the office at nine.

He finally decided that he needed a drink to clear his brain, and headed for Joe the Angel's City Hall Bar.

At this hour the streets were cold and deserted, save for an occasional hurrying taxicab. Malone walked briskly, shivering every step of the way. Shivering, aching with fatigue, and apprehensive at every slight sound.

A faint, pre-dawn mist drifted in from the lake, blurring the edges of deserted office buildings, changing the street into a mysterious canyon, turning every alley into a hiding place of unnamable horrors.

The hour before dawn. Malone suddenly found himself remembering things Grandmother Malone had said, years ago. The last hour before ghosts and ghouls returned to their lairs. The hour when the Wicked One could prowl the earth unchallenged and mark the unwary with his sign.

Not, Malone reminded himself, that he believed in ghosts and ghouls.

He remembered suddenly a young interne who had once confided in him that more deaths occurred in hospitals in the hour before dawn than at any other time of the day.

"Scientific nonsense," Malone announced to the empty street. "Anybody can be a liar, but it takes an education to be a statistician."

He began walking a little faster. Quite a little faster.

When he'd been a very small boy, Grandmother Levinsky had told him stories she'd heard from Polish peasants. Werewolves, who had to return to their natural forms at sunrise, committed their most hideous deeds just before dawn.

A small, mangy mongrel darted out suddenly from an alley between two towering office buildings in pursuit of an even smaller and mangier cat. He ran in front of Malone, barking and yelping. The little lawyer broke into a run. The mongrel changed direction and followed Malone, snapping at his heels.

Joe the Angel was sitting in back of his cash register, adding up the back bar bills of his best customers. There were only two other people in the place: a City Hall janitor, eating cold pork sandwiches, drinking beer, and reading the *Racing Form*, and a recently fired *Tribune* reporter sleeping off a drunk in one of the booths.

It was a pleasantly quiet place, up to the time when Malone burst in, breathless and panting, shoved a stool against the doors, half collapsed on the bar, and muttered something about needing a drink, fast.

Joe the Angel served the drink, fast, but his face had paled at the sight of Malone. He said, "This is on the house. Drink up quick, Malone, and get out of here."

"Can't," the little lawyer panted, trying to catch his breath and gulp the drink at the same time. "Out there? Werewolf!"

The recently fired reporter woke up in time to hear the last word. He propped his chin on his hand and went on listening.

"Malone," Joe the Angel said gently, "you go home and go to bed and go to sleep. I'll call up for a taxi. You never mind about imagining werewolves. You gonna feel a lot better after a good sleep."

"No!" Malone gasped. He glanced apprehensively toward the door.

"Listen, Malone," Joe the Angel said. "You're an educated man. You don't believe in a lot of nonsense." He poured Malone another drink. "This is on the house, too, Malone. And don't you go imagining——"

Out on the sidewalk the frustrated mongrel let loose a melancholy, unearthly howl that echoed and re-echoed the length of Clark Street. Joe the Angel ducked under the bar. For the first time in years Malone spilled his drink. The ex-reporter gave a yell and dived into the back room.

There was a very long interval of almost unbearable quiet. Then the City Hall janitor looked up from his *Racing Form* and remarked that some fool dog must be chasing some fool cat. Joe the Angel came up from under the bar and tried to look as though there hadn't been any interruption in what he was saying. Malone put down his glass, practically untasted. In the back room the ex-reporter passed out quietly under a table, where he was discovered three hours later babbling about witches, wizards, and werewolves.

Malone unwrapped a cigar and managed to light it on the third try. "Quite an experience," he said with a hollow laugh, "being chased down Clark Street by a vicious dog."

"You said werewolf," Joe the Angel said.

"Come, come," Malone said. "You misunderstood."

"You *said* werewolf," Joe the Angel repeated.

"There is no such thing," Malone said firmly. "You've been seeing too many movies."

The City Hall janitor, a Hungarian, finished the last scrap of his sandwich and the last drop of his beer, shoved a few coins across the bar, and slid off his stool. At the door he paused and remarked, "In the old country there are werewolves. One of them destroyed the grandmother of my wife's aunt." He opened the door and went out. The melancholy little dog slipped in between his feet, sat down in the middle of the floor, and began scratching for fleas.

"Imagine being as superstitious as that poor guy!" Malone said with another hollow laugh. He glanced sympathetically at the small dog and said, "Joe, you got any meat scraps around here? A bone, maybe?"

"*You* said werewolf," Joe the Angel said, breathing hard, and ignoring the request for meat scraps or a bone.

"A vicious dog pursued me down Clark Street," Malone said. Again he looked briefly at the mongrel. "A big dog. *This* big. Frothing at the mouth. Probably rabid. Eyes like balls of fire."

Joe the Angel stared long and silently at Malone. He walked out to the tiny kitchen in back, stepping neatly over the legs of the ex-reporter, and returned with a plate of scraps which he set in front of the small dog. Then he returned to his post back of the bar, poured the little lawyer another drink, and drew himself a short beer.

"Malone," he said earnestly, "I been in business here a long time. Twenty-two years to be exact about it. Through prohibition. Through repeal. I work hard, I save money.

Three wives I've buried, seven children I've sent through school. I'm an honest man. I make an honest living."

He drew a long breath. "Understand, Malone. You and me, we're friends. For a long time now, we're friends. Because for a long time we're friends, I tear up the little bar bill you owe me. All you have tonight, it's on the house. A bottle of good bourbon I give you for a present, to take home. Now, Malone, will you please go away and not come back, yes?"

"No," Malone said. He added bitterly, "Friendship!"

Joe the Angel sighed. "Maybe it wasn't, outside, a werewolf. All right, it was, maybe, a dog. But last night you come in and a ghost comes in and sits beside you. Tonight you come in and talk werewolf."

"A dog," Malone said.

"O.K., dog, werewolf, I don't care. But a ghost is a ghost. Malone, my old friend, maybe you don't understand. This is bad for business. So now go away. Go home."

"*No*," Malone said. He added, "Joe, where can I buy some flowers?"

The small dog, having finished up the scraps, howled loudly for more. Joe the Angel groaned. "Very well. You may remain, Malone, my friend. *I* will go home." He began untying his apron.

"Now, wait a minute," Malone said. "We've got to talk this over. Do you believe in ghosts?"

"Me?" Joe the Angel looked at him indignantly. "I am an educated man." He added, "But last night——"

Malone slid off the bar stool and stood as though he were about to address a jury. "Last night you saw the earthbound spirit of a poor, innocent girl who had been framed for a murder rap and sent to die in the electric chair. She bears no animosity against you. She bears no animosity against me. She only seeks our help. She longs only to attain the peace and happiness of her heavenly home. Yet, because she was the helpless victim of a cruel conspiracy that sent her to her death, until she is avenged she must haunt the city of Chicago"—he gulped down the rest of his drink—"beating her poor broken wings against prison bars more grim than any man has devised." He leaned on the bar. "Joe, I know you want to help her."

Juries had broken into tears at the sound of that voice. Joe, made of sterner stuff, simply gulped and said, "You bet I do."

"Fine," Malone said, getting back on the bar stool. "Now, where can I get some roses, hyacinths, and violets at this hour of the morning?"

"Roses, violets, yes," Joe the Angel said. "Hyacinths, no. But gladioli, carnations, pink and white both, orchids, even. In nice baskets, and with ribbons."

"Gladioli, carnations, and orchids will be O.K.," Malone said. "But where?"

Joe beamed. "My brother, Rico di Angelo, opened a very fine undertaking parlor on West Division Street yesterday. A big party. Everybody sent flowers, even the mayor. I dropped in at the party myself. Roses, violets, gladioli, carnations, orchids——"

"I knew you could help me out," Malone said gratefully.

"Only," Joe said, "you have to wait until nine o'clock. That is when Rico opens for business."

"At nine o'clock I'm going to be in my office," Malone said firmly. "And these flowers have got to be at a certain place before then."

Joe sighed and shook his head. "Then you will have to break into Rico's place. It will not be too difficult. Look, Malone." He spread a paper napkin on the bar, wrote down an address, and began drawing a diagram. "Here is an alley. Here is a window. Here is——"

"Never mind," Malone said. He shoved the napkin in his pocket. "I can get in. Will Rico be sore?"

"Be sore? What would he want with all those expensive flowers? Except to sell them back to the florist and have to take a cut on the price."

"I'll pay him," Malone said. "And that reminds me." He reached in his pocket. "How much is that bar bill?"

Joe the Angel looked at him thoughtfully for a minute, then produced the bill. "But remember, Malone. No ghosts in my saloon. And no more talk of werewolves. It's bad for business."

"I'll remember," the little lawyer promised. He handed

over the money and said, "But one thing more. I wish you'd answer a couple of questions."

"For my friend Malone," Joe said, "anything."

"Then tell me," Malone said, lighting his cigar, "how hard have you been hit by this new protection racket, and who have you paid off to?"

There was a silence. Joe the Angel stared at Malone, his mouth set in a grim, hard, straight line. Then he marched to the door and flung it open.

"This time, Malone," he said, "you do go out. Out, and you don't come back."

CHAPTER NINETEEN

"I'm not going," Malone said, "and I think it would be better for everyone concerned if you did answer my question." He almost added, "Let's go somewhere where we can buy a drink and talk this over," before he remembered where he was.

"Out!" Joe the Angel said.

"No," Malone said. He walked over to the door and closed it firmly. Then he stepped back of the bar and said, "This is on the house, what will you have?"

Joe the Angel was not amused. He stood by the door, trying to make up his mind what to do next.

"We've been friends for a long time," Malone quoted, "and I know you don't really think I'm going to turn you in if you do happen to own a piece of the protection racket. I wouldn't even try to muscle in on your share of it. Only, it's costing a friend of mine too much money and I'd like him to be let alone." With a practiced hand, he set a rye bottle back in its place on the shelf and said again to Joe, "Well, what will you have?"

"A little brandy," Joe said hoarsely. He came slowly up to the bar and said, "I do not own any part of this racket, and I do not want to own any part of this racket."

"Too bad," Malone said, pouring out the brandy, "*from all I hear of it, there should be some nice profits involved, with the right management, of course.*" He looked thoughtfully at the end of his cigar. "Maybe we could take it over, you and I."

Joe the Angel gulped his brandy and, breathing hard, dwelt again on the fact that for twenty-two years, through prohibition and through repeal, he had been an honest hardworking businessman who saved his money, buried three wives, and sent seven children through school. He also added that it would not be good for the reputation of Joe the Angel's City Hall Bar if a late customer should come in and find Malone behind the bar serving drinks and Joe the Angel on one of the stools apparently paying for them.

Malone countered with the statement that he had always wanted to be a bartender and that any customers coming in would simply assume that the place had changed hands, if said customers were in a state capable of assuming anything at all. That gave him an idea.

"As a matter of fact," he announced cheerfully, "it is going to change hands. You are going to sell the bar, and I am going to buy it from you."

Joe the Angel raised his eyes to the ceiling and addressed a few well-chosen remarks to be an obscure Italian saint favorably known for dealing with the hopelessly insane. Malone didn't even hear him. He went on thoughtfully, almost dreamily, "That is not a bad idea at all. In fact, it's a very sound idea." He leaned his elbows on the bar, beamed at Joe, and said, "In fact, I'll even let *you* run up a three weeks' bar bill in appreciation of past favors."

"Malone," Joe the Angel said weakly, "I wish you would go away."

"I will go away," Malone said, "as soon as you tell me all you know about the protection racket and sell me your saloon." He added earnestly, "You see if I own this place nobody is going to kidnap and torture one of your seven children, murder your very lovely fourth wife, or chase you up an alley and beat your brains out."

Joe the Angel gasped, "How do you know?"

"I'm psychic," Malone said cheerfully. "A person gets that way running around with ghosts and werewolves." He managed to catch Joe the Angel just before he reached the door, dragged him back to the bar, poured out another brandy, and said gently, "This also is on the house, pal."

Joe the Angel groaned.

"And furthermore," Malone said, "if you don't answer my question———" He stared significantly into Joe's unhappy brown eyes. "Well, if you think you've seen ghosts *yet*———"

"Believe me, my friend," Joe the Angel said, "I will tell you anything you want to know. I will sell you the saloon. I will sell it to you for fifty cents."

"It's a deal," Malone said happily. He fished a quarter, two dimes, and a nickel from his pocket and slid them across the bar. "Next week I'll sell it back to you for sixty cents."

"Maybe the week after that you'll buy it again," Joe the Angel said, "for seventy cents."

"Sure," Malone said, "and then you buy it back for eighty cents. We could keep that up for years and one of us would be bound to make money."

"But not me," Joe the Angel said in a gloomy tone.

"All right, I'll tell you what I'll do," Malone said briskly. "I'll sell you back the saloon for forty cents and take a loss. All you have to do is pay my customary fee for legal advice and services."

Joe the Angel again raised his eyes and requested the intercession of some saint able to deal with crooked Irish lawyers.

"Incidentally," Malone said, "in circumstances like these my fee is usually ten cents." He knocked an inch of ash off his cigar and leaned across the bar. "Look, Joe. As you said, we've been friends for a long time. Ever since I was pushing a hack and you used to slip me a commission now and then for steering out-of-town customers to your speak. I'm not doing you any harm. As a matter of fact, I'm doing this as much to help you as to help out Jake Justus."

Joe the Angel's face reddened with sudden wrath. "My

good friend Jake Justus? You mean they got the nerve to put the squeeze on him, too? The bums!" He reached for the brandy bottle.

Malone pushed it across the bar and said, "This is still on the house. And what bums?"

"My good friend Malone," Joe the Angel said, "I do not know what bums. If I had known I would have told my cousin Benny di Angelo. Or maybe I would have killed them myself, who knows? But one day there comes into my place a man to"—he smiled bitterly—"sell me insurance. I throw him out. The next day he is back, with another friend. I throw them both out. The day after my bartender is arrested selling a glass of beer to a minor. I throw everybody out, and then——" His story was essentially the same one that Jake had told. The arrest of a janitor for selling narcotics. Threats against himself, his children, and his new wife. And all the time the price for "insurance" going up. He ended with a helpless and almost hopeless, "Then what can I do about these bums?"

"Nothing," Malone said, chewing savagely on his cigar, "except pay them. But now I own this place I can do something. I haven't any wives or children to be threatened with bodily harm, and I can beat any framed-up rap of selling narcotics, or selling liquor to minors, or anything else they can think of, including arson, mayhem, or mopery."

"You are making a joke, yes?" Joe the Angel said anxiously.

"I am making a joke, no," Malone said. "I've bought this saloon and I'm going to hang onto it. And if it should be known early in the morning that the City Hall Bar has changed hands, maybe a few insurance salesmen would come around to call on me." He grinned wickedly, "Who knows? I might even be tempted to play along with them."

Joe the Angel gazed across the bar. "Malone," he said, "you are a very bad man, but you are one damn smart lawyer."

"And you," Malone said, "are one damn smart saloon-keeper to sell this joint and get out from under the racket. Shall we have a drink on it?"

He poured two drinks, they shook hands and toasted each other solemnly.

"Now," Malone said, "do you have any idea who is back of this racket?"

Joe the Angel shook his head.

"Did you pay off to——" Malone paused, scowling. He'd started to say, "Jesse Conway." That might not be the right approach, he decided. "Who did you pay off to?"

"A young man," Joe the Angel said. "Thin face. Dark skin. Black hair, very shiny, like on my cousin Mike. Nice fancy clothes. Sometimes a raincoat."

"I think I may have seen him," Malone said, nodding. "You don't happen to know his name?"

Again Joe the Angel shook his head. "Maybe," he suggested, "when he comes to visit you, he will tell you."

"Stranger things have happened," Malone said. "Hell, we may even go into business together. How about the two alleged insurance salesmen who dropped around first?"

"I don't know either of them," Joe the Angel said. "Just bums. One of them I think used to sell slot machine concessions for Brodie."

"Brodie, huh?" Malone said. "Any other names you can think of I might like to know about?"

Joe the Angel shrugged his shoulders. "A thing like this," he said, "there are many rumors, many names. People sit in my place and talk. How much is rumor, I don't know. The names——" He paused. "Malone, I don't want to get anybody in trouble."

"You won't," the little lawyer promised.

"All kinds of names get mentioned in my place," Joe the Angel said. "Brodie. Bill McKeown. Max Hook. Butts O'Hare. How do I know?"

"How about Big Joe Childers?" Malone suggested, relighting his cigar.

"His name was mentioned, yes," Joe the Angel said, "but I think, no. Big Joe——" He shook his head.

"I know what you mean," Malone said. "This isn't the kind of racket Big Joe went in for. And another thing, it's still going on after his death." He looked at his watch. If he was going to collect roses, violets, gladioli, carnations, and even orchids, deliver them to Anna Marie's room, and get to the office at nine, he was going to have to move fast. "Joe, who killed Childers?"

"Ike Malloy," Joe said. "It was in the newspapers."

The little lawyer sighed. "But who hired Ike Malloy?"

"Who knows?" Joe the Angel said. His tone of voice implied, "Who cares?"

Malone poured himself one last drink and said, "I'd like to hire you to run this place for me, Joe. To take full charge, in fact, except of course that any further discussions of protection money should be referred to the new owner."

"O.K.," Joe said. "You pay me a salary to run the place?"

"Sure," Malone told him, "fifty cents."

"It's too much," Joe said, "but I take it."

CHAPTER TWENTY

Out on the street Malone considered the difficult problem of transportation to Rico's. The streetcar would take too long. A taxi would do very well one way, but there still remained the question of explaining to the driver the baskets of flowers at this hour of the morning. Right now Malone didn't want to call any more attention to himself than he could avoid.

He decided on a simple solution; he would borrow Helene's car.

It was a short taxi ride to the near north side apartment hotel. On the way he made up his mind that it would be wiser not to call Helene. The car would be in the hotel garage, the keys would be in the lock, and the attendant knew him. Helene was probably sound asleep by now, and there was no point in waking her. Besides, she would probably want to go along.

He decided on the sedan instead of the convertible. It would hold more flowers. Roses, violets, gladioli, carnations, orchids. The little lawyer hummed contentedly to himself as he made the turn into West Division Street.

Anna Marie was going to be very happy when she opened her eyes. He pictured the times she'd opened them in a particularly cheerless prison cell, and shuddered. But he was going to make everything up to her, a hundred times over.

As he drove, he tried to piece together the meager information Joe the Angel had given him, and to fit it in with what he knew already. The protection racket was widespread and well-organized. What part did it play in the murder of Big Joe Childers and the framing of Anna Marie?

It wouldn't have interested Big Joe. Good, respectable political graft, bookie joints, gambling houses, and what the reform newspapers liked to refer to as Dens of Vice, had been his specialty. Big Joe had always been an honest man, Malone reflected, with a high degree of social responsibility.

Besides, Big Joe would have laid off Jake and Joe the Angel. Very definitely, then, he had to be ruled out.

Malone sighed. All the facts and all the people were in some way linked together, and yet, even the manner in which they were linked didn't make sense. Names, places, facts, and wildly implausible theories revolved in his mind. Finally he came to the conclusion that he could think better after he'd had a bath and a shave.

He parked the sedan carefully in the shadows of the gloomy alley back of Rico di Angelo's new undertaking parlor. For a moment he stood in the alley, listening. Everything was silent. Almost too silent. The whole neighborhood seemed deserted.

Malone reminded himself encouragingly that Rico's place had just opened for business, and there would hardly be any clients laid out inside. He took out the tools he'd borrowed from Fran Herman's brother and went to work on the back door. Five minutes later it opened, and he stepped in.

There was an eerie coldness in the air. Malone shivered, and stood still for a moment just inside the door, his eyes slowly becoming accustomed to the darkness. Then he began moving slowly and stealthily across the room. Suddenly he bumped into something and halted again, breathing hard. The something, he discovered, was a table, unpleasantly long and narrow.

Malone fumbled for a match, found one at last and struck it. The feeble glare showed him that the room had white walls and a white ceiling, with cabinets along two sides, and

Introducing the first and only complete hardcover collection of Agatha Christie's mysteries

Now you can enjoy the
greatest mysteries ever written
in a magnificent
Home Library Edition.

Discover Agatha Christie's world of mystery, adventure and intrigue

Agatha Christie's timeless tales of mystery and suspense offer something for every reader—mystery fan or not—young and old alike. And now, you can build a complete hardcover library of her worldfamous mysteries by subscribing to The Agatha Christie Mystery Collection.

This exciting Collection is your passport to a world where mystery reigns supreme. Volume after volume, you and your family will enjoy mystery reading at its very best.

You'll meet Agatha Christie's world-famous detectives like Hercule Poirot, Jane Marple, and the likeable Tommy and Tuppence Beresford.

In your readings, you'll visit Egypt, Paris, England and other exciting destinations where murder is always on the itinerary. And wherever you travel, you'll become deeply involved in some of the most ingenious and diabolical plots ever invented ... "cliff-hangers" that only Dame Agatha could create!

It all adds up to mystery reading that's so good ... it's almost criminal. And it's yours every month with The Agatha Christie Mystery Collection.

Solve the greatest mysteries of all time. The Collection contains all of Agatha Christie's classic works including *Murder on the Orient Express, Death on the Nile, And Then There Were None, The ABC Murders* and her ever-popular whodunit, *The Murder of Roger Ackroyd.*

Each handsome hardcover volume is Smythe sewn and printed on high quality acidfree paper so it can withstand even the most murderous treatment. Bound in Sussex-blue simulated leather with gold titling, The Agatha Christie Mystery Collection will make a tasteful addition to your living room, or den.

Ride the Orient Express for 10 days without obligation. To introduce you to the Collection, we're inviting you to examine the classic mystery, *Murder on the Orient Express*, without risk or obligation. If you're not completely satisfied, just return it within 10 days and owe nothing.

However, if you're like the millions of other readers who love Agatha Christie's thrilling tales of mystery and suspense, keep *Murder on the Orient Express* and pay just $9.95 plus postage and handling.

You will then automatically receive future volumes once a month as they are published on a fully returnable, 10-day free-examination basis. No minimum purchase is required, and you may cancel your subscription at any time.

This unique collection is not sold in stores. It's available only through this special offer. So don't miss out, begin your subscription now. Just mail this card today.

that the long narrow table was an embalming table. Then the match went out.

Maybe, he reasoned, it would be simpler, and wiser, to abandon this project and break into a florist shop somewhere. He was familiar with the layout of the one he usually patronized, and he could leave payment for the flowers on the counter. In fact, he told himself, that was what he should have done in the first place. He turned around, and at that instant the door to the alley began to open, very slowly.

Malone ducked to the side of the room in one bound. A figure appeared in the doorway, a slight, slender figure wearing a raincoat. It had a flashlight in one hand and what looked very much like a gun in the other.

Even if there was a place to hide in this devilish room, Malone realized, he could never find it in the dark. The flashlight beam began playing around the room, and the little lawyer inched away from it, moving toward the door. Perhaps if the intruder came on into the room, he could slip out unnoticed through the door and make it to the car without being observed.

The intruder showed no signs of coming into the room. That left only one other thing to do. Malone moved to easy striking distance and prepared for a quick, surprise blow. But in that moment the intruder suddenly turned the flashlight squarely into Malone's face.

Momentarily blinded, Malone ducked. He aimed his head at the intruder's stomach and sent him crashing against the doorjamb. He shot a fist into the arm holding the gun, which fell and went sliding across the floor. Then a blow landed on Malone's chin and he went down.

Before he could scramble to his feet again, a third figure came in through the doorway, this one tall and lanky. He tackled the intruder, who also went down.

All Malone could tell of the scuffle that followed was that the tall, lanky stranger seemed to be on his side. He could make it into the alley and to the car now, but a better idea struck him. If he and the stranger between them could hold and subdue the intruder, it would be possible to find out who he was. It might even be possible to find out a few other interesting things.

Evidently, the intruder, seeing that the odds were against

him, decided not to stay. He managed to get loose and get as far as the door. Malone dived at him, but the butt end of the flashlight caught him squarely in the right eye, and he went down for a second time. The intruder vanished into the darkness of the alley.

This time, Malone decided to stay down. He closed his eyes and lay still. It was pleasantly quiet and peaceful now in the room. Perhaps he could just drift contentedly off to sleep, right here on the floor. Rico wouldn't mind. Just a short nap, anyway.

He realized someone was bending over him solicitously.

"Malone," Jake's voice said, tight with anxiety, "Malone, are you hurt?"

"I'm killed," the little lawyer said, opening his eyes. He felt gingerly of his jaw; it seemed to be in one piece. He glared at Jake. "Next time you start a fight, I wish you'd pick on someone my size."

"*I* start a fight," Jake said indignantly. "I should have let him beat you up before I tackled him. Next time I will." He helped Malone to his feet. "What the hell are you doing here?"

"In simple justice," Malone said, "I can ask you the same question."

"I'm here," Jake told him, "because Joe the Angel called me up just as I was starting to go to bed and told me you were on your way here. He added that you were being followed by a man in a tan raincoat and that maybe I'd better come along and look after you."

"I can look after myself, anytime, anywhere," Malone said with icy dignity, brushing himself off.

"Now," Jake said, "explain. Including why you stole Helene's car."

"Flowers," Malone said. "Roses, violets, gladioli, carnations, orchids."

"Malone," Jake said, the anxiety returning to his voice, "are you sure you feel all right?"

"Never felt better in my life," the lawyer lied. He explained the project and the borrowing of the car.

Jake raised his eyes and talked to heaven for a good five minutes about insane, drunken, Irish lawyers.

"I won't argue the point," Malone said, "but while I'm

here, I might as well get the flowers." He paused and scowled. "Why do you suppose he followed *me?*"

Jake yawned. "Maybe he wants you to get a parking ticket fixed for him. Or maybe he's a relative of Rico's and didn't know you meant to pay for the flowers. Anyway, let's get them and get out of here."

He took out a small pocket flashlight. Its beam reflected on the shiny metal of the gun the intruder had dropped. Jake took out a handkerchief and picked it up gingerly. "Might as well take this along. Ballistics might like it for a souvenir. Or it might have fingerprints." He wrapped it carefully and put it in his pocket, and led the way into the front room.

It was filled with flowers, huge gilt baskets of them, vases of them, ornamental display pieces of every size and shape. The air was heavy with their odor. In the center of the room was an elaborate and expensive-looking coffin, evidently placed there for the admiration of Rico's guests.

Malone strolled around the room, admiring the bouquets and reading the cards. "Rico ought to feel proud," he remarked. "Practically the whole City Hall is represented. And some other very notable people." He stopped in front of a large heart-shaped design which had "GOOD LUCK RICO" spelled out in red and white roses and glanced at the card. "That must have set Bugs Brodie back a nice piece of change."

"Pick out your posies and let's go," Jake said. "I haven't had any sleep tonight."

Malone finally settled for two baskets, a vase full of roses, and a set piece made of orchids. "Maybe she doesn't care for dahlias," he said, "but since they came from the mayor, I thought it would be a nice sentiment."

"'*Let's go!*" Jake repeated. He turned toward the door, and as he did so, the beam from his flashlight fell on the display coffin.

Malone, following him, stopped suddenly. "*Jake!*"

Jake looked. There, neatly laid out in the coffin, was the body of the late Jesse Conway.

CHAPTER TWENTY-ONE

Helene met them at the door, dressed in an ice-blue satin robe that swirled around her feet. Her pale hair was loose and shimmering around her shoulders. Her eyes widened. Then she scowled.

"This hour of the morning," she scolded, "and you turn up drunk, you've got a black eye, the collar's torn off your shirt and you're carrying enough flowers to open a florist shop. Fine friends my husband has!"

"I'm your friend, too," Malone said coyly. He carefully selected one perfect orchid and presented it to her with great formality. "Furthermore, I'm sober."

It was true. The last half hour had been enough to sober anyone. But he was tired, he ached in every bone, and his eye was beginning to throb.

Helene pinned the orchid on her robe, "I ought to throw you out," she said. She smiled at him. "Go on in the bathroom and wash your face, and put witch hazel on that bruise on your chin. I'll make you some coffee." She added to Jake, "And you, meantime, tell me what's been going on, or I'll lose my mind."

Jake followed her into the kitchenette. The blue robe rustled pleasantly when she walked. He looked approvingly at her pale, exquisite face, and delicate hands. He admired the sheen of her ash-blond hair. He reflected that he was the most fortunate husband in the United States, if not in the civilized world, and that he ought to do something to celebrate the fact.

"How can I make coffee when you're kissing me," Helene said, a full minute later. "And, damn you, *explain!*"

Jake grinned, lit two cigarettes and handed one to her.

"Malone went out to rob an undertaking parlor, got into a fight with an armed man, and discovered the victim of a murder. That's all."

"Jake, please. Not at this hour of the morning."

"It's the literal truth," Jake said. He filled in the details. By the time he'd half finished, the coffee was perking cheerfully. When he'd reached, "It turned out to be Jesse Conway," the coffee was done.

"I knew I should have gone with you," Helene said calmly. She carried the coffee into the living-room.

Malone was sitting on the couch. He felt a little better, but not much. Helene put the coffee pot and a cup in front of him and sternly ordered him to drink all of it. Then she turned to Jake.

"What do we do now? Phone von Flanagan and tell him the late Jesse Conway has turned up again? And what do we do with the gun?"

"Or," Jake said, "phone Rico di Angelo and tell him he's got his first customer."

"And what do we do with the gun?" Helene repeated.

Malone gulped down a cup of coffee, refilled the cup, took out a cigar, and began slipping off its cellophane wrapper. "I don't think we phone von Flanagan," he said slowly. "No, that's the very thing we don't do."

"Have Anna Marie phone him again," Helene suggested.

"I don't want to wake her," Malone said stubbornly. "I want to have her wake happily and naturally, after she's had all the sleep she needs, and find flowers in her room."

Jake snorted.

"Get someone else to call von Flanagan," Helene said.

Malone shook his head. He held the cellophane cigar wrapper to his lips, aimed it at a wastebasket halfway across the room, and blew. It was a perfect shot. "Practice," he said proudly. He lit the cigar. "Not without consulting Rico di Angelo," he said.

Helene sat down on the arm of Jake's chair. "Of course," she observed, "all we really have to do is wait until Rico opens for business this morning, finds the body, and calls the cops."

"Assuming, he does call the cops," Malone said. He

scowled. "Whether he does or doesn't know anything about the body, I don't want to get him in trouble. No, the person to call is Joe the Angel." He rose and went to the telephone.

He talked at length to a sleep-voiced Joe the Angel, hung up, and returned to the couch. "He'll call Rico, tell him the whole story, and then Rico will call me. Then we'll know better what to do."

Malone poured out a third cup of coffee. He was beginning to feel in better health with every passing moment.

"About the gun," Helene said thoughtfully. "It could have killed Jesse Conway and Garrity."

"It could have killed me, too," Malone said in a sour voice, "if I hadn't socked that guy when I did."

Helene said, "We could wrap it in a pretty little package and mail it to von Flanagan with a note reading, 'This gun may have been involved in the murders which are baffling the police department. Fingerprints may tell who shot it, and ballistics tests may tell whom it shot. Signed, A Friend!'"

"At least von Flanagan would know he had a friend," Jake said. "And then we could all hang around him and hope he'd confide what, if anything, the tests prove."

"Then we'd send another note," Helene said, "reading, 'That gun was taken from a man in a tan raincoat. Fingerprint all the men in Chicago who wear tan raincoats, and you'll have the murderer. Signed, Same Friend.'"

"And," Malone said, "von Flanagan could be happy for days reading up on the psychology of people who send anonymous letters to the police." He flicked at the scattering of cigar ash on his vest.

The phone rang, and Malone answered it. Rico di Angelo was on the other end of the wire, his voice a curious mixture of anxiety and gratitude. "Malone," he said fervently, "thanks. It's a good thing you broke into my place. I'll do something for you sometime. Think what it would do to my reputation to have a body found in my brand-new undertaking parlor!" He added anxiously, "Who put it there? Why pick on me?"

"That's what I'm wondering," Malone said. "Do you have any enemies?"

"No. Me, I'm everybody's friend. Yes. Wait." He paused.

"Malone, I also got other business. Nice little bar, out on Halsted Street. Two, three weeks ago, couple of guys come in to sell me protection. Me, I tell them to go to hell. I can protect myself."

It was the familiar story. The bartender arrested for selling beer to minors. The janitor with marijuana on his person. The repeated visits urging Rico to change his mind. But Rico had been sterner stuff than his brother. He'd not only continued to refuse, but on one occasion had personally thrown his visitors into the street.

"Then," Rico went on, "I am going to open my undertaking parlor. The best one on Division Street. They come back, the bums, and tell me if I don't pay them protection money, something terrible will happen to my nice new undertaking parlor."

"And I think," Malone told him, "that this is it. Can you get rid of the body?"

"Easy," Rico boasted. "I go there right away. I take the body in my new ambulance, drive a long way away, and leave it. An alley, maybe. I put the ambulance away and go home. Nine o'clock I come down and open up for business just like nothing happen."

"Good," Malone said.

"I'm a smart man," Rico said. "These bums figure that is exactly what I will do. Only they think I will do it later, when I come down at nine o'clock."

"That's what I figured," Malone said. "Now, look. After you open up at nine o'clock, see if anyone seems to be watching your place. If anyone is, pretend that you're doing the same thing you did earlier. Drive away in your ambulance. See if they—if anyone—follows you. Then park up an alley and let them approach you. Let them talk. They'll probably offer to forget the whole thing, for cash. Catch on?"

"Sure thing," Rico said gleefully. "Then I knock their heads together, lock them in the ambulance, and call the cops. Malone, you don't need to pay for those flowers. I give them to you."

"Thanks," Malone said. "One thing more. On your way, stop at Joe the Angel's. There'll be a package waiting for you. It contains a gun. Be careful not to touch it, there may be fingerprints on it. Take the gun along and leave it where you leave the body. It's just a little present I want to give the police."

"Malone," Helene said admiringly after he hung up, "you think of everything!"

"Except sleep," the little lawyer said. "But this was worth it." He relit his cigar and said, "There's a chance that some of the tough boys in the police department may be able to find out who's running this protection racket. And if they can't," he added with a wicked grin, "I think I know who can."

CHAPTER TWENTY-TWO

Malone stood back and surveyed the room in which Anna Marie slept. It was, he decided, perfect. He'd arranged the flowers himself, and they turned the room into a bower. There was a thermos of coffee on the bed table, and a note telling her to order anything she wanted from room service and to keep out of sight of the waiter.

He'd considered adding to the note the fact that he loved her but, he'd decided, that had better wait.

Tonight he'd present her with the negligee. Maybe he could pick up a few other trinkets that she'd like.

He tiptoed out of the room after one last glance at her and closed the door very softly.

Back in his own room he looked at himself critically in the mirror. There had been times when he looked worse, but he couldn't remember them. His suit was rumpled and dusty, his shirt was a complete wreck. For perhaps the thousandth time in his life he wondered why he couldn't get into a fight without getting his collar torn off. His necktie—one of his favorites—had been lost somewhere along the way.

His black eye had developed into something really spectacular. The other eye was red-rimmed and puffed from lack of sleep. The bruise on his jaw was an interesting shade of violet. He needed a shave.

The little lawyer stripped to the skin and stood under an icy shower until every nerve in his body tingled. He shaved carefully, wincing when his razor touched the bruise. He considered going to the barber's and having the black eye painted over, then decided against it. It was a magnificent shiner, and he was secretly proud of it.

He selected the dark blue double-breasted suit with the pin-stripe. A proper choice, he thought, for the conservative and respectable businessman he had become. The red and blue striped tie. Finally he looked again in the mirror. The effect was wholly pleasing.

At one minute to nine he opened his office door and stopped whistling to say, "Good morning, Maggie, any calls?"

Maggie dropped her magazine and said, "Good God! What are you doing here?" She looked at him closely. "John J. Malone, you've been fighting again!"

"Just a quiet evening with friends," Malone said airily. "Think nothing of it."

"But," she said, "it's nine o'clock in the morning!"

"Nothing surprising about that," Malone said. "Once in every twenty-four hours it's nine o'clock in the morning. And from now on, that's the hour I arrive at the office. You may not realize it, but I'm a changed man."

She sniffed. "You don't look very changed to me," she commented. She looked at her message pad. "Mick Herman wants his tools back. He needs them in order to pay your fee."

"Tell him the fee can wait," Malone said. "I may need the tools another day or two."

"Judge Seidel wants you to contribute to a benefit."

"Send him ten bucks," Malone said, "and take it out of that last fee for getting a traffic ticket fixed."

"The Toujours Gai Lingerie Shop is sending over that negligee—C.O.D."

"Pay for it out of the petty cash," Malone said.

Maggie looked at him coldly. "There's exactly one dollar

and seventy cents, and two three-cent stamps in the petty cash," she told him.

"Oh, all right." He drew a wadded mass of bills from a trousers' pocket, fished out a hundred dollar bill, and gave it to her. "Pay for it with that. Put the change in the petty cash. And get Mrs. Childers on the phone for me."

He went on into his office and left her staring, bewildered, at the closed door.

Inside his office he tossed his hat on a chair, lit a cigar, and, feeling very businesslike indeed, sat down at his desk to examine the morning mail. Bills. Three envelopes addressed in three different feminine handwritings. An invitation to buy two tickets to a testimonial dinner for a union official. He looked at them for a few minutes, then swept them all into his desk drawer, just as Maggie opened the door and said, "Mrs. Childers on the phone."

He picked up the telephone, leaned perilously far back in his chair, and said, "Good morning, my dear Mrs. Childers. I suppose you wonder why I'm calling you up so early."

"Well," she cooed, "I am just the least little wee bit curious, and I can't help hoping—"

"That's it," Malone said cheerily. "I've decided that since I'm going to devote myself wholeheartedly to your case, I will accept the retainer after all."

"Oh, I'm so *glad!*" she said. "I'll send it over. By special messenger!" There was a brief silence. "Mr. Malone?"

"Yes?" Malone said, his senses sharpening.

"I have just a tiny confession to make. I didn't quite tell you everything yesterday."

Malone sat up straight. "My dear lady, go right ahead. No client of mine ever needs to keep any secrets from me. Your lawyer should be like your doctor, you know. You should tell him everything—absolutely everything." He didn't think for a minute that she would.

"Oh, that's *so* right, Mr. Malone," she said. "I—I'll tell you—it's that, well, there is something else I want you to do for me. Besides finding that unfortunate girl's family, if she had one."

"My services are at your command," Malone said gallantly.

"You're *so* kind!" She breathed over the phone. "I

wonder—maybe, I'd better come down and tell you about it in person."

"That would be fine," Malone said. "Any time this afternoon. Unfortunately, I'm tied up all this morning."

"Four o'clock?"

"Perfect," Malone said. He hung up and wondered what the hell she had in mind. Well, whatever it was, he'd cope with it somehow. He thought happily of the fat fee that ought to be involved.

He stretched, slapped himself on the chest, and reflected that the life of a respectable, hard-working businessman who got to his office at nine every morning was exactly what suited him.

He rose, went to the door, and said, "Maggie, I've got some very serious thinking to do. Under no circumstances am I to be disturbed until I let you know. No matter who or what it is."

He walked over to the couch, loosened his tie, took off his shoes, stretched out with a luxurious yawn, and ten seconds later was sound asleep.

When he woke at twelve he felt like a new man.

There had been a faintly disturbing dream. He sat on the edge of the couch, wriggling his toes and thinking about it. The details of it eluded him, but it had something to do with identical twins. Alike, even to the point of identical fingerprints and cavities in their teeth.

"Silly dream," he told himself. No two things in the world could be exactly alike, except perhaps those two apartments—Anna Marie's and the empty one. He scowled. Silly or not, the dream did have some significance, if he could just put his finger on it. He closed his eyes and tried to think. Twins. The two apartments. *Something.* He felt that an important fact was just beyond his reach of mind, but he could never quite get to it.

At last he gave up. The way to deal with those elusive thoughts, he'd found in the past, was to ignore them. Sooner or later they came along of their own accord.

He put on his shoes, straightened his tie, and walked into the outer office.

"I heard you thinking," Maggie said scornfully.

"I do not snore," Malone said with indignation. He picked up the long white box marked Toujours Gai Lingerie Shop and looked at it lovingly.

"This came," Maggie said. She handed him an envelope.

He opened it and took out the ten one-hundred-dollar bills.

"I knew you'd come to your senses about bribes," Maggie said.

"Strictly business," Malone told her. He stuffed five of the bills in his pocket and handed the rest to her. "Pay the rent and the phone bill, pay your back salary, and fix up the overdraft at the bank. If there's any left over, maybe you'd better put it in the bank, too. We might need it sometime."

He went back in his office and sat down behind his desk.

Maybe the dream was trying to tell him that the two apartments were not exactly alike. He tried to picture them. The windows here. The doors there. The built-in bookcases——

He was interrupted by Maggie, who came in and laid a card on his desk. *Al Harmon*, it read.

Under it was scribbled in pencil, "Special Investigator for the D.A.'s office."

"What the hell," Malone said. He scowled at the card. "Oh, well, send him in."

The man who came through the door was the young man in the tan raincoat.

CHAPTER TWENTY-THREE

"I don't believe you," Malone said hoarsely. He resisted a temptation to duck under his desk.

"Nobody's asking you to," Al Harmon said. "I got credentials." He slapped them down on the desk, smiling unpleasantly. He had thin lips and tobacco-stained teeth.

Malone glanced at them and slid them back. "Then what the hell was the idea of chasing me around last night, and putting a gun on me?"

Harmon sat down, lit a cigarette, and said, "What would you do in the same circumstances, pal?"

"I'd stay home and read a good book," Malone said, "and not go around trailing law-abiding citizens. What does the D.A.'s office have against me, anyway?" Though there was, he reflected, a certain amount of justice on Harmon's side. Under the circumstances, he'd have preferred to have a gun in his own hand.

"Plenty," Harmon said, "as far as I'm concerned. I'm going to be living on soup, milk, and liquor for the next three weeks. You as good as shoved my stomach through my backbone."

"Next time I will," Malone said. He felt of his jaw.

Al Harmon grinned. He took one more puff on the cigarette and used it to light a second one. "Leave us leave bygones be bygones."

"By all means," Malone said. He began unwrapping a cigar. "You've got a nice aim with a flashlight. A nice aim at an eye, that is."

"Occupational skill," Harmon said. "You read about it all the time. Like riveters. And diamond cutters. Where's my gun?"

135

"I don't know," Malone said truthfully.

"Did you take it out of that undertaking joint last night?"

"No," Malone said, just as truthfully.

"Why did you go out to that undertaking joint last night?"

"To get some flowers for my girl," Malone said. "Why did you follow me there?"

"I'm asking the questions," Al Harmon said. "You're giving the answers. You didn't go there because Jesse Conway's body was there, did you?"

Malone lifted his eyebrows. "Jesse Conway!" His voice was shocked and innocent. "You don't mean poor Jesse's *dead*, do you?"

"I've seen healthier people," Al Harmon said. He chain-lit a third cigarette. "Why did you buy Joe the Angel's City Hall Bar?"

"I thought it was a good investment," Malone said promptly. "And I thought it would be cheaper to own a saloon than to patronize one."

"For how much?"

"Fifty," Malone said.

"Fifty what?"

"Fifty cents, fifty dollars, fifty grand," Malone said. "It's none of your business. I'm being very patient with you. Or, I should say, I have been very patient with you." He lit his cigar. "From now on, *I* ask the questions. If you're an investigator for the D.A.'s office, how come you're also collecting protection money for the racket crowd?"

"I've got an old gray-haired mother to support," Harmon said, "and two invalid sisters, and I'm sending ten children through college. A living's a living."

"How come you were seen in one of Bill McKeown's joints with Mrs. Eva Childers?"

"Mrs. Childers is a very charming lady," Al Harmon said. "And also, in the bucks." He added with a slight leer, "Quite a lot of bucks."

"She also happens to be my client," Malone said grandly. "So watch your remarks." He regretted it the moment he'd said it.

Al Harmon regarded him with hard, glittering eyes from under eyelids that wrinkled the way Malone imagined lizards' eyelids wrinkled. "Your client, chum?" He inhaled. "That's very interesting."

"Also, very profitable," Malone told him. "I, too, am sending twenty children through college, and I have four invalid sisters and two old gray-haired mothers. More questions. How do you know Jesse Conway is dead?"

"I—"

"You killed him," Malone said pleasantly, slipping one hand under his desk for the buzzer that would signal to Maggie, "Help! Fast!"

"Malone," Al Harmon said, "do I look like a murderer? Do I talk like a murderer, chum?"

"No," Malone admitted. "You look like a rat and you talk like a skunk, but you don't look like a murderer." He held one finger close to the buzzer. Harmon grinned at him and didn't make a move. "I asked you, how do you know Conway is dead? Did you see his body?"

"Yes."

"Where?"

Al Harmon said, "Try and find out. And what's it to you?" He started another cigarette.

"You wouldn't know Jesse Conway was dead because you moved his body, would you?" Malone said nastily. "Or because you found it in Anna Marie St. Clair's apartment?"

He was on his feet five seconds ahead of Al Harmon. "Were you looking for the body when you went there?" He went on fast, "Or were you looking for something else? You left in kind of a hurry, didn't you? Why? Did something startle you?"

"How do you know?" Harmon said.

"I'm still asking the questions," Malone said. "And you'd better sit down, because there's going to be a lot of them." He sat down himself, and picked up his cigar.

Harmon sank into his chair. "Listen, Malone. I don't believe in ghosts."

"I do," the little lawyer said. "I saw this one. Now. What's the straight dope about you being a special investigator?" He added, "A better word for it, I suppose, is private spy."

Al Harmon lit his next cigarette with hands that shook just a trifle. "You know the cops haven't been able to touch the protection racket. Not a thing to go on. Sure, a lot of wild rumors floating around. But not even a complaint. Nobody would admit he was a victim. As rackets go, this was a beaut."

Malone nodded. "And a number of night clubs, joints, and just plain saloons changed hands. Most of them had been run by honest guys who never had any trouble with the police until all of a sudden a tip would come along that so-and-so was selling reefers."

"You haven't been doing badly by yourself," Al Harmon said.

"I get around," Malone told him. "After the tip was followed up, so-and-so was arrested, the evidence would mysteriously disappear, so would the witnesses, and some high-powered mouthpiece would spring so-and-so from the can. Shortly after, so-and-so's joint would quietly change hands." He scowled. "Couldn't the cops trace the tips? And how about the new ownership of so-and-so's joint?"

"No luck," Al Harmon said. "The whole business worked smooth as anything you could name. Not because the cops were in on it, either. Believe me, it's a honey." There was admiration in his voice.

"Now," Malone said, "about the D.A.'s office."

Al Harmon grinned. "They decided to find out who the boss was and smash the racket. Could be somebody wants to run for governor. So I drifted in from Detroit, looking for an easy way to make a living."

"Detroit, eh?" Malone said. "I wondered why I didn't recognize you. I know most of the local boys."

"The only tip I had," Harmon said, "was The Happy Days place on Clark Street. I hung around there, and after a while I was in, as a collector."

"Who's the boss?" Malone said.

"I don't know. Nobody seems to know."

"Why did Jesse Conway call himself Ambersley?"

"He did a little of the fancier collecting. He didn't think it was smart to use his own name. He wanted to get out of it, but he couldn't. With that mob, once you're in, you're in."

"Which might have been a reason for his sudden death," Malone said.

"Doubt it," Harmon said, shaking his head. "They needed

him. But since he did get it, they decided to use his body to frame that tough di Angelo guy. Only di Angelo outsmarted him." His eyes narrowed. "You wouldn't have had anything to do with that, would you, pal?"

"I did not," Malone said promptly. "I told you, I went up there to get some flowers for my girl."

"I'm sucker enough to believe you," Al Harmon said. "Maybe I'm sucker enough not to tell the boys you were there last night. In that case, maybe you and me could do some business together."

"Possibly," Malone said. "Especially if you tell me why you were following me."

"Listen, chum," Al Harmon said. "I figure this whole business ties up together somehow. Jesse got his in that dame's apartment. Big Joe got his in The Happy Days saloon. Both times that ghost—I mean, when guys thought they saw a ghost—you were around. O.K. So last night I know the body's been moved to di Angelo's. I didn't do it myself, I was just casing the joint. Then I spot you in Joe di Angelo's making a lot of chin music. Am I crazy to follow you?"

"No," Malone said. "Let's have a drink." He fished a bottle out of the file drawer marked "Important Papers," found two glasses and poured.

"Thanks, pal," Al Harmon said, lighting a cigarette. "And you bought Joe the Angel's bar because you figured you could trap the racket guys."

"You have a nice, logical mind," Malone said admiringly.

"You'll probably get bumped off," Al Harmon said. "But maybe I'll help you. Then maybe we'll both get bumped off. Those guys mean business. Officially, I'm here to tell you, as new owner of the Joe the Angel's, to kick in."

"Officially," Malone said cheerfully, "I've told you to go to hell. Have you any leads at all to the guy behind it?"

"No. But I've got a hunch. I'm not telling it to you, because you'd say I'm crazy. Maybe I am. But if I'm right, it's going to be the biggest surprise in your life." He rose, said, "So long, pal, be seeing you," and left.

Not until after he was gone did Malone remember he'd forgotten to ask one important question.

When Al Harmon went into Anna Marie's the night before, why had he gone *upstairs* first?

CHAPTER TWENTY-FOUR

Jake Justus strolled through the dark and empty Casino and reflected that it was the most beautiful place in the world. To some others, a night club seen in the early morning, with chairs piled on tables, only the most essential lights burning, and cleaning women moving around with their mops, pails, and evil-smelling cleaning fluids, was eerie and depressing. Jake felt otherwise. Day or night, morning or afternoon, crowded or empty, the Casino was beautiful.

He loved it almost one-half—well, almost one-quarter—as much as he loved Helene.

Nobody in the world was going to take it away from him.

He looked at the deserted and unlighted stage and thought about some of the people who had appeared there. Angela Doll. Gypsy Rose Lee. Lou Holtz. Milly Dale. Jay Otto.

The name of Jay Otto stirred an unpleasant recollection. A murder on the Casino's opening night hadn't been exactly a premonition of success. He remembered Allswell McJackson and his one appearance on that stage, after the murder of Jay Otto. It had brought down the house, but Allswell McJackson had never appeared again on that, or any other, stage.

The recollection brought his mind back to the present difficulties. Now, as then, there had been murder. Again the Casino was involved—though indirectly this time.

He walked slowly backstage to his office. It was a small, cluttered, shabby room. Helene wanted to have it decorated, but Jake liked it the way it was.

He wondered how Helene had made out with Eva Childers, and wished again that he'd been able to keep her out of this dangerous business. Fat chance he'd had, though.

If there was excitement anywhere, Helene could unerringly find her way to it.

Jake sat down behind his desk, lit a cigarette, and tried to push the worries out of his mind. The morning papers were piled on his desk, a telegram lay on top of them. He opened it almost disinterestedly.

> FLYING TO CHICAGO. DO NOTHING UNTIL
> YOU HEAR FROM ME.
>
> LOU BERG

What the hell? Jake frowned at the wire. Lou Berg, one-time band leader, was now an important Hollywood producer. He'd made his first hit at the Casino. "Do nothing until you hear from me." Do nothing about *what?*

He gave up trying to figure it out and turned his attention to the papers.

Anna Marie had landed on the front pages with even more splash than at the time of her arrest and trial. There were pictures of her as she had appeared when "Alive." There were complete rehashes of the story of Big Joe Childers' murder and of the trial. There was an interview with the pastor of an important church, with the head of an organization for the investigation of psychic phenomena, with a prominent medium, and with Dr. Ellsworth LeGeorge, the eminent psychiatrist. Jake grinned happily.

Anna Marie was doing all right for herself!

Again he stared at the wire. "Do nothing until you hear from me." Had Lou Berg gone insane?

He was still worrying about it when Helene arrived. She'd done a very special job of dressing to lunch with Eva Childers, and he looked at her with appreciation. A wide navy blue felt hat framed her lovely fragile face and pale, shining hair. There was a scarlet scarf at her throat, and she carried an enormous scarlet handbag.

"There's a smudge on your nose," he said critically.

She made a face at him and sat down on the corner of his desk. "Mrs. Childers did not hire Ike Malloy to murder her husband," she announced, "nor did she frame Anna Marie for the crime. She has nothing to do with the protection racket.

The man in the tan raincoat is just a casual acquaintance. She never met Jesse Conway. She never has been in Anna Marie's apartment in her life. There was a key to it among Big Joe's effects, and she threw it away. And here's the afternoon paper."

"Wait a minute," Jake said, pushing the paper aside. "How did you get her to say all that, none of which I insist on believing."

"I asked her," Helene said calmly. She lit a cigarette. "It might even be true. Except that she didn't seem to be talking to a casual acquaintance when I eavesdropped on her yesterday." She grinned. "It was really rather wonderful. I started right out by asking her very tactlessly if she believed in ghosts."

"Does she?" Jake asked.

"No. Especially Anna Marie's ghost. But she turned pale. And she said Anna Marie didn't have any reason to haunt *her*. That's when she slyly confided that she didn't hire Big Joe's murderer."

Helene took out her compact and began powdering her face.

"For Pete's sake," Jake said, "go on."

"I learned just one more important thing from Eva Childers," Helene said. "She's a very worried woman. Worried, and scared. The question is, what's she scared of? Including or excluding ghosts."

"Could be the police," Jake said.

"Could be," Helene agreed. "Could also be a murderer." She snapped the compact shut and slipped it in her purse. "Don't you want to read all about how two horrid men tried an extortion scheme on an honest undertaker named Rico di Angelo, and how the bright undertaker neatly trapped them and turned them over to the police?"

"No," Jake said. "I'd rather wait and hear Rico tell it." He added, "Have either of them talked?"

"Not yet," Helene said. "According to the paper, they're sitting tight and yelling for a lawyer."

"Who will probably be Malone," Jake said with a grin.

"Don't you want to read how the late Jesse Conway's body was found up a lonely alley, together with a nice shiny gun with no fingerprints on it, that hadn't been fired and that, according to ballistics tests, didn't shoot Jesse Conway."

Jake sighed and reached for the paper.

"Von Flanagan," Helene said, "must be having fits. It's bad enough——"

She broke off at the sound of high-heeled footsteps in the corridor. "Hello, Milly."

Milly Dale came in and sat down. Her face was very pale. "Mr. Justus, I'm through. I'm taking the six o'clock to New York."

Jake stared at her. "Milly, you can't do that to me. You're the biggest hit the Casino has had in months."

"I don't care," she told him. "I don't even care if I never land another job. Not after last night."

Jake groaned. It was a possibility he hadn't figured on.

"Now, Milly," Helene said, "you're too sensible to let a thing like that upset you."

"Besides," Jake added hastily, "it was probably just a practical joke."

"I saw her," Milly Dale said firmly. "It wasn't anybody dressed to look like her, it was *her*."

"You can't actually believe in ghosts," Jake said in what turned out to be a hollow voice.

"I certainly do," she said.

"But——" Jake picked up the paper. "Look at the publicity. Think what it'll do for the Casino. Think what it'll do for you. Look. Every one has your picture. 'Milly Dale, lovely young singer, who was on the stage when—' and so on! Two column cuts!"

He launched into a fervent speech about her future career, not forgetting to include Hollywood and vast sums of money.

"Well——" Milly Dale said.

"Besides," Helen put in, "Anna Marie St. Clair didn't have anything against you. You were her best friend. She wouldn't want to hurt you."

"No——" Milly Dale said. Then, "Only I won't sing that song again. It was hers. And I won't do that girl-with-the-gun number any more. I'm tired of it."

Jake drew a long breath of relief. "Sing anything you

want. I'll get special arrangements made for you, that's how much I like you."

A little color had come back into her face. "Maybe it is good publicity at that."

"You're a very bright girl," Jake said.

She smiled at him. "You know, that story they made up, that Anna Marie was jealous of me—it wasn't true. Sure I knew Big Joe. I guess I was the best friend he had. But he adored Anna Marie."

She sighed reminiscently. "He wouldn't even let her know when he was sick."

"I can't imagine Big Joe ever being sick," Jake said.

"He was. Some kind of trouble with his stomach. It worried him a lot. But he wouldn't let me tell her. I tell you, he worshiped that girl. If he'd ever known she was two-timing him——"

Helene gasped. Her eyes were suddenly bright. "She was!"

Milly Dale shrugged her shoulders. "Anna Marie was human. Nobody could blame her if she fell for a guy."

"*Who was it?*" Helene said.

"Why?"

"Listen," Helene said. "It may be important. Terribly important. You've got to tell me."

"I don't know why I shouldn't," Milly Dale said, reaching for a cigarette. "Considering it's all over and done with. It was——"

There was a sound in the corridor. There was a shot. Running footsteps and a door banging shut.

Helene looked at Milly Dale sprawled across Jake's desk in a widening pool of blood, and her face turned white.

"That," she whispered, "makes five."

CHAPTER TWENTY-FIVE

When a hastily summoned and breathless Malone arrived at von Flanagan's office, he found a purple-faced and furious police officer, an indignant and protesting Jake, and a pale and anxious Helene.

"Perfect nonsense," Malone said, without waiting for a word from anyone. He flung his hat and topcoat on a chair. "Why would Jake shoot his star act?"

"And if I did," Jake said wildly, "where's the gun?"

"You had plenty of time to get rid of the gun and then call the cops," von Flanagan said. He folded his arms across his massive chest. "I'm not accusing you. I'm not arresting you. I just brought you here for questioning."

"Questioning!" Jake said. "The third degree!"

"I never use no third degree," von Flanagan roared. "I use psychology."

"Don't you dare bully my clients, you big ape," Malone said.

"Don't you interrupt me, you shyster." Von Flanagan turned back to Jake. "I'm not saying you did, and I'm not saying you didn't. I'm just saying, if you didn't, do you know who did, and if you did, why did you?"

Jake sighed wearily. "I didn't. And I don't know who did. It's just exactly the way I told you. We were talking, someone fired from the corridor and was out of the building before I could get a glimpse of him. I don't even know if it was a him. Could have been a her."

"It sounds possible," von Flanagan said, "but how do I know it's the truth?"

Helene leaned forward and flashed a smile at him. "But that's just what happened," she said. "And you don't think I'd lie to you, do you?"

145

She had, on numerous previous occasions, but von Flan-\
agan had never been able to resist Helene. He said gallantly,
"No, I don't."

"There," she said, "that proves Jake couldn't have done
it." She sat back in serene self-confidence and lit a cigarette.

"But," von Flanagan said, "when a dame gets murdered,
and there's only two people with her, and they had time to
get rid of the gun before they called the cops, a guy is bound
to get suspicious." He looked thoughtfully at Jake.

"I protest," Malone said, "against this false accusation."

"Shut up," von Flanagan said. "In fact, suspicious enough
to make an arrest."

Malone said, "We'll sue you!"

This time von Flanagan ignored him. "The newspapers
and the commissioner are raising enough hell as it is," he
went on. "I can't have another murder without at least making
an arrest, even if it turns out I was wrong." He sat back
complacently.

"Von Flanagan!" Helene said in a shocked voice. "You
wouldn't do that to us!"

Jake said, "Look here, damn you——"

Malone roared something about throwing friends to the
wolves.

The scenes was interrupted by the door opening. A
plain-clothes man came in and said, "Ballistics reports that
the bullet in the dame came outa the same gun that killed
Garrity and Jesse Conway." He went out again.

"Well," Jake said, rising, "it's been nice knowing you. I
have an alibi for at least one of those murders. We'll be
running along now."

"No, you don't," von Flanagan said. "Maybe I can't
arrest you, but I can question you and, by God, I will. And
remember, withholding information from me is against the law."

"I'm just as anxious to find the murderer as you are,"
Jake said angrily. "She was a swell singer and a good kid. I
liked Milly Dale."

"Any idea who might want to shoot her?"

"No," Jake said, "nor why she should be shot in my
office, right at that particular time."

A meditative gleam came into the big police officer's

eye. "Maybe she was just about to tell you something important about somebody, and the somebody had been following her around in case she did just that, and bumped her off before she got a chance. Because you said she was talking to you. What were you talking about?"

Jake scowled. "At the minute she was shot, she was just about to tell us the name——"

"The name of the man behind this protection racket," Helene said quickly. She gave Jake a look that meant, "Watch what you say," and nodded almost imperceptibly toward Malone.

Von Flanagan nodded slowly. "Jesse Conway was mixed up in the racket," he said. "Garrity was just a small-time politician who got himself a fat appointment. But there must be some connection there."

He groaned. "Jesse Conway gets killed in the apartment of that dame, St. Clair. Then he gets planted in an undertaking parlor. Then he turns up in an alley. He moved around about as much after he was dead as he did when he was alive. And there was a gun by him that didn't shoot anybody, and so far we haven't been able to trace it yet. Now this girl gets shot. And she was the St. Clair dame's best friend. Did you ever see such a lousy mess?"

"Try psychology," Malone said.

"Oh, go to hell." Von Flanagan moaned.

"I'd better go to my office instead," Malone said, looking at his watch. "I've an appointment at four."

Helene rose and said, "We'll drop you." To von Flanagan she added consolingly, "Don't worry."

"It's always darkest just before it rains," Malone said. "And it never rains but it gets dark."

Out in the car Helene said, "At least he didn't say anything about closing the Casino. Malone, who might have wanted to murder Milly Dale?"

"I don't know," Malone said. "There's still a bare possibility it hasn't anything to do with the other murders."

"You forget the bullets," she pointed out.

"That's right," Malone said, "but I don't see what the connection can be."

"Milly was a nice girl," Helene said. "I can't believe she was mixed up in any rackets."

Malone said thoughtfully, "What was she talking about just before she died?"

"Malone," Helene said hastily, stepping on the gas. "Are you going to help von Flanagan solve his crimes?"

"I am," Malone said, "but not for von Flanagan. Now tell me. Milly Dale——"

"Who's your appointment at four with?" Helene said.

"Nobody important," Malone lied.

She stopped the car in front of Malone's office building. "See you tonight, Malone."

"Wait a minute," Malone said from the sidewalk. "What was Milly Dale talking about?"

"It's too long to tell you now," Helene said. "I'll tell you tonight."

"Just for that," Malone said indignantly, "I won't tell you who the man in the tan raincoat is. And I know." He was across the sidewalk before she could say a word.

"The nerve of him," Helene said. She swung around the corner and headed south.

"What was the idea of all that?" Jake said. "And where are we going?"

"We're going to see Anna Marie," she told him.

"Why?"

"For the same reason we couldn't tell Malone what Milly Dale was talking about."

"Maybe I'm dumb," Jake began, "but——"

"You are," she said, "if you don't see that Malone is crazy about her. How would Malone like to be told that she was two-timing Big Joe?"

"He ought to be told," Jake said.

"Later," she said firmly. "We've got to talk to her first. Then, if anyone tells him, she does."

Jake sighed. "Women!"

They parked the car and took the elevator to the floor on which Malone's hide-out room was located.

"You're sure Anna Marie wants visitors?" Jake said.

"She's getting them, anyway," Helene said. She knocked on the door.

There was no answer. She knocked again. At last she turned the knob. The door was unlocked.

There was the profusion of flowers, just as Malone had arranged them. There was the little parade of cosmetics. There was the thermos bottle.

But no sign of Anna Marie.

CHAPTER TWENTY-SIX

"Mr. Al Harmon called," Maggie reported as Malone came in from the corridor. "He wants you to defend two men charged with attempted extortion. Their names are—wait a minute"—she pawed through papers on her desk—"Earl Wilks and Louis Perez. You're supposed to go down and talk to them."

"Fix up an application for a writ of *habeas corpus*," Malone said. "I'll go see them later. Got an appointment at four."

He slammed his office door behind him, dropped his hat and coat, walked over to the window, and stood there looking out. A dreary mixture of rain and sleet was falling on the dingy, soot-covered roof tops outside. Windows in office buildings opposite him were dull, yellowish blurs.

He was tired, and the murder of Milly Dale had depressed him. Partly because he'd liked and admired the pretty little dark-haired singer and hated to think of her being dead—especially, of her dying so unpleasantly. He remembered the two dates he'd had with her and sighed regretfully.

Then, too, Malone hated to see anyone murdered, even when he got a fat fee for defending the murderer. There had been times when he agreed that the victim deserved what he got, and that the world was far better off without him. But murder seemed such a—well, such a sudden way to die.

This murder in particular depressed him because it was confusing. Nothing connected with the whole case seemed to fall into any pattern, and he was beginning to wonder if it ever would. So far, it was a crazy quilt. Everything sewed together, but no design showing.

Two men had known that Anna Marie St. Clair was alive. Both of them had been killed, with the same gun. Was it *because* they knew Anna Marie was alive?

It suddenly occurred to him that there was one important thing Anna Marie had never explained to him. Concealing the fact that she had not gone to the electric chair had been a difficult and risky job. If it had gone wrong, both men would have been in a bad jam.

He could understand the hold she had had over Jesse Conway. She could have proved that he'd allowed her to be framed. But Garrity—that was something else.

He walked to the desk, picked up the phone, and called an old friend at the *News*. "Ed? Malone. Do me a favor. Find out who got Garrity his appointment as warden. And anything else you may have on him. Especially dirt. Call me back, and thanks."

He felt better after he'd hung up. At least he was doing *something*. He walked over to the washstand, splashed cold water on his face, dried it, and brushed his hair. He sat down at his desk and concentrated on looking businesslike.

There was that long, flat, white box, marked Toujours Gai Lingerie Shoppe. Maybe after he'd finished with Mrs. Childers, he'd slip over to the hotel and give it to Anna Marie. No, he'd wait till tonight. He wanted to see her try it on. He put the box away in the closet.

But maybe he'd slip over and see her for a minute on his way to interviewing his two new clients. It seemed like a very long time since he'd seen her. He counted on his fingers. A little over seven hours. Practically an eternity.

He was so absorbed in thinking of Anna Marie that he almost forgot to look businesslike when Eva Childers came in. The sound of Maggie opening the door reminded him just in time. He sprang to his feet and greeted Mrs. Childers gallantly.

"My dear Mrs. Childers! I find that I owe you an apology!" He ushered her into the most comfortable chair, offered her a cigarette, and lighted it for her. "It was inexcusably thoughtless of me to let you come all the way to my office, in this weather, when I could just as well have come to your home. Forgive me!"

"Don't think of it," Mrs. Childers said. "I wouldn't dream of taking you away from your office when I know how busy you must be."

"Never too busy to call on such a charming lady," Malone said.

She flushed a little, not very becomingly. She wasn't, Malone reflected, very pretty. Except in the way small women give an impression of being pretty, unless they are downright ugly. It wasn't anything about her features nor her coloring. Simply that her face was too shrewd. She was shrewd about business and gullible about flattery, Malone decided. Her clothes were obviously expensive and looked as though they had been chosen for her by someone else. All save her little flowered hat, which would have looked better on someone ten years younger.

"You must have been years younger than your late husband," Malone said, admiration in every sirupy syllable.

He sat down behind his desk, began unwrapping a cigar, and said, "I'd hoped to have some good news for you soon. I thought I had a very good lead to where Miss St. Clair's family might possibly be—if she had one. Now, I haven't."

He paused very deliberately to light the cigar. "My lead was a very good friend of Miss St. Clair's. She would know, if anyone would."

"Yes?" Eva Childers said, a little breathlessly.

"Unfortunately," Malone said, with maddening slowness, "my lead was shot and killed this afternoon." He crumpled up the cigar wrapper and dropped it near the wastebasket. "Milly Dale. You may have heard of her."

Eva Childers turned white, and fell back in her chair. She murmured something that sounded to Malone very much like, "Hell!"

"My dear lady!" Malone said, "I had no idea it would be such a shock! Let me get you a—something to steady your nerves a little——"

He hoped to heaven there was a clean glass. There was. He opened the file drawer marked "Confidential," took out the bottle Maggie had labeled, "For Important Clients Only," and poured a good ounce and a half into the glass.

"Thank you," Eva Childers said. "I really don't ordinarily drink, but——" She took it in one gulp.

"Did you know Milly Dale?" Malone asked, putting the bottle away.

She shook her head. "But I knew of her. I knew she'd been the best friend of that—poor girl. I'd hoped she could help us not only in locating the family, but in—something else——"

"Yes, yes?" Malone said hopefully.

"Of course, I do want to locate the family," she said. "I feel that I owe them a great debt. But I know you'll succeed."

"I shall try," Malone said. He remembered that the thousand dollars wouldn't last forever and added, "Though it's going to take a little time and may not be too easy. Anna Marie may not have been her real name, you know."

"Please remember, Mr. Malone," she said, "if at any time you need any money for expenses——"

"I'll let you know," Malone told her. The search for Anna Marie's Aunt Bess, he reflected, was going to take a long, long time. "Now, my dear Mrs. Childers—about this other business——"

She clasped her hands on her knees and looked up at him trustingly. "Mr. Malone, I want you to find out who did murder my husband, and did frame that poor, innocent girl."

Malone knocked ashes off his cigar. He scratched his right eyebrow. Finally, he said, "Why?"

"It's my duty," she said finally.

"Ike Malloy did the actual shooting," Malone reminded her.

"But I want to know who hired him."

Again Malone said, "Why?"

"Mr. Malone," she said, "I am in a very unpleasant position. My testimony at her trial helped to convict that poor girl. Now that it's known she was innocent, I appear in a very unfavorable light. Some people may even think that I was responsible myself."

"I see," Malone said. "Go on."

"If I succeed in bringing the real murderer to justice,"

she said, "I will feel that I have redeemed myself in the eyes of the world—and in my own eyes."

It was a flimsy reason, Malone thought, but he knew he wouldn't get a better one. He decided Mrs. Eva Childers ought, with her style of language, to be writing political speeches.

"It's going to be difficult," Malone said, "because it happened so long ago. If I try—you'll have to help me with information."

"If you will," she said, "I'll tell you everything I know."

Malone doubted that last statement. "All right," he said. "Did Big Joe have any personal life that isn't common knowledge."

"No. Only myself and his—and that poor girl. We haven't any children."

"Any relatives who might want to inherit his dough?"

"Only me."

"Any enemies?"

"A man like Mr. Childers always has enemies. But you probably know more about them than I do."

Malone nodded. "Do you know of any threats against his life?"

"None."

"Did he leave anything that might tell us something? Letters, papers, perhaps a diary?"

"No."

Malone sighed. "This certainly isn't very much to go on."

"I know. Don't you see? I haven't anything to go on, really. That's why I've come to you—for help."

She rose and lifted her hands in an appealing little gesture.

"Dear Mrs. Childers," Malone said warmly, "you must just leave everything to me."

After she'd gone, he wondered if she'd expected him to kiss her.

He wondered about some other things, too. First, just what was she up to? What per cent of her story could he believe, if any? Had she really expected to get some useful information from Milly Dale, and, if so, what? And why hadn't she tried before?

Big Joe's diary. That was another funny thing. A few weeks before his death he'd told Anna Marie that he'd destroyed it. Why did he? People seldom destroy diaries just for the hell of it. He was still puzzling over it when the phone rang.

"Malone? Ed. I couldn't dig up much dirt on Garrity. Suspected of some petty theft a few years back, nothing ever came of it. Left a wife and three kids."

"And who got him the job?" Malone said.

"His brother-in-law. Brother-in-law and evidently his best pal. Big Joe Childers."

CHAPTER TWENTY-SEVEN

"It's after four," Jake said, looking at his watch. "I don't think we ought to wait any longer."

"I do," Helene said firmly. "She may walk in any minute."

Jake scowled. "But——" He paused. "Maybe we ought to be looking for her, instead of waiting for her. How do we know she isn't in trouble?"

"We don't," Helene said, "and I'm just as worried as you are."

"She can't have run away," Jake said, "because she left all her things. She could have been kidnaped. She could have been lured away from here and—"

"Stop it!" Helene said. She added in a softer tone, "We've been all over that twenty times. Anyway, don't forget no one knew she was here except Malone and ourselves."

"If we could be sure of that," Jake began. He looked at her and said, "Oh, all right. But I'll show you who's the head of this family. We'll wait five more minutes, and then we'll——"

"There's someone at the door," Helene said.

Jake breathed a sigh of relief.

The door opened. It wasn't Anna Marie who walked in, it was Malone.

For a long moment no one spoke. Then Malone said, "What the hell!"

"We thought Anna Marie might be lonely," Helene said, "so we came up to keep her company."

"But where is Anna Marie?" Malone said hoarsely. *"Where is she?"*

"She isn't here," Helene said.

"I can see she isn't here. But where is she? Where did she go?"

"I don't know," Helene said. "She was gone when we got here. The door was unlocked, so we came in and waited for her."

"I'll call the police!" Malone gasped. He reached for the telephone.

"You can't do that," Jake reminded him.

Malone put down the phone. "But we've got to do something. We've got to go out and look for her."

"That's what I've been saying," Jake said. "But where do we start?"

"Maybe she left a note," Malone said, clutching at a straw.

"We've looked," Helene told him.

The little lawyer groaned. "If anything's happened to her——"

The door opened, and Anna Marie walked in. She stared at the three visitors and said, "Well! Surprise!"

She had on a plain brown coat and galoshes. She wore a scarf tied over her head to protect her from the rain. Not a wisp of her tawny hair showed, and there wasn't a speck of make-up on her face. No one in the world would have recognized her.

Helene commented, "I've always said, leaving off make-up is as good a disguise as putting it on."

Anna Marie laughed, her silvery little laugh. "I hope you weren't upset when you found I wasn't here. I got terribly tired of being cooped up here, after being cooped up somewhere else for so long. So I went for a walk. I left the door unlocked so I could get in when I came back—I didn't have a key."

"We were just beginning to get a little worried," Malone said very casually.

Helene looked from Malone to Anna Marie and back again. She was thinking hard. Malone, she reminded herself, was a grown-up man. He'd taken some bad blows before. Anyway, there might be an explanation, there *had* to be one. It might as well be given in front of Malone.

She met Jake's eyes for a moment. Jake nodded and looked away.

"What's the matter?" Anna Marie asked. She slipped off her coat and untied her scarf. Her smooth hair tumbled over her shoulders. "You look as though you'd seen a ghost."

Helene didn't smile. She drew a long breath and said, "Malone, I wasn't going to tell you this until I'd talked to Anna Marie. But, now that you're here——" She turned to Anna Marie and said, "This afternoon when Milly Dale was murdered, she had just told us you'd been two-timing Big Joe. She was all set to tell us the name of the boy friend when the shot was fired."

"It's a lie," Malone said immediately.

"Thanks, Malone," Anna Marie said. "It *is* a lie."

"See," Malone said, "she admits it." He glared at Helene. "We've been friends for a long time, but——"

Jake said, "Malone, you can't use that kind of language in front of my wife."

"I haven't used any language in front of your wife," the little lawyer said. "I mean, not so far."

"He's a prophet," Helene said, "and he knows your vocabulary."

Anna Marie said, "There isn't any reason for anybody to get sore. Mr. and Mrs. Justus are good pals of yours, Malone, and if they thought I was a two-timing bitch, they wanted to do something about it. On the other hand, they're right guys and while they'd only met me last night, they wanted to give me a chance to square myself. Malone, you ought to be ashamed of yourself."

"I am," Malone said. He fixed his gaze on the end of his cigar. "Helene, I'm sorry for what I called you."

Jake said, "You hadn't called her anything, yet."

"Shut up, Jake," Helene said. "He can dream, can't he?"

"I apologized," Malone said, "so why don't you two get the hell out of here and never come back." He sat down on the edge of the bed and looked at the floor.

"Please," Anna Marie said. "Would you guys mind my putting this record straight? Since the whole thing's my fault, anyway."

"I will," Jake said, "if you'll let me black the other eye of that damned Irish shyster lawyer."

"Try it," Malone said.

Helene and Anna Marie looked at each other, shook their heads in feminine resignation, and shrugged their shoulders.

"If you're really going to black Malone's other eye," Helene said, "let's rent the Stadium and sell tickets. If you aren't, let's listen to what Anna Marie has to say."

"I say," Anna Marie said, "let's have a drink."

She brought out the bottle of scotch Malone had given her and managed to round up four glasses. She poured four drinks, sat down on the arm of the one easy chair, and said, "Also, let's talk."

They looked at her. She was very pale, even, Malone thought, more pale than a ghost. It wasn't just the lack of make-up, either. She had on a lavender wool dress, her tawny hair shone over her shoulders. Her eyes were a pair of dark, deep shadows.

"Sure, they said I two-timed Big Joe," she told them. "Milly Dale didn't lie to you—she was just repeating what they'd told her. The name she was gong to give you, just before she was killed—that was told to her, too. Understand? It was part of the same thing."

"Part of what same thing?" Malone asked.

"They—or he—or she—had to get Big Joe and me into a fight," Anna Marie said. "A fight that witnesses would over-hear. It wasn't enough for me to think Big Joe was running around with Milly Dale. Hell, he'd have talked me out of that in three minutes flat. He had to think I was playing games with somebody else. So——" She turned her head and smiled. "You know what I'm getting at, Mrs. Justus."

"Call me Helene," Mrs. Justus said.

"O.K., Helene. Now, look. Suppose some guy went to

Big Joe and said, 'Your little pittipat is playing pattycake with a cute tomcat.' What would you do if you were Big Joe?"

"Beat the guy into a raw pulp," Helene said.

"But suppose somebody convinces a gal pal of mine, who is also a gal pal of Big Joe's, all under strictly clean circumstances, of course, that the same thing is true. What do you do if you're the pal?"

"You mean the gal pal," Malone muttered.

"*You* shut up," Helene said. She added, "I'm afraid, in those circumstances—I'd have told Big Joe."

"A woman would have," Malone muttered. "A man would have kept his mouth shut."

"Let's leave the battle of the sexes out of this," Jake said. "It all boils down to, somebody wanted to get Big Joe sore at Anna Marie, so he planted a story that Anna Marie was two-timing Big Joe with Milly Dale—who liked both Anna Marie and Big Joe. He planted it so well that not only Big Joe but Milly Dale believed it. The point is, what boy friend did he or she pick?"

Anna Marie shook her head and said, "I don't know. How could I know?"

"The *real* point is," Malone said, "why did somebody shoot Milly Dale just when she was about to tell what this alleged or imaginary guy's name was?"

Anna Marie stared at him. A sudden light came into her eyes. "Because," she said, "someone would have checked with him and found out the story wasn't true. Though that wouldn't have been reason enough to—kill anyone——" Suddenly she buried her face in her hands. "I'm sorry—perhaps I shouldn't have walked so far this afternoon—I'm not used to it——"

"My poor baby!" Malone said. He lifted her as though she were six years old, laid her tenderly on the bed, and began rubing her hands.

She lifted her eyelids and whispered, "Malone—you don't believe that story is true?"

"Just malicious gossip," Malone said. He kissed her gently on the forehead. "And even if it were true——"

Helene signaled Jake toward the door. They tiptoed out, and no one noticed when they closed the door after them.

Out in the car, headed north, Jake said indignantly,

"You might have known the story wasn't true. And you might have known Malone wouldn't believe it."

Helene said nothing. She swung the car viciously around a corner.

"Someday," Jake said, catching his breath, "you women will learn to mind your own business."

Helene whispered a mild profanity under her breath.

"But I love you just the same," Jake murmured.

"Because I'm beautiful, or because I'm bright?"

"Neither," Jake said, "but the word I had in mind begins with the same letter."

Helene was silent all the way to the Michigan Avenue bridge. The bridge was up, and she stopped in a long line of futilely protesting cars.

"Jake," she said thoughtfully, "do you believe in hunches?"

"Sure," he said. "I used to keep rabbits in them when I was a boy back in Iowa. Rabbit hunches."

"Damn you," Helene said, "I'm serious."

"Or," he said, "do you mean, like the prophet who sat on his hunches and——"

"Jake, *please!*"

A chorus of indignant honks reminded her that the barrier had gone up and the line of cars was moving again. Helene started up the convertible and began inching along. Jake glanced at her, at her pale, lovely profile outlined against the dark fog outside the car. He had one of those sudden moments of wishing there were only two people in the world, Helene and himself.

"Darling, what's the hunch?"

She gave him one brief glance. "Jake, I love you!"

"That isn't a hunch, that's a miracle. Shall we stop off at the Drake Bar?"

"No."

"Shall we stop at Pierre's, Rickett's, or Armen's?"

"No. No. And No."

"Home?"

"Home."

She'd made the left turn on Ohio Street and swung up on North Wabash before she said, "Since you're so anxious to hear about my hunch, this is it. What Milly Dake was about to tell us isn't important. What she did tell us, is."

"Well," Jake said at last, "what was it?"

"That's the trouble," Helene said, "I can't remember. Except, it's something about a gun. And I don't know why— but it has something to do with—Bill McKeown!"

CHAPTER TWENTY-EIGHT

"A very good friend of mine is a judge," Malone said, "or should I say a friend of mine is a very good judge. Anyway, he can spring you guys in the time it takes him to sign his name, as soon as I say the word. Bail money is stacked up neatly in front of him, ready to be collected. Only"—he looked at his watch—"the judge likes to go home early. So you'd better make up your mind, quick."

He looked at his new clients. They were goons, he decided, but a little above the average. Postgraduate goons. Perez was a little skinny man with a snaky look about him, black hair, black eyes, and a sallow complexion. Earl Wilks was a big goon, six-foot-four in his socks, if he wore socks, and wide as the south side of a barn. Wilks, Malone decided, was ninety-nine and forty-four hundredths per cent brawn, and the rest was brains. And the one difference between Wilks and Perez was that the latter didn't even have the brawn.

"Of course," he went on, "that don't mean you won't have to stand trial. Though, come to think of it, there might be a way to fix that up, too." He paused there and waited.

Perez and Wilks looked at each other uneasily. Wilks nodded to Perez. Then Perez said, "I'm an American citizen and I know my rights. Nobody can keep us in jail for doing nothing. Me and my pal here was just walking down an alley, peaceable as you please, and we seen a guy parking a hearse and starting to open it up. Naturally, we stepped up and asked the guy what was the idea. And for that we get pinched. How come there's a law against citizens being curious?"

"That depends," Malone said. "It depends on whether when you approached the driver of the hearse you said"—he pulled a sheaf of notepaper from his pocket—" 'O.K., Rico, open up. We know what you got in that hearse,' and that when Rico said, 'There is nothing in this hearse and none of your, deleted, business, anyway,' you, Mr. Perez, made the statement, 'Don't give us no monkey talk, Rico. Kick in or we'll call the cops and tip 'em off you're trying to get rid of a hot body,' whereupon Mr. Enrico di Angelo replied, 'Hot or cold, there's no corpse in this hearse.' Whereupon you threatened Mr. Enrico di Angelo with severe bodily harm if he did not open up the hearse."

Malone paused and said, "Be sure to interrupt me if you have any corrections."

Louis Perez and Earl Wilks looked at each other and at Malone. Neither of them said a word.

"At this point Mr. Enrico di Angelo made the statement, 'You make a move and I murder you two bums,' and Mr. Perez made the statement, 'We ain't got all day. Quit stallin' or we call the cops,' to which Mr. di Angelo replied, 'You call the cops! I call the cops.' "

Malone flipped a page in the sheaf of paper. "At this point a brief altercation ensued in which both Mr. Perez and Mr. Wilks were loaded, while unconscious, into the hearse and secured there. Mr. Enrico di Angelo then drove to the nearest police station and lodged the following complaint."

Malone paused again and said, "Shall I read you the complaint? Or are you sufficiently familiar with it?"

Earl Wilks began hoarsely, "Listen here, Malone——"

Malone folded the sheaf of blank papers, put them in his pocket, and said, "It was a lucky coincidence Rico happened to have a reliable witness and a stenographer hidden in the front seat when he went out for a harmless little ride this morning in a perfectly empty hearse. Only it won't be so lucky for you if this case ever comes to trial." He added, "Of course if the stenographer's notes should disappear, and the reliable witness should leave town, and Rico should decide to quit the whole thing——"

Louis Perez and Earl Wilks exchanged another glance. Then Perez said, "How much?"

"That depends on who's paying it," Malone said.

Earl Wilks opened his mouth to speak. Louis Perez kicked him in the ankle, and he shut it again.

"Or," Malone said pleasantly, "there's just a chance that it might not cost you a cent. You or anybody else. If you'd consent to have a little private conversation with me, of a highly confidential nature, of course, and help me out in the matter of a little information I need, I might be able to arrange the whole thing for free."

There was a moment's silence. Then Perez said, "Mind if me and my pal talk it over first?"

"Go right ahead," Malone said pleasantly, "only I don't want to keep my friend, the judge, waiting too long."

The two men withdrew to a far corner of the visitor's room and held a consultation. Malone waited patiently, meanwhile making a concertina from a cellophane cigar wrapper. At last they returned, and Perez said, "O.K., Malone, we take you up on it."

Malone rose from the uncomfortable straight-back chair and said, "That's fine, boys. I'll rush this through, meet you outside, and we'll go somewhere and talk this over."

It was a surprisingly short time later that he greeted Earl Wilks and Louis Perez, climbed into a taxi with them, and gave the address of his office.

"Everything's fixed," he reported, "including getting rid of the evidence. You'll never be bothered about this again."

Louis Perez said, "See what comes of having a smart lawyer, Earl?"

Earl muttered something under his breath, and conversation lagged until the cab deposited them in front of Malone's office building.

It was just barely dusk, but the low-hanging clouds and the continual drizzle of rain and sleet had plunged the city into a murky darkness. The three men hurried across the sidewalk and paused just inside the lobby. Earl Wilks took

Malone by the arm. Perez said, "You're sure you got rid of that evidence, Malone?"

"Everything's attended to," Malone assured him. "You haven't a thing to worry about."

Louis Perez beamed and said, "Well, we haven't a thing to tell you, either. Hold him, Earl, while I flag a cab."

Earl pulled Malone's arms behind his back with an iron grip on his thumbs and said, "I wouldn't advise you to move if you don't want to bust a coupla arms."

Louis added, "We don't want to do you no harm, we just want you to stay put till we get outa here."

"I thought you'd take it this way," Malone said joyfully.

Earl didn't see the six-foot-one, two hundred and twenty-five pound Rico di Angelo snaking his way along the wall of the deserted lobby. But he did feel the blow on the back of his head. That was all he felt, for a while. Similarly, Louis Perez didn't see Bill, the aged elevator man, waiting in the shadows of the door to trip him with a sudden thrust of the foot, but he sprawled on the marble floor just the same.

"Nice work, pals," Malone said, rubbing his thumbs. "Let's load them into the hearse and get going." He added, "I sure would have been in one hell of a spot if they'd decided to come up to my office in a nice peaceable manner and spill me a lot of nice, irrefutable lies."

Rico di Angelo hauled Perez over his shoulder and carted him out through the alley entrance. He returned and dragged Wilks out by the collar. Malone tucked a ten-dollar bill in the old elevator man's hand and followed Rico. A moment later the shiny new hearse was roaring up Clark Street.

"Take it easy," Malone said. "Are you sure they're locked in safely?"

"Safe as in a tomb" Rico said. "Watch, Malone. All my life I want to drive through a red light without getting the pinch!" The hearse shot across Ohio Street, scattering traffic and pedestrians.

"One more like that," Malone said, "and you will get pinched."

"Never," Rico said. "In this beautiful new hearse, we don't get arrested. The cops they stop us, they say, 'Where

you think you're going, a fire?' and we say, 'No, a funeral.'
Good-by cops. Look, Malone, another red light! Whee!"

The hearse careened madly across Chicago Avenue, skidding around the front end of a streetcar and narrowly dodging
a truck. Malone closed his eyes and tried to convince himself
that he was asleep and having a particularly bad nightmare,
and that he'd waken any minute now.

"At this time of day it's especially fun," Rico said. "Lots
of traffic." The brakes screamed and horns honked wildly on
all sides as he made the turn into Division Street.

An incredibly short time later the brakes screamed again,
and the hearse slid to a shuddering stop. Malone sat very
still, his eyes closed, trying to get just one long breath.

"I drive good, yes?" Rico said proudly.

"Wonderful," Malone said. He climbed out of the front
seat and stood still for a moment, enjoying the feeling of solid
and motionless ground under his feet. "Wait a minute, Rico,
and I'll give you a hand."

"I carry them O.K.," Rico said, unfastening the back of
the hearse.

Malone leaned against the side of the hearse and watched
while Rico opened the back door of his establishment, switched
on a blindingly brilliant light, and dragged the two limp
forms inside. Then he followed and closed the door behind
him.

Suddenly he felt a pang of sympathy for the two cap-
tives. The back room of Rico di Angelo's undertaking parlor
had been frightening enough last night, in the darkness.
Now, with the lights on, it was ten times worse.

"All new," Rico said proudly, "and everything the best.
Malone, maybe you like a drink of wine while I lay them
out?"

Malone nodded. Rico opened a cupboard and brought
out a bottle of red wine and a glass. Malone gulped half a
tumbler full—it was sour stuff, but heady—while he watched
an expert job of undressing two unconscious men and stretching them out on the tables.

Rico covered both tables with sheets, got a glass for
himself, and said, "Now, we wait."

They didn't have long to wait. Only half the bottle of red

wine was gone when Louis Perez stirred faintly, moaned, stirred again, and finally pushed the sheet away from his face. He stared at the ceiling, lifted his head and stared at the walls with their instrument cases, and sat upright with a blood-curdling yell.

"Now, now," Rico said, "you are in a very fine establishment. Everything new." He waved a hand at the cases of instruments. "See? Everything new and shiny. Never used yet." By that time Wilks was conscious and watching him with silent horror. "All the best modern methods, if I do embalm you."

"You can't embalm me," Wilks gasped. "I'm *alive!*"

"I never embalmed a live man yet," Rico said, "but I can try." He beamed. "It is a very simple process. First I——"

Perez let out another yell, slid off the table, clutching at the sheet, and said, "Malone, you're our lawyer, get us out of this."

Malone shrugged his shoulders and said, "Mr. di Angelo has a one-track mind. He seems to have made it up that you ought to answer any questions I want to ask you."

Rico grinned, took just one instrument from one of the cases, and twirled it unpleasantly on one finger.

"Did you shoot Jesse Conway?" Malone asked.

"No." It was a duet.

"Did you move his body?"

"Yes." Another duet.

"Look, Malone," Perez said, wiping the sweat from his face. "We ain't brains. We're just thugs. We do like we're told, see?"

"Like putting the pressure on for protection dough?" Malone said.

"Sure, that's it. We get the names and addresses, and we do the advance work. This here business was just an odd job. A certain guy slips us a fancy key and tell us to go to a certain address and move out a stiff. He meets us, we give him back the key, he gives us another key and tells us to park the stiff out here in the swell coffin. Then he tells us to watch this guy who runs this undertaking joint, a guy who'd given us a lot of trouble in the past, and see if he tries to snake the stiff out and stash it in some alley. O.K., we do, and it looks like this guy does, and we make the pitch according to directions, only it turns out this guy has laid a trap for us, and look at all the trouble it caused." He added indignantly. "The bastard."

Rico di Angelo spat out seven words in Italian.

Louis Perez countered with nine words in Spanish.

Rico advanced, the shiny instrument swinging on his finger.

"Malone!" Perez shrieked. "Don't you let him!"

"Lay off, Rico," Malone said.

Earl Wilks sat up and made a number of unpleasant comments on the probable ancestry and personal habits of everyone else in the room.

"Shut up," Malone said amiably. "And go on with what you were saying, Louis. Never mind the interruptions."

"I told you everything," Louis Perez said. "Lemme go home now."

"What's the name of the guy that told you to move the stiff, slipped you the key, and worked out the details?"

"Guy name of Art Harvey, Al Harmon, or Abe Haycraft. Sometimes calls himself Alex Hazlitt."

"Does he usually give you your orders?"

"No."

"Who does?"

"I can't tell."

Rico sighed and said, "Son of a bitch! Malone, you let me handle him. Maybe I put in the embalming fluid first, and then draw off the blood. You lie down on the table, bum!"

"*No!*" Perez yelped. "Malone, get me out of here!"

"In due time," Malone said. "Give me the name."

"I can't. I'd be killed."

"And if you don't," Malone said, "you'll probably be embalmed alive. I don't want to rush you. Make up your mind." He turned to Rico and said, "If you've got a couple more glasses, maybe the gentlemen would like a glass of wine."

"Sure thing," Rico said, going over to the cupboard.

"Malone—" Perez began.

A car roared past in the alley. One of the back windows shattered with a loud crashing of glass, and something landed on the floor.

Malone took one glance and yelled, *"Duck!"*

"Gun!" Perez howled. "Must have gun!" He dived at the heap of clothes on the floor, made a quick grab and stood swaying, naked as a clam, clutching his gun in one, unsteady hand.

"Out, you damn fool!" Malone shouted at him. Earl Wilks raced for the back door, Rico almost beat him to it. Malone grabbed the dazed Louis Perez, flung him into the alley, and fell on top of him.

There was a moment of blinding light, in which the earth seemed to shake violently. There was a blasting roar, followed by an almost intolerable silence. Malone closed his eyes and wondered if there was enough money in the bank to give him a fine funeral.

He heard running footsteps in the alley. They paused close by him for a moment, then ran on again.

He opened his eyes, just as the back room of Rico di Angelo's new undertaking parlor burst into flames.

Malone pulled himself to his knees. He could see Rico leaning against the back wall of a garage, stunned and staring. He could see Earl Wilks, sprawled on the pavement.

He had to get away from here, fast. The fire department and the police department would be here at any moment. This was no time to answer questions. He managed to get to his feet, estimated that he could make it to the end of the alley. But there was one thing he had to do first.

He hauled Louis Perez out of the reach of the flames. Then he stood over the half-conscious man and said, "Tell me. The name, the *name!*"

Already he could hear sirens shrieking in the distance.

Louis Perez stared at him with glassy eyes. Blood bubbled from between his lips. He gasped, "Name——name—— Guillermo. . . ." His eyes closed.

CHAPTER TWENTY-NINE

"Rico," Malone said, "Rico, are you all right?"

"Sure," Rico said, "it's O.K. I got insurance."

"That isn't what I mean," Malone said furiously. The approaching sirens were very close now. "How do you *feel?*"

Rico looked at the two forms lying in the alley and said, "I feel fine."

Malone hastily examined Earl Wilks. The big gangster was unpleasantly limp, his mouth was open, and a thin trickle of blood ran down his chin. But he was alive. So was Louis Perez. Alive but dead to the world. Malone ran back to where Rico stood half dazed, still staring at the flames.

"Listen, Rico," Malone said earnestly, "get this straight in your mind. You didn't see me today. You've been out here all afternoon. After these two goons got out on bail they came out here to talk to you, in a nice friendly fashion, of course, about forgetting the whole business, and no hard feelings on either side. While they were talking to you, somebody tossed a bomb through the window."

Rico nodded. "I get you, Malone," he said, "but their clothes, Malone. Would they be having a nice friendly talk with me laid out on the embalming tables with all their clothes off?"

"Hell!" Malone said. He could hear one of the fire engines making the turn into Division Street. He thought fast. "Rico, do you have any clothes in your establishment?"

"Sure," Rico said proudly, "laying-out clothes. Everything the best. All dress suits and tuxedos."

"That does it," Malone told him. "Look, here's your story. These guys were holding you up. They were forcing you to let them change clothes here—change into your clothes—so that they could make a getaway. Therefore they were wearing September morn costumes when the bomb sailed in through the window. All the clothes involved are burnt to ashes by now, anyway, so there's no way of proving or disproving anything." He added hastily, "And if these guys talk when they come to—well, the explosion drove them out of their heads. Nobody'd believe the story they'd tell anyway."

"I fix everything," Rico said. "Scram, Malone."

Malone said, "Good luck," and raced down the alley. He reached the next street just as a fire engine roared into the alley from the other end. Another raced past him, headed toward Division Street, and a third came screaming down Division Street itself. The wailing of a police-car siren began to join the chorus somewhere in the distance, and suddenly the whole neighborhood, dark and deserted a moment before, was full of people.

Malone leaned against the door of an enlighted poolroom and tried to catch his breath. He realized suddenly that his heart was pounding and that he ached in every limb. The street in front of him was behaving in a matter no self-respecting street would intentionally adopt, making rapid changes from vertical to horizontal and back again and occasionally going into a sideways spin. Malone closed his eyes.

It was several minutes before he opened them again. The street had evidently repented its misbehavior and had settled down to normal. The little lawyer examined his reflection in the glass door against which he had been leaning. His clothes were a mess, the navy blue pin-stripe suit had been ripped and torn in half a hundred places. His face was black with soot and dirt.

The neighborhood was alive now not only with curious spectators but with police. Squad cars went slowly around the block, flashing their spotlights in every direction. Other policemen on foot were going over every square inch of territory, their flashlights in their hands.

"The damn fools," Malone thought. Didn't they realize that by now the car from which the bomb was thrown was probably halfway to Gary, Indiana!

An ambulance shot out of the alley. Malone hoped Louis

Perez and Earl Wilks wouldn't be conscious enough to talk for at least a day or two.

There still remained his problem of getting away from the scene. A policeman with a flashlight was coming dangerously near to his sanctuary. Malone flattened himself against the side of a narrow entry way toward which the policeman was coming, and waited. The flashlight suddenly blazed on the door at the end of the entry way, and at the same moment, in one swift silent move, Malone ducked behind the policeman's back and was safely out on the sidewalk.

Malone had been brought up in a neighborhood where the average small boy learned to dodge policemen at least a year or two before he learned his alphabet. He headed south in the direction of Chicago Avenue, adroitly ducking into doorways and disappearing in the shadows of buildings whenever a squad car came unpleasantly close. Two blocks of this and he was safe.

He was on a badly lighted residential street in a neighborhood that changed abruptly from Italian to Polish. He was weak and exhausted and walking with difficulty. He wished that a taxicab would come along and rescue him.

Once, in fact, he sat down on the curbstone, mopped his brow, and muttered, "There's as much chance of finding a taxi on this street as there is of finding a snowflake in a haystack." He thought that over for a moment and amended it to, "Finding a needle in hell."

He finally reached Chicago Avenue at a point just east of its junction with Milwaukee Avenue. There wasn't much chance of finding a taxi here, either. It was nearly seven o'clock but the eastbound streetcars were still jammed to the doors with homebound workers.

Anna Marie must be starving for her dinner by now, Malone reflected, starving and, he hoped, worrying about him. But he couldn't arrive looking like this. He'd better go to Jake and Helene's first.

He thought it over and decided that a streetcar would be the safest bet. He caught the first one that came along, shoving his way through the crowd, catching a precarious foothold on the step, and finally inching his way into the vestibule where he dropped his fare in the box, clutched a pole, and stood hanging onto it for dear life.

The crowd thinned out rapidly along the way. By the time the car crossed Wells Street it was half empty. Malone still stood there clutching the pole. The car was between Clark and State Streets when a fellow passenger said sympathetically, "What happened, bub? Been in a fight?"

"Uh-uh," Malone said. He opened his eyes, saw where he was, and prepared to get off. "I was blown up in an undertaking parlor."

The other passengers laughed appreciatively. Malone climbed down the steps, shook his fist in the direction of the streetcar, and said, "Damn it, I *was* blown up in an undertaking parlor! I can prove it!"

He walked over to the sidewalk, leaned against the wall, and waited until a taxi came along. He climbed in, relaxed against the cushions, and gave the address of the apartment hotel where Jake and Helene lived.

The cab driver was another sympathetic soul. He said, "Been having a little trouble?"

"It wasn't any trouble to me," Malone said.

He decided the wisest policy would be to use the back elevator and not expose himself to more sympathetic questions as he walked through the lobby. Any minute now, he told himself, his head would clear. It would keep on getting more and more filled with fog right up to a certain point and then, miraculously, everything would be right again. But it was getting very foggy now.

He clutched the side of the elevator for support. The name Louis Perez had gasped out kept beating an annoying percussion accompaniment to the thoughts that whirled madly through his mind. The name didn't seem to have anything to do with what had happened so far. It was a name he had never heard before and hoped he would never hear again.

Maybe the name was important. Maybe that was why Louis Perez had whispered it just before lapsing into unconsciousness, or maybe——maybe psychology or something——or just maybe——

Malone staggered out of the elevator, its door clanging shut behind him revived him for a moment. He started down the corridor toward Jake and Helene's apartment, only occasionally pushing the wall away with the flat of his hand.

Ten feet from the door he halted. A short, paunchy man with sleek black hair was being welcomed by Helene at the door. For a moment Malone stood there, undecided. But the familiar-looking stranger seemed harmless, at least at this distance. And the floor and walls were beginning to play merry-go-round now. He wasn't at all sure he could find the back elevator again, or that he could trust it if he did find it. He groped his way to the door, pounded on it, and nearly fell in when it was opened.

"Malone," Helene gasped. "What happened to you? Were you robbed?"

"No," Malone gasped. "I was bombed."

Jake grabbed him by the elbow and said, "Hello, Malone. You remember Lou Berg, don't you?"

"Sure do," Malone muttered. He aimed at the ex-band leader's outthrust hand and missed it by a good six inches. Jake steadied him.

"Call——*her*——" the little lawyer gasped. "Tell her—— late to take her to dinner——can't have her worry—" The room was spinning now. "Send to the hotel——for clean clothes—— razor——get cleaned up——go meet her——" He pitched forward. Jake caught him just in time.

"Funny thing," Malone whispered, "for a minute—thought I knew who—but can't remember name now——"

The walls stopped spinning and mercifully turned black.

CHAPTER THIRTY

"It's just a mild concussion," the doctor said. "Coupled with shock and exhaustion. He'll be up and around in a day or two." He tucked the sheet around Malone's chin, put a little box on the table. "Give him two of these if he wakes up. What happened to him, anyway?"

"I don't know," Helene said truthfully.

"From the symptoms," the doctor said, "I'd think he'd been in an explosion, but of course——"

Malone lay very still and kept his eyes closed.

"I don't suppose you have any idea how it happened?" the doctor said.

Helene opened her mouth to speak, then shut it again.

"Well, don't worry about him," the doctor told her. He picked up his bag. "A little rest and quiet, and he'll be all right."

Jake frowned. "There's a chance we'll have to go out and leave him alone. Shouldn't we get a nurse in?"

"No need for it," the doctor said. "Once he's taken those capsules, he'll stay asleep for twelve hours. I'll come in in the morning."

Malone repressed his indignation. Feed him capsules, would they! Keep him asleep for twelve hours! He'd show them!

He heard a low murmur of voices from the next room, and the opening and closing of a door. He waited craftily until he was sure the doctor couldn't be called back and then moaned softly.

Helene and Jake were at his side in two seconds flat. Malone opened his eyes and looked dazed. "Where—am—I?" he said in a feeble whisper.

"You're here," Helene said, taking his hand.

"Where's—here?"

Jake said, "Malone, what happened?"

The little lawyer blinked and looked bewildered. "What happened to who?"

"To you," Jake said.

This time Malone didn't answer. He simply looked blank and faintly puzzled.

"For Pete's sake," Helene scolded, "don't bother him with questions now. Let it wait until he's had some sleep."

Malone gave her a faint smile of gratitude.

"You just need a nice little nap," Helene said soothingly. "And then you'll be perfectly all right again. You take those two little pills the doctor left for you."

Malone nodded obediently, inwardly seething. Nice little nap! Twelve hours! Be perfectly all right again! Why, the female Judas!

He opened his mouth, let her slip in the capsules, and managed to anchor them under his tongue. He took one small sip of water and closed his eyes.

"He'll be asleep in no time," Helene whispered. "Let's get out of here and not disturb him."

Malone heard them tiptoe to the door, heard it close very softly. Then he hastily took out the capsules and tucked them under his pillow. There! Now, it was just a question of waiting until they left.

It was pleasant to lie still and think. His head throbbed, and he felt weary. Wide awake, though. Wide awake, and able to cope with any situation that might come along.

It occurred to him that Jake and Helene might try to take matters into their own hands. Anna Marie would have to be warned.

He listened for a moment. There was a very faint murmur from the next room. He propped himself on one elbow, wincing at the effort, reached for the telephone on the bed table, called his hotel, identified himself, and gave Anna Marie's room number.

"Listen," he said in a very low voice. "I've got to talk fast, so get all this straight. I want you to send down for some dinner, then get into bed. Jake and Helene may turn up and try to get you to go somewhere or do something. I don't know where or what. They'll tell you I've been hurt and I'm asleep, but don't believe them. It's a trap. Tell them you're very tired from last night and you've gone to bed and you're going to sleep. Stay right in your room and wait for me, I'll be along as soon as I can."

He hung up the phone, feeling very pleased with himself. He'd fixed *that* business all right!

Someone had gone to pretty great lengths to make sure that Earl Wilks and Louis Perez wouldn't talk. Why? If what Al Harmon had said was correct, they wouldn't be able to give much dangerous information about the protection racket. Only the name of their immediate contact. Or had they been in the inner circle, so to speak? Was the name Perez has

174

gasped out the name he, and Al Harmon, and a lot of other people, had tried to learn?

Guillermo. Who the hell was Guillermo? Malone puzzled over it. He knew practically all the large- and small-scale racketeers in the city, at least by reputation, and he'd never heard of anyone named Guillermo. He felt that somehow it ought to connect up with something in his mind, and it didn't.

Had the bomb been thrown because Perez and Wilks could tell something else of importance? As far as he knew, they hadn't been tied up with Ike Malloy. But could they have known who planned the murder of Big Joe Childers?

There was a third, and distinctly disquieting, possibility. The bomb hadn't been thrown because Louis Perez and Earl Wilks were in the back room of Rico's undertaking parlor, but because he himself was there.

He didn't like the idea, but he couldn't discard it. Malone scowled and asked himself what *he* knew that might make him dangerous. The hell of it was, he suspected, that he did know something important. If only he could remember——

The name, Guillermo, was important, but he couldn't think why. Something Helene had told him was important. Something to do with Milly Dale. If it would only come back to him. He wished he could call Helene and ask her, but he was supposed to be asleep.

Milly Dale. Something Helene had told him *before* Milly had been killed.

Just some one fact that he'd forgotten—that was all he needed now to pull everything together.

He lay very still, his eyes closed, thinking. Little by little facts began to fall into their proper place in his mind. The name, Guillermo, and the fact about Milly Dale belonged side by side. They were twin facts. Identical twins.

Suddenly he knew the answer.

He wished Jake and Helene would hurry up and clear out. Now that he knew he wanted action. He told himself to be patient, and waited.

Out in the other room Helene said, "I wish I knew what happened to Malone. He said he'd been bombed." She turned to Jake and said with a wan smile, "Have you heard of any good bombings lately?"

"No," Jake said, "but I think we will." He turned to Lou Berg, and said, "What the hell was the idea of that telegram? 'Do nothing till you hear from me!' Do nothing about what?"

The ex-band leader said to Helene, "Your old man's losing his grip. Too bad. Always hate to see a fine mind go to pieces."

"Damn you," Jake said indignantly, "tell me what you mean."

"Greatest exploitation idea I ever heard of!" Lou Berg exploded. "We'll première the picture in the Casino. Has a picture ever been preemed in a night club? Not that I know of."

"What picture?" Jake said.

Lou Berg rolled his eyes and said, "Diagrams I have to draw him yet! Listen, Jake. Tomorrow morning I'm planing on to Hollywood. Already I'm wiring writers. We'll rush into production the greatest ghost picture ever made."

A light was beginning to dawn in Jake's mind. "So that's what it's all about."

"Modern setting. Ghost is a beautiful girl. Then we give it terrific publicity. Invitation-only première in the Casino, the night club where a huge audience of people once saw an actual, honest-to-God ghost! Not just one person saw the ghost, dozens did. Hundreds. First authentic case like that in history."

He paused and looked at Jake, his eyes narrowed.

"Look, Jake. Tell me. It wasn't all just a publicity stunt for the Casino, was it?"

Jake said, "It was not just a publicity stunt for the Casino."

"Not that the box-office customers would care," Berg said. "If only somebody could have gotten a picture of her. Spirit photograph, I suppose it would have to be." He sighed. "Oh well, you can't have everything."

"In this set up you seem to have damn near everything," Jake said, "except the ghost herself. How would you like to have her in the picture?"

Lou Berg said, "Are you kidding?"

"No," Jake said. "Why shouldn't a beautiful ghost have a screen career?"

"Jake," Helene said, "you're a genius!" She looked reproachfully at Lou. "And you said he was slipping."

"I'm beginning to think he's nuts," Lou said. "What d'ya mean, Jake? Get somebody to impersonate this ghost and try to pass it off as the real thing?"

"I mean, use the real thing," Jake said. "As I understand it, a ghost can materialize any time or anywhere it wants to. This one would probably be tickled pink to materialize in Hollywood. Maybe she can't act, but who cares? There's a *real* exploitation!"

"I'll be damned!" Lou Berg said. He was silent for a moment. "You aren't kidding, are you?"

"I am not," Jake said firmly.

"How the devil do you go about getting in touch with a ghost?"

Jake said, "I imagine the thing to do would be to hang around places she seems to haunt. If that don't work, we could always call in a medium." He added, "If you could get her to Hollywood, you might have trouble photographing her, but——"

"I know cameramen who could photograph anything," Lou Berg boasted. He scowled. "It'll be a hell of a contract to draw up, but I got nothing but the best lawyers."

Helene looked at Jake and her eyes said, "Jake, you're wonderful and I love you!"

There was a loud knock on the door. Helene opened it apprehensively. The knock had had a familiar sound.

Von Flanagan stepped into the room and said, "Where's Malone?"

Helene thought for approximately two seconds and then said, "In there," pointing to the bedroom, "but you mustn't try to wake him."

"Wake him? What's the matter? Is he sick?"

"He had a collapse," Helene said very solemnly. "He didn't get any sleep last night. He got into a fight with somebody and got all banged up."

"Nothing serious," Jake said. "The doctor said it was nervous exhaustion and gave him a couple of sleeping pills. I doubt if you could wake him if you tried."

Von Flanagan opened the bedroom door, peered in at

the motionless man, and closed the door softly. "Poor guy.' Hope he feels O.K. How long has he been sleeping?"

Jake and Helene looked at each other, "Since—oh, I don't know exactly," Helene said. "It's been a long time. You remember Lou Berg, don't you?"

"Sure," von Flanagan said. "Suspected him of murdering a radio producer once. Wouldn't blame him if he had, some of the programs we hear." He turned back to Helene and said, "Would you say Malone had been sleeping since before six o'clock?"

Helene thought, nodded, and said, "Yes, he could have been. We've been sitting here talking for simply ages. You know how it is—talking about old times."

"What happened at six o'clock?" Jake said very casually.

"It was sometime between six and seven," von Flanagan said. He mopped his brow. "Malone sprung two clients this afternoon. Two mugs that tried to put the pressure on an undertaking parlor. They left the jail with Malone."

Helene said quickly, "He must have come directly here from getting them out of jail."

"Go on," Jake said.

"Well, about six o'clock somebody throws a bomb in the undertaking parlor, which catches fire and burns all to hell. Three guys are out in the alley. The owner of the joint—he ain't hurt, just bruised—and the two mugs. One of 'em died in the hospital, the other's hurt bad. And no sign of Malone."

He sighed deeply and said, "The things people do to make life hard for me!"

"A murder by bomb must be a hard problem to solve," Helene said sympathetically.

"That ain't it," von Flanagan said. "One of the mugs carried a gun. They gave it back to him when he was released, he has a permit for it. Damn fools in the department didn't check it while they had it. O.K., the gun's on him when he's killed, and it's turned over to me. I send it to ballistics, and what do I find?"

"All right," Helene said, "what do you find?"

"It's the gun that killed Jesse Conway, and Garrity, and the Dale girl," von Flanagan said, his face beginning to turn purple. "And now the guy's gone ahead and died in the hospital, and I can't even question him!"

"That is too bad," Jake said.

"It's too bad," von Flanagan said, "but it ain't the worst of it. At the time the Dale girl was killed the guy was in the jail and so was the gun that killed her." He glared at the three people in the room as though it were in some way their fault. "It's not only too bad," he repeated in a roar, "it's impossible!"

CHAPTER THIRTY-ONE

Malone waited till the murmur of voices ceased and the door to the corridor closed. He waited until, from far down the hall, he heard the elevator door clang. Then he waited ten minutes more, just to be on the safe side.

He sat up experimentally. Then he swung his short, hairy legs over the side of the bed. Finally he stood up and took two steps.

No doubt about it, he felt fine.

He felt under his pillow for the two capsules, and considered leaving them on the table with a caustic note. His feeling of resentment returned in full force. No, he'd drop them down a drain, and let Jake and Helene be mystified about how he could have gotten up, dressed, and gone out with a double dose of sedative in his system.

He wrapped Jake's bathrobe around him and went out to the kitchen, the robe trailing on the floor. He filled the coffee pot with water, put in a double measure of coffee, and put the pot on to boil. Then he returned to the bedroom to dress while it was cooking.

A lot of cold water on his face made him feel even better. He examined his clothes and made up his mind that when he located the man who'd thrown the bomb, he would stick him for the price of a new Finchley suit and a Sulka tie. But these would have to do until he could get back to his hotel and change into something else.

While he dressed he thought over von Flanagan's revelation. It wasn't hard to figure out what had happened. The man who had thrown the bomb, or had arranged for it to be thrown, had decided to kill two birds with one bomb. Get rid of a troublesome individual—whether himself, or Perez, or Wilks—and plant responsibility for the three murders.

It might have worked, too; if the bomb thrower hadn't overlooked—or hadn't known—the fact that at the time Milly Dale was murdered, both Louis Perez and his gun had been safely in jail.

Save for that, it would have been a simple matter to race into the alley after the explosion and switch guns on a dead, or dying, man. Probably making sure, at the time, that he was dead or dying.

Malone scowled. He remembered the footsteps in the alley at the time he was lying, half dazed and stunned, on the pavement. That's when it must have happened. If he'd only opened his eyes——

If he had, he might not be here now.

Rico may have seen the man. No, Rico would have told him. And if the man had thought that Rico had seen him, Rico would be dead now, too. The murderer made some foolish mistakes, but they weren't due to squeamishness about multiple killings.

Not that it mattered any more whether Rico had seen him or not. Malone didn't need to be told, now.

The coffee was done by the time he'd finished dressing. He sat out in the kitchenette and drank every drop of it.

He borrowed a topcoat of Jake's. It came nearly to his ankles, but it hid his tattered clothes. He pulled his hat brim over his black eye, and went down the freight elevator.

Out on the sidewalk he stood for a moment, deciding on his next move. He didn't want to talk to von Flanagan on the telephone, but something had to be done about that gun. And he had a hunch he was going to need von Flanagan's help before the night was over.

He walked over to State Street and headed south until

he reached a Western Union office, where he wrote a telegram to von Flanagan.

CHECK OWNERSHIP GUN PLANTED ON
LOUIS PEREZ. THIS IS URGENT.

MALONE

To be on the safe side, he sent it both to von Flanagan's office and to his home.

Maggie always got the address and phone number of everyone who ever visited the little lawyer's office, and she kept a spare notebook of them at her home, for just such emergencies. Malone stopped in a corner cigar store, called Maggie, and got Al Harmon's number. Then he called Al Harmon.

"Jeez," Al Harmon said, "I thought you were dead, pal. I thought you'd been blown into such small pieces they couldn't find a trace of you in the ruins."

"I was," Malone said, "but I pulled myself together. Can you meet me in my office in ten minutes?"

"I've got a date with a blonde," Harmon began.

"This is urgent." He hung up.

He called a cab and reached the office ahead of Harmon. While he waited he called Eva Childers.

"I just may be on the trail of something," he told her very casually. "Can you tell me the name of your late husband's doctor?"

She hesitated a moment. "Why? Is it important?"

"It may be," Malone said.

"Well—it was Dr. Fitzgerald. Why do you want to know?"

"I'll tell you," Malone said, "when I tell you who hired your husband's murderer." He hung up and waited for Al Harmon, deep in his thoughts and not happy with them at all.

Al Harmon came in breezily and said, "This had better be important, pal." He looked at Malone and said, "You don't look half bad."

"Not half as bad as I feel," the lawyer growled. "Sit down." He scowled at the top of his desk. "Are we still working together?"

"We were the last I heard. By the way, I don't suppose

181

you'll ever be able to collect from those two mugs now. Too bad. I'd thought maybe you'd split the fee with me."

"I'm thoroughly ethical," Malone said primly. "I never split fees." He took out a cigar and began unwrapping it. "I may be able to wind everything up, for you and me both, if you'll tell me a couple of things."

"Chum," Harmon said, chain-lighting a cigarette, "I'm the original quiz kid. Ask anything you like."

"What were you talking about with Mrs. Childers in The Happy Days saloon, and when you went to the St. Clair girl's apartment last night, why did you go *upstairs* first?"

Al Harmon stared at him for a moment in sheer amazement. Then he grinned.

He said, "I'm beginning to think you've got second sight. O.K., here's the works." He leaned back in his chair. "While I was mousing around this protection racket, I tumbled to a couple of things. One, Big Joe had heard about it, and he didn't like it. It was the sort of thing he wouldn't stand for, especially not in his territory. I had a hunch Big Joe found out who was back of it. Two, Big Joe was killed in The Happy Days saloon. Catch?"

Malone nodded and said, "You cast two and two upon the waters and it came back cake."

"Right, pal. So I figure, suppose the babe isn't guilty. Suppose Al Harmon makes like a detective, finds out who is guilty, saves the babe, and is a hero all over the place—just as a little sideline to the main job, see? Only it don't work out so good."

"So," Malone prompted him, "you decided to go to work on Mrs. Childers."

"Right again. But I had the murder all figured out, see. Big Joe wanted to smash this nice, profitable racket. He got bumped, and his girl friend got framed. Her lawyer, who was mixed up with the racket, helped frame her. Why frame her? Well, she must have known too much about the racket. Big Joe probably confided things to her."

"Only," Malone said, "if she did—why did she keep her mouth shut after he was killed?"

"At that point," Al Harmon said cheerfully, "I am stuck." He lit another cigarette. "And when I first went to work on

Mrs. Childers, I was stuck. As far as she was concerned, the verdict was correct, the case was closed, everything was settled, and the hell with it." He paused.

"And yesterday?" Malone said.

"Yesterday she comes looking me up at The Happy Days. She sees everything different now. Her eyes have been opened. Justice must be done. I say, O.K., and pressure her to give with the facts. The facts she gives me you can put in your right eye and still have room for a camel. While we're having this pleasant little chat over a couple of short beers, something happens which throws The Happy Days crowd into a spin. We beat it out, she tells me she'll see me later, and scrams."

"What was the incident that occurred?"

"This babe comes in," Al Harmon said, "Mrs. Justus. Her angle is, she's supposed to be meeting her husband there. As if a guy in his right mind would pick a joint like The Happy Days to meet his wife in. Especially one that looks like her." He whistled admiringly and blew a kiss toward the ceiling.

"Never mind that," Malone said. "Go on."

"Well, Justus was one of the guys in The Happy Days when Big Joe was shot. He gave a lot of trouble afterward. Now she turns up. Acts nosy as hell. Finally she asks where the john is and heads down the hallway. Everybody scrams. The relief bartender and the relief bouncer come in, and a new batch of customers. Because the bunch that were there happened to have been the same bunch that were there when Big Joe got shot. Actually, I don't think a damn one of 'em knows anything about the murder, but that bunch don't ask for trouble if it can duck."

Malone thought of Helene, alone and unprotected, in The Happy Days saloon, and cold sweat broke out on his forehead. He knocked the ash off his cigar and said, "So you didn't learn anything from Mrs. Childers?"

Al Harmon sighed and said, "I'm doing an awful lot of talking, pal."

Malone rose, got the bottle out of the file drawer, and poured two drinks.

"Thanks," Al Harmon said. "I do like to meet a guy who

can take a hint." He downed his drink, lit a cigarette, and said, "Big Joe kept a diary from the time he was a kid. Always kept it hid. After he got bumped, all the volumes from about the year one turned up in a safety deposit box. All, that is, except the last one."

"It looks," Malone said thoughtfully, "as though he had a hiding place for the current volume, and as soon as he finished one, he put it in the safety deposit box. Question is, where is that last volume?"

"Brother," Al Harmon said, "if you can answer that one, I'll give *you* a drink."

"Could he have destroyed it?"

"Now, I ask you," Harmon said, "when a guy has saved all his diaries since he was twelve years old, does he throw away the last one?"

"Suppose he decided to stop keeping a diary?"

"Then why not burn up the whole bunch and save paying for the safety deposit box?"

"All right," Malone said wearily. "It must be somewhere."

"O.K. So Mrs. Childers slips me her husband's key to this chick's apartment. She's searched every inch of the official Childers' residence, and it ain't there. It ain't in what used to be his office. Well, I get hold of a pal of mine who really can search. He could find a——"

"A camel in your right eye," Malone said.

"Right. I figure Big Joe ain't gonna leave his secret diary around where his girl friend can find it. He also has the top floor apartment. So, we start there and, brother, we *search!* Finally we give up. We don't start on her apartment because— there was a slight interruption."

"I know," Malone said. He frowned. "I think the diary will turn up."

"Anything else you want to know, pal?" Al Harmon asked.

"No. But a couple of things I want you to do," Malone told him. "You've got official papers and I haven't, and I've got an idea and you haven't. So maybe you'd better call on Big Joe's doctor and ask him a few questions."

"No need," Al Harmon said, grinning. "I can tell you right now. Big Joe had cancer of the stomach. He'd have been dead, anyway, in a few months."

Malone sat silent for a long moment. "How do you know?"

"When I got this idea of mine," Al Harmon said, "I didn't miss a thing. I went over Big Joe's life like I was going to write his life story to be played by Don Ameche. I know how many fillings he had in his teeth, when he had his eyes tested last, and the lovelife of his cook. Naturally, I talked to his doctor." He paused. "But, so what?"

Malone didn't answer.

"Nobody murders a guy because he's got cancer of the stomach, unless he happens to be a terribly good pal, and in that case he doesn't frame the guy's girl friend for the murder."

"That's right," Malone said. He added, "Well, I thought it might be important."

"What's the other thing you want me to do?" Al Harmon asked.

"You know the layout of The Happy Days saloon. Duck over there to spend the evening. You know the door leading to the alley. Unlock it, and see that it stays unlocked. That's all. And hang around."

"I'll be there," Al Harmon said. He rose, poured himself another drink, and walked to the door. "You know, pal," he said, "sometimes you puzzle me." He went out.

For a few minutes Malone sat at his desk, his head resting on his hands. He felt tired and indescribably depressed. A lot of things were going to happen before the night was over. He knew all about them, and he didn't like any of them.

At last he called Anna Marie. "I'll be over pretty soon. Get all dressed up, we're going out." He resisted the impulse to call her "darling."

He took one drink, put the bottle back in the file drawer, and went out.

But he didn't go straight to his hotel. He called a cab, drove to Anna Marie's apartment, and said, "Wait here." He went to the second floor apartment, and the cab driver had to wait a long time before he came out again.

CHAPTER THIRTY-TWO

"I hate leaving Malone all by himself," Helene said in a worried voice.

"He'll be all right," Jake told her. "The doctor said he wouldn't bat an eye until tomorrow. Besides," he added, "Malone's a big boy now."

"But suppose he did wake up?"

"He won't."

"Maybe that bomb was intended for Malone. Suppose the murderer goes up to the apartment while we're gone, and Malone is asleep and helpless——"

"For Pete's sake!" Jake exploded. "In the first place the murderer wouldn't know he was there. In the second place he wouldn't be able to get in."

"And in the third place," Lou Berg said, "from all I remember of Malone, he could take care of himself even if he was asleep."

Helene sighed and was silent. She swung the big car and headed south. "Jake, you said you'd stop by Malone's hotel and pick up his mail." She nudged him.

"That's right," Jake said. "We'll go there first." As she parked the car, he said, "You two wait here, I won't be a minute."

He took the elevator up to the floor where Malone had lived for years, and where he maintained a room to hide out important witnesses. He knocked softly on the door of the latter room and called out softly, "It's me, Jake Justus."

"I'm in bed," Anna Marie called back.

"Get dressed then, quick. This is something important," Jake said.

"Wait a minute."

He heard footsteps, and a moment later the door opened. Anna Marie stood there, wrapped in a deep rose bathrobe, her hair loose over her shoulders. There was the remains of dinner on a tray, the pillows were propped up against the head of the bed, and a book lay face down on the covers.

Jake went in and sat down on the arm of the one easy chair.

"I know it's early," she said, "but you've no idea how tired I am. Everything that's happened has exhausted me— and last night was just too much. I thought that as soon as the dinner tray went downstairs I'd turn out the light and sleep just hours and hours."

"You thought wrong," Jake said. "You've got some very important things to do."

She frowned and said, "Where's Malone? I was going to leave a note for him, telling him I'm sleeping."

"Malone's been in a little accident."

Her eyes widened prettily with surprise and horror. "Tell me!"

"Now don't be worried," Jake said hastily. "He's all right. He's up in our apartment. The doctor gave him some sleeping pills and told us he'd sleep till morning and be perfectly all right in a day or two."

"But what happened to him?"

"I don't know," Jake said. "He'll tell us when he wakes up." He decided against adding what he did know about the bombing of Rico di Angelo's. "The important thing is that he's all right."

She drew a long, quivering breath of relief. "I was really scared for a minute!"

"Now," Jake said, "about you."

"Please, Mr. Justus."

"Jake."

She smiled. "All right, Jake. I'm really desperately tired. And even if I weren't I couldn't go anywhere—*appear* anywhere—without Malone."

"You've got to," Jake said.

"No."

He sighed. "Look, your whole future depends on it." He went into details. Lou Berg. Hollywood. Exploitation.

He even included the première at the Casino. "When Lou finds out that you're not a real ghost, he's going to be surprised, but he isn't going to be sore. It's just as good exploitation when the whole story finally breaks."

"But——" She frowned.

Jake went on hastily, "When you finish with this—little business—of yours, you're going to have to do something with your life. What would you have done a year ago if somebody had offered you a chance like this?"

"I'd have jumped at it," she said. She paused. "Can't it be done tomorrow night?"

"No. I know Lou. He's impatient."

"Let me think for a minute." She sat down on the edge of the bed, lit a cigarette, and stared at the end of it. At last she looked up, smiled at him, and said, "O.K., you win."

"Good girl," Jake said. "Get dressed, and we'll work out some plans."

"You'll have to leave the plans to me," she told him. "But I promise they'll be good ones." She looked at her watch. "Where can I phone you, a little later?"

Jake thought for a moment and said, "The Casino."

"You'll hear from me. I'll tell you where I'll be and what to do."

"When you're a Hollywood star," Jake said, "don't forget to send me your autograph." He grinned at her and went out.

On his way to the lobby a thought struck him. Anna Marie might try to phone Malone. He paused in a phone booth, called the apartment hotel, and left strict orders not to put any calls through. Malone, he reflected, would probably sleep through the last trumpet, doped as he was, but Jake wasn't taking any chances.

Lou Berg grumbled, "It sure took you long enough to pick up a little mail at the desk."

"Ran into someone I knew," Jake said smoothly. He caught Helene's eye and nodded slightly.

She smiled at him, started the car, and said, "Well, guys, where to?"

"The Casino," Jake told her. As she started the car, he added, "Best floor show in town, and no cover charge."

Berg said, "Used to have a great band there, once. Fella by name of Lou Berg."

"Personally," Jake said, "I thought his band was strictly a stinker."

They squabbled amiably all the way to the Casino. The floor show had just started, and by the time their drinks arrived it had reached the spot where Milly Dale had always appeared.

Helene suddenly said, "Jake!"

He reached across the table and gripped her hand, hard. "I know," he said, "she was a swell kid."

"It's not only that," Helene whispered. Her eyes were bright with excitement. "I've remembered."

"You've remembered what?"

"Yesterday, when I was in The Happy Days saloon, and I heard Bill McKeown warning her not to sing that song—the strip-tease one about the gun."

"Bill McKeown's a good egg in some ways," Jake said, "but he has no taste in music."

"Damn you," Helene said, "that isn't it. Jake, don't you remember—she dropped that song and didn't sing it for a long time. I think night before last was the first time she'd sung it since—just after Big Joe Childers' murder."

Jake stared at her. "I don't get it." He scowled. "The 'Girl-With-The-Gun.' Did Milly Dale shoot Big Joe Childers and frame her friend Anna Marie? Then who shot Milly Dale?"

"I don't know," Helene said. "I don't know who shot who or why, but I do know that song has something to do with it, and I know Bill McKeown has." She added, "Why the hell did Malone pick this particular night to get himself blown up in a bombing!"

"Don't be impatient," Jake told her. "We can talk to him tomorrow."

"There's been too many murders," she said firmly. "There might be another one. We ought to do something now."

"Look," Lou Berg interrupted. "I don't mind you two going ahead and having a good time, but with me, this is strictly business."

"That's right, Helene," Jake said.

She sighed and was silent.

"And if that ghost of yours was going to show up," Berg went on, "it would've been in that spot where the other babe sang. So, where do we go now?"

"We stay here," Jake said. "Last night it appeared during the second floor show. And this is as good a place to get drunk in as any you can name."

"We ought to go to the apartment and see how Malone is," Helene said.

"*No*," Jake said very positively.

The second floor show was half through when Jake was called to the telephone. When he returned, Lou Berg said, "She didn't show up this time, either. Your ghost must be playing a different circuit."

"We'll find her," Jake said confidently. "Right now, we're going somewhere else. The Happy Days saloon." He turned to Helene. "Maybe you're right. Maybe someone should be there with Malone. Suppose we drop you at the apartment and join you there later."

"Oh, no," Helene said. "You don't put that over on me. You said yourself he'd be perfectly all right. If you think for one minute I'm not coming along——"

"Helene," Jake said, "be reasonable."

"Jake," she said, "be sensible. Don't argue with me. You always lose."

"I don't like it," Jake said unhappily. "It isn't safe."

"It as safe for me as it is for you. I don't have any particular desire to be a widow."

"Hell," Lou Berg said, "lay off the argument and let's get going. I know Helene. She'd be safe in a den of wildcats, but heaven help the wildcats."

Helene flashed him a grateful smile and slid into her coat. Jake sighed and gave up.

It was a short drive to The Happy Days. Helene parked the big car on Ontario Street, just off the alley, and they walked around the corner.

At the door Jake made one last try. "Maybe you'd better stay in the car and keep the motor running in case we want to leave in a hurry."

She didn't even answer that one.

The Happy Days was far from crowded. The bartender was polishing glasses, the bouncer stood leaning against the wall. A couple at one of the tables were drinking beer and arguing. A lone customer in one corner was drinking a gin rickey and playing solitaire. And Al Harmon was leaning against the bar.

"Jake," Helene whispered. She dug her fingers into his arm.

"I see him," Jake whispered back. "The young man in the tan raincoat. But remember, as Lou pointed out, we're here strictly on *business*." He led the way to a booth.

The bartender stared at them, so did the bouncer. Helene waved cheerily at the bartender, who came slowly over to their table.

"Three ryes," Jake said.

After the ryes had been brought, Al Harmon strolled very casually over to their booth and leaned on it.

"Friend of yours is down the hall talking to Bill McKeown," he said. "Lawyer, name of Malone."

Helene almost upset her drink. Jake said, "That's impossible. He's in bed, full of sleeping pills, and he won't wake up for hours."

"You're all wrong, pal. I talked to him myself, about an hour and a half ago."

Helene's lips set in a firm line. "The damned Irishman! I should have made sure he *swallowed* those capsules!"

Jake started to rise. "He's in no condition to be out and around."

"I wouldn't interfere," Al Harmon began.

The front door opened, and von Flanagan came in. He had a plain-clothes man with him. He saw Jake and Helene and Berg, glared at them, and said, "How the hell do you manage to turn up everywhere?" He walked to the bar and said, "Where's McKeown?"

The bartender jerked his head toward the hall and said, "Office."

The police officer and the plain-clothes man strode down the hall. Jake, Helene, and Lou Berg followed. As they reached the door, they heard Malone's voice.

"Louis Perez told me," Malone was saying. "You can't get out of it, McKeown."

Von Flanagan walked in. Malone looked very tired and pale, his eyes were bloodshot, and he was swaying slightly. Von Flanagan ignored him as he tossed a gun on the desk.

"Is this your gun, McKeown?"

Bill McKeown said nothing.

"Talk!" von Flanagan said.

"You might as well admit it," Malone put in. "He's had it traced to you."

Suddenly Bill McKeown's eyes stared at something over their shoulders. Von Flanagan gave one quick glance.

There in the semidarkness of the hallway, framed against the dark wooden door of the room marked "Ladies," was the pale, misty, beautiful vision of Anna Marie St. Clair.

Von Flanagan gave one blood-curdling yell and fled toward the front of the building, followed by his plain-clothes man. Lou Berg stared in open-mouthed admiration.

No one noticed Bill McKeown's fingers closing over the gun.

CHAPTER THIRTY-THREE

"Now, von Flanagan," Helene said, "it's just psychology. You didn't really see anything."

"I suppose *they* didn't see anything, either," the big police officer grunted, pointing to the bartender, the bouncer, and the few customers, who were huddled together out on the sidewalk.

"It's *mass* psychology," Helene said firmly.

The plain-clothes man said uneasily, "There's nothing in the police manual about dealing with cases of this kind."

"Malone wasn't scared," Helene said.

"Who said anything about being scared?" von Flanagan said. "I was startled, that's all." He peered anxiously down the hallway. There was no sign of Anna Marie. Jake, Al Harmon, and Lou Berg were staring at the place where she had been.

"Even if it were real," Helene said, "I never thought you'd let a mere ghost intimidate you."

"I don't believe in ghosts," von Flanagan said. He jerked his head toward the hallway and said, "Go ahead, Mike. I'll follow you."

"I don't believe in ghosts, either," the plain-clothes man said, "but *I'll* follow *you*."

Helene sniffed, said, "Shame on both of you," and led the way down the hallway. Von Flanagan and Mike trailed after her.

There was a sudden movement at the far end of the hallway. Malone came backing out of McKeown's office. Jake and Lou Berg suddenly moved away from the door.

Von Flanagan forgot all about ghosts and/or psychology, and yelled, "Hey! What's going on here?"

Bill McKeown came out of his office. The gun was in his hand.

"Don't make the mistake of trying to rush me," he snarled.

"You crazy fool," von Flanagan said in a very quiet voice. "You can't get away. You can't shoot down six people before somebody grabs you."

"No," McKeown said, "but I can shoot her first." He had the gun about six inches from Helene and pointed at her.

Jake said, "Damn you, McKeown—" and started to make a move.

"Don't, Jake," Helene said quietly. "He means it."

"You're a sensible babe," McKeown said. He moved around to the alley door, always keeping the gun aimed squarely at Helene.

"Now, listen," von Flanagan said. He spoke very patiently. "There's no reason for you to try and make a break. I'm not arresting you for anything. I simply came in to establish ownership of the gun. Even if you admit it's yours, that isn't enough for me to arrest you for murder."

Al Harmon added quickly to McKeown, "Don't be a dope, pal. He can't hang a murder rap on you."

Bill McKeown laughed harshly and didn't say a word.

Malone said wearily, "Unfortunately, I made the mistake of letting him know I had other evidence. Not only enough to hang a murder rap on him, but a few other things. Including extortion by intimidation, perjury, first degree arson, and illegal transportation of a dead body. I'm sorry I didn't keep my big mouth shut until I had a couple of cops along."

"You can't get away," von Flanagan said to McKeown. "I've got this place surrounded. You'll be stopped before you get ten feet from the door."

"Not with this beautiful babe along, I won't be," Bill McKeown said. He grinned evilly at Helene. "I bet you're a good driver. Wanna take me for a little spin?"

"Why you—" Jake began, starting forward.

Al Harmon grabbed him by the arm. Jake wheeled and swung on Harmon, who staggered back against the wall.

"While you boys scrap it out," McKeown said, "the babe and me are leaving. Don't worry, she's not going to get hurt. Not if she's a good girl."

He opened the door. Jake made another frantic move and again Al Harmon grabbed him, this time by both arms.

"Thanks, Al," McKeown said. "Let's get going, babe." He stepped out sideways, keeping Helene in front of him. "Don't try to come after us if you don't want the babe to get shot."

The door swung shut.

The alley was dark and deserted. Helene looked around. Not a soul in sight. The gun nudged her in the ribs.

"Where's your car?" McKeown demanded.

"In the garage. We came in a taxi."

"C'mon. I said, where's your car?" The gun nudged her harder.

"Right down here. On Ontario Street."

"Head for it. And no tricks, now."

Helene walked down the alley, crossed the sidewalk, unlocked the door of the car, got in and slid under the wheel. McKeown followed her and slammed the door.

"Where to?" Helene said, starting the motor.

"Straight ahead across Clark Street and keep going west. South on Wells Street, west on Washington Street, and then head right along unless I tell you different."

The big car shot forward, dodged Clark Street traffic and swung into the comparative quiet of West Ontario Street.

"You're a pretty cool character," McKeown said, glancing at her.

"Maybe it's because I'm not scared," Helene said, slowing for an intersection.

It was almost true. She had been nearly paralyzed with terror in the moment when she stepped into the alley. But the fear was practically gone now, and in its place was growing a serene confidence that she'd think of some way out of this jam.

She stole a glance at her passenger. She'd always thought the big, perfectly dressed man was handsome. She didn't think so now. There wasn't the slightest doubt in her mind that he would shoot, if he had to.

They'd reached Washington Street before McKeown said, "They're probably following us. It's up to you to lose them, if you want to get home safe."

"You've got a lot of confidence in my driving ability," Helene said, "but I'll do my best."

"I liked the way you dodged that truck," Bill McKeown said.

Conversation lagged.

A few minutes later Helene said, "Would you light a cigarette for me, please?"

"Sure," McKeown said. "Anything to oblige a beautiful babe."

She waited until it was between her fingers before she said, "It's none of my business, but frankly I think you're making a big mistake. Von Flanagan hasn't enough on you to bring you to trial."

"How about Malone?"

"Hire him for a lawyer. He wouldn't use his own evidence against his own client."

"I don't trust lawyers."

"I shouldn't think you would, after Jesse Conway."

"Jesse was O.K., only he was beginning to crack up. I don't know why Malone started messing around in this in the first place, but he was getting to Jesse."

"How do you know?"

"I was tipped off."

"Why did you kill poor Mr. Garrity?"

McKeown said, "Look, you just tend to your driving."

They had reached Oak Park when Helene said, "How far west do you want to go, California?"

"I'll tell you where to go," McKeown said.

Conversation lagged again.

They passed through a succession of west-side suburbs. Suddenly Bill McKeown said, "Turn right when you get to the highway."

"Thank goodness," Helene said as she made the turn. "I was beginning to think we'd wind up in Iowa, and then Malone would add a Mann Act rap to the collection he's hung on you."

"You think you're pretty smart, don't you," Bill McKeown said.

"Um-h'm. And my friends think I'm cute, too. Why did you tell Milly Dale not to sing that 'Girl-With-The-Gun' song?"

"None of your damn business."

"You should have been a music critic," Helene said. She was silent for a few miles. "Tell me, why did you murder Milly Dale?"

"Shut up."

"Was it because——" She broke off suddenly. "Never mind. I'll ask Malone, after you're safely in Australia or somewhere."

The highway had entered the Forest Preserve. For a few miles it would be a gently curving drive through the woodland, then it would emerge as a streamlined highway again. The Preserve, so beautiful in spring and summer, was a desolate, dreary, and almost frightening place at this season of the year, and this hour of the night. The trees were dark, gaunt skeletons; the ground below was covered with mud, water, and heaps of wet, rotting leaves.

It had been a long time since they had passed a car on the highway. Helene had had a number of ideas and dismissed all of them as impractical. Such as telling McKeown the door on his side wasn't shut tight, and, as he released the handle to slam it shut, swerving the car and dumping him on the pavement. Or, stopping the car suddenly, so that his head would bang against the dashboard.

She'd also considered scaring her passenger into a faint by a series of rapid skids. That had worked once before when there had been an unwelcome gangster in her car. But Bill McKeown didn't look like the type that would scare easily.

It was just as she entered the Forest Preserve that she looked in her rearview mirror and suspected that a car was following, its lights turned off. For a moment she wasn't sure. There was just a shadow not far behind.

Suddenly she stepped on the brake, then released it. The moment of glare from the tail-light reflected on the headlights of the car behind her. Three headlights. Then it was a police car.

"What'd you do that for?" McKeown demanded.

"Sorry," Helene said. "I thought I saw a cat in the road."

He muttered something about women drivers, then glanced over his shoulder.

"No more games," he said. "I saw it, too. Step on it."

The big car shot ahead, swerving crazily on the wet pavement.

"They don't dare shoot," McKeown said, "because if they did, they might hit you."

"And you don't dare shoot," Helene said serenely, skidding around a curve, "because if I relaxed my hold on the wheel, for two seconds, at this speed, the car would go climb a tree. It's a tie." She swerved the car again, viciously.

"Stop that," McKeown said.

She glanced anxiously in the rearview mirror. She seemed to have lost the car behind.

"I can't help it," she said, going into another side-to-side skid. "I'm not a very good driver, and I'm scared."

Bill McKeown swore, looked over his shoulder, and said, "Slow down and jump out. I'll take over the car."

Helene gave the gearshift a quick shove. The car stopped, instead of slowing down, with a sudden, bucking motion. She opened the door, jumped, and ran blindly toward the security of the trees. Behind her she could hear McKeown's vain attempts to start the car. A dripping branch slapped her across the face, a vine tripped her and sent her sprawling into a puddle of mud.

She heard the other car come roaring close and stop. She heard voices. *Jake!*

Somehow she got to her feet, stumbled back in the direction of the road. Bill McKeown had given up trying to start the car, had leaped out and was running up the highway. Five men piled out of the other car. Jake, Malone, von Flanagan, the plain-clothes man, and the man in the tan raincoat. Von Flanagan yelled to McKeown to stop.

McKeown turned just long enough to fire one shot. Jake stopped dead in his tracks and grabbed at his ear. Helene screamed. McKeown fired again. She heard the bullet zip past, close to her. There was a third shot, and the man in the tan raincoat staggered and fell forward. McKeown kept on running.

The plain-clothes man drew his gun, stood still, held his elbow close to his side, steadied his gun hand in the palm of his other hand, took aim, and fired. McKeown stumbled. The plain-clothes man fired again. McKeown fell.

Helene ran out into the road and gasped, "Jake! You're hurt!"

Jake felt of his ear. "Just a scratch. Darling——"

She leaned her head against him, he put an arm around her. It felt very firm and very comforting.

The plain-clothes man came back from examining McKeown. "He's dead," he reported.

Von Flanagan rose from examining Al Harmon. "And he isn't. Radio for an ambulance."

Malone said, "Well, there you have it, all tied up in one neat little package. Head of the protection racket. Murderer of Jesse Conway, Garrity, and Milly Dale. To say nothing," he added, "of Big Joe Childers."

"Wait a minute," von Flanagan said. "Even if the guy's dead, we need *evidence* to close the case."

"As far as the protection racket is concerned," Malone said, "you'll probably find plenty of evidence when you fine-toothcomb that private office at The Happy Days. Al Harmon may be able to give you some additional evidence when he comes to." He added, "I hope he isn't hurt bad."

"Bullet grazed his scalp," Mike, the plain-clothes man said. "Not much harm done."

Malone nodded. His knees were beginning to behave a little strangely. He braced himself with one hand against the fender of Helene's car and fumbled in his vest pocket with the other hand. "Has anybody here got a cigar?"

Mike beamed, produced a cigar, and said, "My niece got married yesterday. These are good cigars. Three for a dime."

"Thanks," Malone said, leaning against the car. "Now, all I need is a drink. Let's all go back to The Happy Days."

"I'd like to know one thing first," Jake said. "Helene, how did you fix the car so McKeown couldn't use it?"

"Easy," Helene said. "I threw it into reverse going at a high speed, and stripped the gears."

"Women drivers!" von Flanagan said.

CHAPTER THIRTY-FOUR

The Happy Days was deserted, save for a white-faced, nervous bartender and Lou Berg. Even the bouncer had vanished.

Lou Berg was sitting at the bar, nursing a drink, and watching the spot where Anna Marie had disappeared like a cat watching a mousehole. He turned around as the party came in and reported anxiously, "She hasn't appeared again."

"Don't worry," Jake said. "She will."

There was a bit of fresh white bandage stuck on the lobe of Jake's ear. Another bandage adorned Al Harmon's head. More bandage covered Helene's skinned knees, her beige wool dress was torn and covered with mud, and there was a scratch on one of her pale, smooth cheeks. Malone, his black eye even more prominent against the whiteness of his face, was walking as though he expected every step to be his last.

"Run into any trouble?" Lou Berg asked casually.

"A little," Jake said, just as casually.

"What happened to McKeown?" Berg said.

"Mike shot him," von Flanagan said. "Shot him dead. Mike's a good shot."

The bartender made a strange little gurgling noise in his throat.

"You should worry," von Flanagan said to the bartender. "Nobody's going to hang a thing on you, if you play along with us and show me where McKeown's private records are kept."

The bartender nodded and started toward the hallway.

"That can wait a few minutes," Malone said, sagging into a chair. "We all need a drink, and we all need it fast."

Von Flanagan muttered something about being on duty. Malone looked at his watch. It was near midnight. "If you don't get time-and-a-half for overtime, at least you're entitled to have a drink in your overtime. Besides, I'm paying for it. Sit down and shut up."

They sat down at one of the tables. Lou Berg brought his drink over from the bar and joined them. Malone gave an order to the bartender.

"The Commissioner is happy as an ant at a picnic," von Flanagan said. "Malone, how the hell did you know?"

"I didn't," the little lawyer growled. "I was just bluffing." He saw the bartender approaching with a tray and paused.

The bartender had just reached the table when suddenly his face turned even a shade more white. He gave a half-strangled moan and his knees began to buckle. Malone resourcefully grabbed the tray just as the bartender slid to the floor in a faint.

"He wasn't a very good bartender, anyway," Helene said.

No one paid any attention to her. Von Flanagan looked down the hallway, yelped, and started to rise. Malone grabbed him by the arm and pulled him back to his chair. Al Harmon sat paralyzed and staring. Jake and Lou Berg were both gazing at the hallway, Jake with admiration, Lou Berg with delight.

The lovely vision of Anna Marie St. Clair walked, with an almost floating motion, in the darkness of the hallway. She seemed a pale, gray shadow, ethereally beautiful. There was a faint smile on her face.

"Please," Lou Berg cried, "don't go away again!"

Malone rose as Anna Marie came into the bar and moved another chair up to the table. She sat down and began removing her gloves. Everyone stared. The bartender sat up, shrieked, and shut his eyes.

"Get up," Malone said, nudging him with a foot, "and bring one more drink."

The bartender scrambled to his feet and made it to the bar in two jumps.

"You mean, you can *drink?*" Lou Berg gasped.

"Sure," Anna Marie said, "and I can smoke, swear, and spit. Would you like to pinch me?"

He gave her a long, thoughtful, almost calculating look. Then he turned to Jake.

"I didn't think you'd do a thing like this to me, Jake," he said resentfully. "You told me she wasn't anybody made up to look like her. You told me she was the real thing."

"She is the real thing," Jake said, grinning. "The *real*, real thing. She's Anna Marie St. Clair, all right, but she's alive."

Von Flanagan and Al Harmon said, "What the hell!" almost in the same breath.

Jake rose and said, "Malone, you make the explanations. I'm going to phone the newspapers and give them the best story they've had since the Chicago fire."

By the time he returned from the phone booth, the story had been told to the group at the table. Anna Marie sat, calm and unconcerned, while everyone looked at her, amazed and almost incredulous. The bartender's eyes were like a couple of billiard balls.

"Little Girl," Lou Berg said earnestly, "you have a very great future ahead of you. I will personally supervise it."

"She can sing, too," Jake said. "And I have a hunch she can act."

"Who cares?" Lou Berg said in a dreamy voice. "Did I say anything about can she act or can't she act? I got the best directors, they could teach a baboon to act. Sometimes they do." He drew a long, rapturous breath. "Little Girl, there's a plane for Hollywood at six in the morning, and we're going to be on it. I'm making the reservations right now." He almost raced to the telephone booth.

Anna Marie smiled at Jake. "He might at least have asked me if I wanted to be a movie star."

"He didn't need to," Jake said.

"You're right." She turned to Malone. "I'm sorry——"

"I'm not," Malone said. "I'm glad. It's very much for the best. More, perhaps, than any of you know."

His voice was strangely flat, with something more than weariness alone. He took out a cigar and slowly began unwrapping it. Helene resisted an impulse to reach out and pat his hand. She'd seen Malone before on occasions when he'd trapped a murderer, and she knew exactly how he felt.

No one spoke until Lou Berg had come back to the table, beaming.

"Photographers and reporters at the airport," he announced. "Here, and when we get to Hollywood. Little Girl, you are going to be very rich and very famous." He signaled to the bartender and said, "This is on me."

"Now," Helene said, "Malone, will you please tell me, *how did you know?*"

"I had an eye on Bill McKeown from the beginning," Al Harmon said, "but I never could pin a thing on him. How did you do it?"

Malone lit his cigar, with a hand that trembled only a little. "Louis Perez made a dying declaration that McKeown was head of the protection racket," he said. "And——" He remembered just in time that he had not been, officially, on the scene of the crime. "Rico di Angelo heard it. Furthermore, Rico saw the murderer."

He puffed hard on the cigar. "McKeown preferred to do his own murdering. After he'd thrown the bomb, he switched guns with Louis Perez. He didn't see Rico in the alley and assumed that he'd been caught in the building. Otherwise, he'd have killed Rico. He didn't know Louis Perez would live long enough to make a dying declaration or he'd have attended to that."

The little lawyer made a mental note to tip Rico di

Angelo off quick as to what he had and hadn't seen. After all, he told himself, this wasn't going to be actual testimony at a trial, so he wouldn't be asking Rico to commit perjury.

"McKeown had some bad breaks," Malone said, "and he made some bad errors. He didn't know Louis Perez and his gun were in the jailhouse at the time he killed Milly Dale—when she was on the point of telling his name as the name of the man behind the protection racket. Otherwise, he wouldn't have planted his own gun on Louis Perez."

He caught Helene's eye across the table. She smiled at him.

"The thing that really tipped me off," Malone said, downing the last of his drink and waving for another, "was that McKeown had ordered Milly Dale not to sing that strip-tease song about the girl with the gun. It was just a coincidence, of course, that the gun song happened to be one that would have made it plain to everybody that Anna Marie St. Clair couldn't have shot Big Joe Childers."

Von Flanagan looked searchingly at Anna Marie. His eyes moved slowly from her feet to her head. "*That's* the thing I should of thought of!"

"That's what we all should of thought of," Malone said bitterly. "That's what was the one bad link in the chain of evidence that framed Anna Marie. But nobody could guess she'd show up at The Happy Days in a costume that wouldn't have allowed her to conceal as much as an extra hairpin." He glanced at her, and glanced away, quick. Six o'clock was when the plane left for Hollywood. "That, plus the dying declaration of Louis Perez, was all I needed."

He sat back and flicked cigar ash inaccurately toward the ash tray.

"He killed Milly Dale because she was about to reveal that he was head of the protection racket," Helene said thoughtfully. "But Malone, why did he——" She paused. "Jesse Conway. And Garrity. And——"

"Because," Malone said quickly, "both of them knew the truth about Big Joe Childers' murder and the frame-up of Anna Marie. He put them on the spot by telephone calls that would send them rushing to me, and then rubbed them out."

"The frame-up," von Flanagan said, "that's what I don't

get. I get his killing Big Joe Childers because Big Joe had tumbled to the protection racket and wanted to put it out of business, but why pick on her?"

"Frustration," Malone said. "He had a psychological reason."

"Psychology," von Flanagan said, "that I can understand."

The little lawyer stared at an imaginary spot on the table. "He had two reasons, as far as Big Joe was concerned," he said in a low voice. "You know one. The other was jealousy. Bill McKeown wanted Anna Marie St. Clair, and he couldn't get her. He tried hard enough, but she always turned him down cold. She was loyal to Big Joe. McKeown knew he couldn't get her even with Big Joe out of the way, so he framed her for Big Joe's murder. You can check that with Anna Marie herself."

He lifted his eyes to hers. "That's right, isn't it?"

She nodded. Her face was very pale.

"It pleased him to have her framed for the murder of her boy friend," Malone said. "You can see, von Flanagan, it was just a matter of psychology."

"Psychology, hell," von Flanagan growled. "I say the guy was crazy." He rose and said, "I better get back there and start digging out that evidence." He nodded to the bartender, who started toward the hallway.

Al Harmon rose, said, "I'm in on this, too," and followed them.

Helene waited until they were out of earshot before she asked, "Now, you Irish shyster, how did you *really* know it was Bill McKeown?"

"For the reasons I gave von Flanagan," Malone said. "Do you think I'd lie to a policeman?" He added, "When Louis Perez was dying, he told me the name of the head of the protection racket. Only he said, 'Guillermo.' That had me stuck for a while."

"Guillermo," Helene repeated thoughtfully. "That's——"

"That's the Spanish version of William," Malone said. "Perez was Spanish. When he was dying, he instinctively lapsed back into his native tongue. As soon as I remembered that Guillermo meant Bill, I had everything straight." He stretched, yawned, and said, "The bartender's busy, so we might as well go home. Anna Marie, I'll get a cab, help you pack, and see that you get to the airport by six."

Everyone rose. Lou Berg said ecstatically, "She's a wonderful Little Girl. She's going to have a great future."

Malone went out to the sidewalk to hail a cab. Rain was falling in a thin, unpleasant drizzle. Only a few weary drunks were staggering up Clark Street. Electric and neon signs shone dismally in the rain.

He felt a hand on his arm, and turned to see that Helene had followed him to the sidewalk.

"Malone," she said, "when are you going to tell us what *really* happened?"

He looked at her for a minute. "The chances are," he said, "that I never will."

CHAPTER THIRTY-FIVE

"Malone," Anna Marie said softly, "just because I'm going to Hollywood—it doesn't mean——"

Malone sat back in the darkness of the cab and said, "I'm afraid it does. But don't let that bother you."

He glanced at her, at the way her smooth, tawny hair caressed her shoulders, at the pale, delicate line of her cheek, at the way dark, curling lashes framed her eyes. Something happened to his throat that kept him from speaking for a moment.

Suddenly she looked out the window and said, "Malone, we're going in the wrong direction."

"I've got to stop somewhere before we go to the hotel," Malone said. "Don't worry, I'll get you to the airport on time. Time, and time to spare."

He patted her hand and said, "You're a wonderful Little Girl with a great future ahead of you, and by all means, don't let me stand in your way."

"But Malone——"

"Never *mind*."

"I've got to talk to you."

"Later." There was one way of keeping her from talking until he wanted her to talk, and he used it, fast. The cab was slowing for a stop before she could catch her breath.

Then she said, "I don't *have* to go to Hollywood. I haven't signed any contracts."

Malone thought of the little house in Winnetka, or possibly Willmette; the house that would be like a jewel box. He thought of the diamond-studded key he'd have made. He thought of Anna Marie.

The cab stopped. He reached for the door handle. "You're going to love Hollywood," he told her.

She stepped out, looked at the building in front of her, and gasped. "What's the idea of bringing me—*here?*" She'd almost said, "home."

"I left something here," Malone said. "I hope you don't mind."

"Why should I? After all, I used to live here."

"That's right," Malone said in a flat, emotionless voice. "We may be a few minutes," he said to the cab driver. "Please wait."

Anna Marie said, "I'll wait in the cab."

"No," Malone said.

He looked at her. Again the breath caught in his throat, almost in a sob, just at the sight of her. "It isn't very long until six o'clock. I'd like to have you with me for every minute." He added, "You're not afraid to go in there with me, I hope."

"Of course not," she said. She laid a hand on his arm. "I wouldn't be afraid to go anywhere with you." She walked up the steps by his side.

Malone flung open the door, ushered her in, and said, "I'm sorry—I don't know where the light switch is for the hall."

She reached in and clicked the light switch. The hall and stairs were suddenly flooded with light. "Thanks," Malone said, "I'd hate to go up these stairs in the dark."

He had taken three steps when she caught at his arm.

He turned and looked down at her. "Malone," she said, almost whispering, "there's nothing upstairs."

Malone stared down at her. Suddenly he caught her face between his hands and kissed her, almost roughly, on the lips, the forehead, the cheeks, and the chin. He covered her face with kisses just as he had covered it more than once in his dreams.

He said, "Anna Marie, I don't care what you do to me as long as you don't lie to me. Now, come on upstairs."

He put his arm around her and led her up to the second floor. The door to the upstairs apartment was slightly ajar. Malone pushed it open and reached for the light. The bare, unfurnished room seemed fairly to blaze. Malone glanced around it, remembered the room below, and shuddered.

Anna Marie stood close by the door, watching him. He walked over to the door to the kitchenette and reached up to the top of it.

"I should have brought along a chair to stand on," he complained, "but I think I can make it."

He ran his hand along the top of the door. A thin strip of wood sprang up as his fingers touched it. He reached in, stretching and standing on tiptoe, and drew out a small black book, on the front of which was printed "One Year Diary."

Anna Marie sprang at him, her eyes blazing. He caught her by the shoulders and held her fast.

"Why bother?" the little lawyer said.

She relaxed against his shoulder. He kissed her very tenderly and said, "You're going to Hollywood, remember? And the diary ought to be burned, anyway."

Anna Marie stood flat against the wall, bracing herself with the palms of her hands. She whispered, "How did you know it was there?"

"Because I dreamed about identical twins—identical in *every* respect, even to the fillings in their teeth. You made a hiding place for Big Joe in the apartment downstairs, but when the time came that he wanted to hide his diary from you, he made one just like it in the upstairs apartment. The two apartments were exactly alike in every other way, so naturally they would be alike in the matter of a hiding place."

"He told me—that he'd destroyed the diary," Anna Marie whispered.

"He told you that," Malone said, "to spare you the trouble of looking for it. Because he was writing things in it that he didn't want you to see. He hid it from you just as he hid those notes for a letter that never was written." He paused, smiled bitterly, and quoted, " 'Anna Marie—Forgive me for what——' " He broke off, stared at her, and said, "You knew what he was going to do that called for your forgiveness."

She said nothing, but stood there watching him, her face as expressionless as the wall.

"Do I need to read you the last pages of Big Joe's diary," Malone said, "or do you know what he must have written? Do you need to be reminded that Bill McKeown was your lover? Do you need me to tell you that you were the real brains behind the protection racket?"

She said hoarsely, "You can't prove a thing!"

"I'm not trying to prove anything," Malone said. "I don't need to. Because Bill McKeown's dead. I'd sort of like to think you're sorry, but I know you aren't." He glanced at her. "You were in love with him, once. Or—were you?"

Her lower lip curled unpleasantly. "He didn't try to save me from the electric chair—remember?" She took a cigarette from her purse and lit it. There was bitterness and resentment in her voice when she spoke again. "He wanted the money. He wanted to have the racket all to himself. There's a lot of good-looking dolls running around loose, but damn few rackets as sweet as this one. If he hadn't——" She paused. "Hell, yes, I'd have killed him myself."

"With your own little lily-white hands," Malone said. He sighed. "Hate isn't good for people, Anna Marie. You've hated too many people in your lifetime."

He began walking up and down the unfurnished room, his cigar held limply between his fingers. "Maybe von Flanagan ought to be in on this. He's the guy who's reading the book about psychology. Me, I just make it up as I go along. Hate, and ambition. That's a bad combination."

Anna Marie looked at her watch and whispered, "I've got to pack. It's getting late."

"I'll help you pack," Malone said. "I'll get you to the

plane on time. You'll get to Hollywood, and you'll be a big success, but I don't think you'll be happy there. I don't think you'll be happy anywhere. Remember the dream you had, when you thought you were going to the chair? It was a dream of glory. A magnificent gesture. You dreamed of being noticed. And the statement Garrity gave the press at your order. 'Anna Marie died at midnight, with a smile on her lovely lips——' You're going to be a success as an actress, Anna Marie."

"Please," she murmured. "Malone, don't hate *me.*"

Malone said, "I'm crazy about you, and you know it. You're the one who's been doing the hating, as long as you could remember. You hated your father for deserting your mother. You hated the people in Grove Junction who had all the things you wanted. You hated grandmother, because all she left was a mortgaged house, a garnet necklace, and a pair of silver earrings."

"Other girls," Anna Marie began. Her voice broke off suddenly.

"Other girls had things you wanted," Malone said. "Expensive clothes, and a house without a mortgage. And dates with boys whose parents approved of them. I can understand why you hated them. I can understand why, later, you hated Bill McKeown. I can't understand, though, about Big Joe Childers." He looked at her closely, his eyes narrowed. "Or maybe I can."

"There isn't any point in this," she said. Her voice was a faint whisper. She looked around for a place to put out the cigarette, finally dropped it on the floor, and stepped on it.

"No, there isn't," Malone said. "But we've a little time left, and I'd like to hang on to every minute of it. It doesn't matter now, but I'd like to reconstruct what did happen."

She sat down on the windowseat, looked out through the soot-streaked window, and said, "Go ahead."

"You were framed for Big Joe's murder," Malone said. "You were arrested for it. Bill McKeown's brother told you not to worry. Jesse Conway turned up as your lawyer, and *he* told you not to worry. You didn't really believe either of them, but you had to play along with them. They promised you an acquittal, and they promised to cover up your part in the protection racket."

"You're guessing," Anna Marie said faintly.

"Of course I'm guessing," Malone said, "and stop me if I guess wrong. It wasn't until after the conviction—hell, even after you were sentenced—that you realized Bill McKeown had given the orders to let you *stay* framed."

She turned to face him. "Malone, what could I do?"

"That's just it," Malone said. "You couldn't do a damned thing. You knew who'd framed you—you must have known by that time. But you couldn't find the proof, not while you were sitting in that cozy little cell in the deathhouse."

"Don't!" She shivered.

Malone took her face very tenderly between his hands and kissed her. "It's over now," he said. "You're free."

He opened the window, tossed his cigar end out, took out a fresh cigar and began to unwrap it. "You couldn't even talk to anybody. Warden Garrity saw to that. Your own lawyer wouldn't come near you. You were trapped."

Again he began pacing up and down the unfurnished and chilly room. "One person guessed. Milly Dale. But she didn't dare speak. She didn't even dare sing that song, the 'Girl-With-The-Gun' number, after Bill McKeown told her to lay off—because some smart person might have realized it proved you couldn't have shot Big Joe."

Suddenly he wheeled around to face her. "The night Ike Malloy was killed and made his confession, Jesse Conway and Bill McKeown had to work fast. There was a chance the confession might in some way involve them. It didn't, but it exonerated you, and Bill McKeown wanted you safely and quietly out of the way. *He sent Jesse Conway up to the prison to make sure you were executed. And you knew it.*"

"I only guessed it," Anna Marie gasped.

"I'm guessing, too," Malone reminded her. "This is guess night, on the Malone hour." He felt deathly weary, almost ill. "It's a curious thing how traits come out in a person's personality at a time like that. Maybe von Flanagan could explain it. Like the way the hatred came out in yours, and the decency came out in Jesse Conway's, at the last. Because, when it came right down to it, he couldn't see you go to the chair, and he forced Garrity—who had his own reason for wanting you to die—to play along. He was sure he could keep you from talking, once you were free. But he didn't see far enough ahead to realize you would turn things around and trap *them*." He felt his face muscles moving into a smile. "Why *did* you decide to play ghost, Anna Marie?"

She rose and stood facing him. The light glared on her white face. "It was a gag," she told him. "A little fun—scaring a few people."

Malone shook his head and said, "No."

"Well—all right, you had it O.K. I'd guessed who hired Ike Malloy and framed me. I thought I could scare someone into turning up the proof."

Malone shook his head again and said, "It's still no."

Anna Marie shrugged her shoulders and said, "It's your question, you answer it."

"It was a damned convenient way to keep out of the public eye," Malone said. "If Jesse Conway, and Warden Garrity, and, eventually, Bill McKeown had been murdered shortly after your release, the police might have asked some embarrassing questions. Only by playing ghost could you get away with it."

"Get away with what?" A harsh note had come into her voice.

"Why," Malone said amiably, "getting rid of the people you hated, grabbing off all the money you could, and quietly disappearing." This time he intended the smile. "You were luckier than you thought you'd be. You discovered you didn't have to disappear quietly—you could reappear publicly with your face all over the front pages and a chance at a Hollywood career."

"Go on," she said coldly.

"Anna Marie," Malone complained, "don't use that tone of voice with me. I'm only telling you what happened. You got in touch with Bill McKeown as soon as you got back to Chicago. You told him you were alive, and you told him how and why. You pretended you didn't know anything about his part in the frame-up. But you warned him that Jesse Conway was about to crack. You put Jesse on the spot for Bill McKeown by calling him and telling him to come to your apartment.

You told McKeown that Garrity was ready to spill the whole story, and you put him on the spot by calling him, telling him to drive to Chicago and to get in touch with me right away." He paused and relit his cigar.

"You told me you were guessing," Anna Marie reminded him.

"But I'm guessing right, now," Malone said, not looking at her. "Jesse Conway wouldn't have come to your apartment unless you asked him to. I can do a little more guessing, and correct me if I guess wrong. Milly Dale knew about you and Bill McKeown. She may have suspected the real truth. You went out the day of her death and talked to McKeown. You told him to follow her and make sure she wasn't going to talk. When he was afraid that she was going to talk, he killed her. In a way, you put her on the spot for him, too. Killing Louis Perez and Earl Wilks was probably his own idea, but it wouldn't have been necessary if it hadn't been for you."

She walked out into the middle of the room and said, "There's a telephone in the apartment downstairs in case you want to call the police."

"Why should I," Malone said, "when you're a wonderful Little Girl with a great future ahead of you? It would break Lou Berg's heart, and I like Lou Berg. What good would it do him, for instance, if I told the police and the world the reason Eva Childers set not one, but two men, on the trail of what had actually happened to Big Joe—that she hated you, suspected the truth, and wanted the world to know it."

Anna Marie said very calmly, "Then you know who hired Ike Malloy to murder Big Joe and frame me."

"It's all in the diary," Malone said, slapping the little book with the palm of his hand. "There's only one person in the world it could have been. Big Joe Childers himself!"

He turned and faced her. "That's why he started to write a letter beginning 'Forgive me.' He wanted you to read it— afterward. Because he loved you, even on the day when he'd arranged his own murder—but arranged for you to suffer and die for it. And you knew all the time, didn't you? And Jesse Conway knew. And Garrity knew because he was Big Joe's brother-in-law, and Big Joe had confided in him. And Bill McKeown knew."

Anna Marie murmured, "What are you going to do about it, Malone? Tell the story to the whole world?"

"Why should I," Malone said again, "when such a number of otherwise useless people died to keep it from being told? It would be a shame for their deaths to be wasted as much as their lives were. What good would it do for me to tell Daniel von Flanagan that Big Joe Childers was heartbroken and desperately ill, that he knew he could live only a few more months, that he'd discovered that the girl he adored was cheating on him, and even worse than that, that she was the brains behind a particularly nasty racket."

"I was completely innocent as far as Big Joe's murder was concerned—and Jesse Conway—and Garrity——" She looked at him stony-faced. "You can't prove that I put them on the spot for Bill McKeown. You can't prove that I so much as talked to Bill McKeown after I came back to Chicago."

"I'm not trying to prove anything," Malone said, still pacing the floor, "but Bill McKeown was an Irishman and he wasn't frightened when he saw what might have been your ghost back at The Happy Days. He was startled, that's all." He paused, smiled at her, and said, "Well, that's it. I'll burn the diary. You'd better hop in the cab, go back to the hotel and pack, if you're leaving for Hollywood on the six o'clock plane."

She looked at him with wide uncomprehending eyes. "Why, Malone?" she said. "I mean—why don't you——?"

"You haven't murdered anybody," Malone said.

She said, "There's something about—being an accessory before the fact."

Malone said, "Don't keep that cab driver waiting too long. He might start cruising around for another fare."

She shrugged her shoulders, walked to the door, paused there, and said, "You still haven't answered, *why?*"

"For the same reason Big Joe Childers started to write you a letter beginning 'Forgive me,'" Malone said. "I love you, too. Now you'd better go." He closed his eyes.

For a moment he felt her arms around him, her lips against his. Before he could reach for her she was gone. He opened his eyes and saw briefly a shadowy gray form fleeting down the stairs. He heard the downstairs door open and close, he heard the cab start. He knew he would never see her again.

He paused and looked back at the unfurnished and desolate room, then he returned and started slowly down the stairs. He had reached the bottom step when the front door opened and Al Harmon came in.

"I thought you'd come here, pal," Al Harmon said, lighting a cigarette. "Look, that blonde isn't sore at me after all, and she's got a friend for you."

CHAPTER THIRTY-SIX

It was three in the afternoon when the door of Malone's office opened and Maggie looked up from her magazine.

The little lawyer came in, a trifle wearily, but his eyes, including the blackened one, were bright. He greeted Maggie with a cheerful nod and said, "Any calls?"

"Nothing important," she said, "just a couple of prospective clients with a lot of money."

He ignored her and glanced at the newspapers on her desks. They told of the brilliant job Daniel von Flanagan of the homicide squad had done in smashing the protection racket and finding the murderers of Big Joe Childers, Jesse Conway, Warden Garrity, Milly Dale, and Louis Perez. The story explored the fact that the murderer had not lived to stand trial, but commended Captain von Flanagan just the same.

There was also a story of what an inspired reporter called, "The Greatest Hoax in History"—ex-ghost at the airport on her way to Hollywood. There might also have been a story about a well-known Chicago lawyer being arrested after a fist fight in a South Chicago saloon, if Malone hadn't done a quick job of contacting a friend of his on the *Herald-American*, and bribed his way out of the South Chicago jail.

"Take a letter to Mrs. Eva Childers," Malone said. "Tell her that Anna Marie St. Clair's only relative is a Mrs. Bessie O'Leary in Grove Junction, Wisconsin. Tell her the murderer of Big Joe Childers has been discovered and that the case is closed. Send her a bill and leave the amount blank, and let her use her own judgment."

He started toward the office door. "Anything else?" Maggie said.

"Yes," Malone said. He went into the office, opened his closet, took out the long, flat, white box, and carried it back to Maggie's desk.

"Send this back to the Toujours Gai Lingerie Shoppe," he said. "Call Miss Fontaine and ask her if she has the same model in rose in——"

He paused and closed his eyes for a moment,—"size sixteen."

Maggie made a note, sniffed scornfully, and said, "By the way, did I hear anybody make any remarks about getting to any office by nine o'clock in the mornings, or was I dreaming?"

"That," Malone said happily, "was yesterday. Believe me, Maggie, I'm a changed man."

He went into the office, closed the door, and in five minutes was sound asleep.

from Sue Grafton
author of "A" IS FOR ALIBI

"B" IS FOR BURGLAR
A Kinsey Millhone Mystery

KINSEY MILLHONE IS ...

"The best new private eye."   —*The Detroit News*

"A woman we feel we know, a tough cookie with a soft center, a gregarious loner."   —*Newsweek*

"Smart, sexual, likable, and a very modern operator."
          —*Dorothy Salisbury Davis*

"A stand-out specimen of the new female operatives."
          —*Philadelphia Inquirer*

"Thirty-two, twice divorced, and lives in a fifteen-foot-square room in a converted garage ... On the road she stays in crummy motels because she's cheap. She likes people for good reasons. She's smart but she makes mistakes ... I like Millhone."   —*The Detroit Free Press*

Finding wealthy Elaine Boldt seems like a quickie case to Kinsey Millhone. The flashy widow was last seen wearing a $12,000 lynx coat, leaving her condo in Santa Teresa for her condo in Boca Raton. But somewhere in between, she vanished. Kinsey's case goes from puzzling to sinister when a house is torched, an apartment is burgled of worthless papers, the lynx coat comes back without Elaine, and her bridge partner is found dead. Soon Kinsey's clues begin to form a capital M—not for missing, but for murder. And plenty of it.

And coming in May from Bantam "C" IS FOR CORPSE